A LURKING PRIMROSE

Also by Suzette A. Hill

The Francis Oughterard mysteries

A LOAD OF OLD BONES
BONES IN THE BELFRY
BONE IDLE
BONES IN HIGH PLACES
A BEDLAM OF BONES
THE PRIMROSE PURSUIT
DEADLY PRIMROSE *

The Rosie Gilchrist mysteries

A LITTLE MURDER
THE VENETIAN VENTURE
A SOUTHWOLD MYSTERY
SHOT IN SOUTHWOLD
THE CAMBRIDGE PLOT

Southwold mysteries

A SOUTHWOLD MYSTERY
SHOT IN SOUTHWOLD
SHADOW OVER SOUTHWOLD

* *available from Severn House*

A LURKING
PRIMROSE

Suzette A. Hill

SEVERN
HOUSE

First world edition published in Great Britain and the USA in 2024
by Severn House, an imprint of Canongate Books Ltd,
14 High Street, Edinburgh EH1 1TE.

severnhouse.com

British Library Cataloguing-in-Publication Data
A CIP catalogue record for this title is available from the British Library.

ISBN-13: 978-1-4483-1184-2 (cased)
ISBN-13: 978-1-4483-1185-9 (e-book)

All Severn House titles are printed on acid-free paper.

Typeset by Palimpsest Book Production Ltd., Falkirk,
Stirlingshire, Scotland.
Printed and bound in Great Britain by TJ Books,
Padstow, Cornwall.

Praise for the Francis Oughterard mysteries

"Delightful . . . will leave series fans and newcomers alike
eager for the next installment"
Publishers Weekly Starred Review of *Bones in High Places*

"Includes well-drawn characters, especially the acerbic
Primrose and her savvy pets"
Booklist on *A Deadly Primrose*

"The pets are the stars of this twisty, sardonically
humorous adventure"
Kirkus Reviews on *A Deadly Primrose*

"Jaunty . . . Those in the mood for silly fun will be delighted"
Publishers Weekly on *A Deadly Primrose*

"Diverting . . . blithely mixes cozy elements with black farce"
Publishers Weekly on *A Bedlam of Bones*

About the author

Suzette A. Hill is a graduate of the universities of Nottingham and Newcastle, and taught English literature for many years at Reading College before retiring to Herefordshire.

www.suzetteahill.co.uk

Author's Note

The events of this tale are set in the Lewes area of Sussex in 1960–1961. They are recounted mainly by the chief protagonist Primrose Oughterard, the assertive sister of the late Reverend Francis Oughterard, who, when living in Surrey, had been remiss in slaying one of his parishioners, the cloying Elizabeth Fotherington . . . an unfortunate gaffe which had caused the perpetrator much dismay and severely interrupted his hitherto blameless life. The crime remained undetected (though known to his crony, Nicholas Ingaza, and to Primrose), but was somewhat offset by his own death when gallantly rescuing a church stalwart found hanging from a gargoyle. (See *A Bedlam of Bones*, the last of the 'Bones Quintet').

Despite such heroism, Primrose is fearful that her dead brother's misdeed be exposed, and that her own 'impeccable' reputation as Sussex artist and trustee of the local prep school, damaged. But being insatiably nosy she cannot resist the lure of the peculiar and perplexing, and her 'essential researches' invariably lead her into choppy waters. As with her previous exploits, this current one is monitored and occasionally discussed by her cat and dog, pets once belonging to the dead brother. At times both they and Primrose allude to previous adversaries – for example MacManus, the bovine police superintendent, or the egregious Hubert Topping featured in *The Primrose Pursuit*.

Except in chapters one and eleven, the arch-controller of this narrative keeps a tactful silence.

ONE

Summoned by Mr Winchbrooke, headmaster of Erasmus House, the local prep school for boys, the staff were gathered to discuss a development of 'vital urgency', a development which apparently could jeopardize the institution's whole future. This alert had caused even the most blasé of masters to show a quizzical interest. Eyebrows were raised, pens laid down, and copies of *Sporting Life* and *Rugger News* stashed back into briefcases.

However, on being told that the school was due for a visit from Her Majesty's inspectors, startled interest changed to weary annoyance. After all, a periodical inspection was surely par for the course, and while tiresomely intrusive it was hardly a real threat.

'Oh, I shouldn't think it is much to worry about,' Thomas Briscoe, the deputy head, said carelessly. 'It's bound to be just a formality.'

'No,' Winchbrooke snapped, 'it is not just a formality. They will be mounting a full reconnaissance, and the fate of the school hangs upon its outcome.'

'But, Headmaster,' his deputy murmured, 'surely you exaggerate. Erasmus House has impeccable form. We're one of the oldest establishments in the county, and our cricketing record is second to none. Admittedly, one of Eastbourne's copious prep schools has recently had to close its doors. Surplus to requirements, I imagine – though of course it *may* have been precipitated by their matron and gardener being caught *in flagrante* in the tool shed, and—'

'Well, we are certainly safe enough in that respect,' interposed the maths master, laughing. 'I doubt if our pair would be capable.'

There were titters of merriment, while Winchbrooke glared.
'This is no time for flippancy or coarse speculation. This is a
serious matter requiring serious thought.'

'But I can't see what the problem is,' his deputy persisted.
'After all, the school passed the last inspection with flying colours;
the chap awarded us praise and ticks all round.'

'Yes, and he has since been dismissed for incompetence,'
Winchbrooke said dryly. 'Besides, that was five years ago. There
are new brooms at the helm now' – George Pierce, the English
master, winced – 'and I gather this is to be an intensive operation
lasting the best part of a week and with at least two inspectors
involved, possibly three. Huh! No doubt eager beavers demanding
changes and intent on making their mark at our expense. The
head of St Crispin's at Worthing told me that their presence had
pushed him to the brink of a nervous breakdown and that he is
now seriously considering retirement . . . Mind you, in my
opinion, that's a consideration not before time.' A malevolent
gleam entered Winchbrooke's eye. 'Anyway,' he continued,
'apparently these days it's not enough to be steady and old
established, one must be *dynamic* and *thrustful* and prepared to
be radical in the name of "progress". Absurd. Tradition is what
the parents like, which is why they fork out the money for their
dubious offspring. Erasmus House has always prided itself on
practising a calm conservatism. *Noli scapham agitare*, that's our
motto.'

'No, it isn't,' Richard Sayer, the history master, said. 'It's
"Fortune favours the inventive". Always has been. One gathers
that, back in the 1880s, Lord Pinkswade was always mumbling
it to himself.'

Winchbrooke scowled. 'My compliments on your remarkable
memory, Sayer. Naturally my words were not to be taken literally, but not rocking the damn boat has always worked well in
the past and there is no reason for us to change our policy now.
However, you are quite right to quote our founder's words. Yes,
we must be inventive in preserving the status quo and foiling the
disruptive forces of *thrusting* radicalism. A sober adherence to
the tried and tested is our way, and none of this pandering to the
whiz-kid whims of jumped-up "educationalists"!'

There was silence accompanied by a vague nodding of heads. The headmaster spread his hands and announced, 'So, gentlemen, that being decided, let us now adjourn to discuss tactics, and to drink to our success with two bottles of the excellent bourbon which young Dickie Ickington's *judicious* grandfather has so kindly provided.' He gave a gracious leer.

'Who is Dickie Ickington?' murmured the new geography master to his neighbour. 'And what's his grandfather got to do with things?'

'Sickie-Dickie is a precocious third former, and his grandpa the distinguished High Court judge of uncertain temper and a preference for bourbon over Scotch,' whispered his companion. 'Will tell you more later. Quick, he's moving!' They hastened after the headmaster into the adjacent study and, jostling for position, proffered eager glasses.

'But the judge has his uses,' the neighbour continued. 'He relieves us of Sickie from time to time, and as President of the Board of Trustees (nominal of course, he never presides), his name heads its list in the school prospectus. Another carrot for would-be punters; it confers a legal gravitas.' He paused, and then added, 'Actually, he's a total bastard.'

Ten minutes later, and with bourbon under their belts, the assembled staff relaxed and began to devise ways of presenting the school as a dynamic standard-bearer to modern liberalism – that is to say, fearsomely forward in all but fact.

'How about enrolling girls?' the science master suggested. 'After all, in America co-ed schools are all the rage, and over here there's always the Millfield lot and those peculiar Bedales buggers. If we said we were thinking of widening our clientele, the inspectors would certainly think we were up with the times.'

Winchbrooke winced and shook his head. 'We are a boarding *preparatory* school, not one that caters for adolescents. It would mean having to provide pinafores for the girls and space for their skipping ropes and dolls' houses. As it is, there is barely enough storage for the boys' train sets and football clobber. Besides, we should be expected to employ a dance teacher. All far too expensive.'

'That would be the reality, Headmaster, but we are not talking about realities, are we?' Briscoe pointed out. 'It's all to do with appearance – with creating a favourable *impression* so that the inspectors disperse duped but satisfied.'

Winchbrooke flushed slightly and cleared his throat. 'Yes, yes, you are right. I was being thoughtlessly literal; in my position one gets so used to grappling with harsh practicalities that it becomes second nature! But in any case, Thomas, if I may say so, I don't think "duped" is quite the right term, do you? A little raw for our purpose, surely. All that is needed is to create a subtle . . . a subtle *aura*, what one might call—'

'Stagecraft,' ventured the new geography master. 'A scene of flimsy props which can easily be dismantled once the audience leaves.'

'Exactly,' Briscoe said approvingly.

The headmaster blinked. Exactly? No, it wasn't *exactly*. Stagecraft was hardly the most subtle of metaphors – though at least a term less crude than 'duped'. He gave the geography master a wintry nod, sipped his whisky and invited more ideas. 'But mind you, we don't want any mention of taking girls,' he said grimly. 'They could hold us to it, and then we'd really be up the spout!'

There followed a plethora of suggestions: some facetious, some feasible. But the first to receive a consensus as being both useful and manageable was the idea of replacing the paintings currently adorning the walls of the main corridor with those of a more abstract and challenging style. The present ones were of Sussex churches and placid sheep – though an occasional cow could be seen ruminating in the distance – but sheep were the principal incumbents. It was thought that the inspectors might find these a trifle soporific and dated.

'But actually, the boys quite like them,' the maths master said, 'and they give some of the sheep nicknames – disgusting mostly – but the originals can easily be put back once the inspectors have left.'

All agreed that such a substitution would give visual evidence of the school's lively appreciation of modern art, and would be the first things to confront the visitors when they arrived. The new pictures would establish the tone of things to come, and with luck ensure immediate ticks.

'Excellent,' Winchbrooke declared, 'but there are a couple of problems, i.e. the cost of their purchase and the reaction of our renowned artist, Miss Primrose Oughterard. She might be piqued.'

Somebody murmured that Primrose Oughterard was frequently piqued and that one more pique was neither here nor there, and that the real hurdle was economic. Was the school prepared to purchase a set of flashy daubs to be jettisoned once the danger of dissolution had passed?

'We wouldn't have to purchase,' George Pierce explained. 'They can be hired. There's a man in Brighton – Ingaza I think his name is – rather an enterprising chap. He owns an art gallery and occasionally will rent out pictures to those needing to impress their boss or future in-laws. You know the sort of thing, a stag's severed head or a fake Dali or Picasso. I am not saying he is cheap, but it would certainly be cheaper for us, and simpler, than buying the wretched things.'

'Good idea, Pierce. I'll leave it to you to pursue matters,' Winchbrooke agreed.

'Ah, but that still leaves Miss Oughterard,' interrupted Briscoe. 'How do we handle her?'

The headmaster's rising spirits wilted. The prospect of having to explain to the artist that her pictures were surplus to requirements (albeit temporarily), and had been relegated to the cellar was not a happy one . . . But then he brightened as he saw that such a challenge could perhaps be averted. 'As you all know, Miss Oughterard is one of our more active trustees and periodically comes to talk to the boys and to judge their paintings. But her next visit isn't due for nearly two months, and the trustees held their AGM only last Wednesday. So I am not expecting to see her here for several weeks, by which time the inspectors will be gone and her pictures reinstated.'

He began to look vaguely cheerful and asked for further views, declaring that, 'At all costs we must outflank the foe!' This was a rallying call which was met with dutiful grunts – except from the new geography master, who, still hurt by Winchbrooke's earlier coolness and eager to find favour, cried, 'Hear! Hear!'

TWO

The Primrose version

After the unsettling events of the previous year (murders and God knows what), life in Lewes has been mercifully quiet, and I have been able to attend to my rustic painting without let or hinderance. This has been most satisfactory, that is to say extremely lucrative. Some punter from Mayfair with a yen for rural nostalgia ordered two large canvasses to adorn his hallway ('sheep and churches are so calming after all those bloody Picasso reproductions,' he had enthused). And that nice Inspector Spikesy – such a relief after the ghastly MacManus – has commissioned yet another sketch for his wife's birthday. They already have three . . . Is she an ovine addict, I wonder? Not that I care. After all, provided they hand over the lolly, one can hardly complain.

Yes, trips to the bank's deposit counter have been quite frequent of late and, apart from the machinations of the town clerk, life has been proceeding smoothly. In fact, to be perfectly frank, rather too smoothly. What you might call satisfying but a trifle *dull*. Thus, when Charles Penlow rang to say that there was a nice new couple at Needham Court (empty for some time after the disturbing demise of its owner) and asked if I would care to join them for tea one afternoon, I was intrigued. Who were these incomers? Refugees from Hull or Tunbridge Wells? Or did they hail from somewhere more exotic – inner Chelsea perhaps, or even an embassy in Washington or Tehran? Interesting.

Thus, on the prescribed date I donned my second-best hat – naturally, one doesn't like to overdo things – and set off to join Charles and Agnes Penlow at Podmore Place, their partially renovated ancient pile just outside Lewes.

*   *   *

As my tyres negotiated the hazards of Podmore's long drive – the bumps, flintstones and craters of its raddled surface – I thought wryly of the considerable money that must have been spent on the imposing orangery that now graces the manor's southern aspect. It had been Charles's pet project, his pride and joy, and on which no expense had been spared . . . except the expense of tarmacking the drive or making the cistern in the downstairs lavatory less capricious. Still, one has to admit that the result is splendid: elegant, stylish and *warm*. Feeling the cold as I do, it is this last feature that really draws me. As to actual oranges: as yet it houses only two trees, but those having fructified fill their owners with reverential pride. More specimens are soon to be ordered . . . a process which no doubt will further retard the drive's repair.

Tyres seemingly intact, I parked next to an important-looking Jaguar which (my hosts' car being a battered shooting brake) was presumably the guests'. Approaching the front door, I encountered Duster, the Penlows' lugubrious cairn terrier. Grey of coat and grey of temperament, Duster does not greet one with unalloyed enthusiasm. But neither does he growl or bark; he merely stares, making an assessment. If you pass muster, he will accompany you inside. If not, he stalks to the nearest flower bed and lifts his leg or squats malignly. This time I was evidently deemed acceptable, for he trotted quietly at my heels into the porch.

Here I was met by Charles, who said that the new people – a Mr and Mrs Hamlyn – were dying to meet a local artist of such distinction. 'Ah, but will they buy my paintings?' I asked *sotto voce*.

'We'll work on it,' he muttered and, taking my coat, ushered me into the drawing room: a room which like the orangery had received meticulous attention, and also like the former was large, inviting and warm (not so the hall and loo – cloistered places which for eight months of the year were arctic). In front of the blazing fire and amidst the subtle aroma of Turkish cigarettes, introductions were made and pleasantries exchanged.

I soon learnt that, contrary to my assumption, Douglas and Daphne Hamlyn had come from a place neither distant nor exotic,

but Eastbourne a mere twenty miles away, and where they had
settled from abroad two years previously.

Well, I thought, better than many at any rate . . . And it must
be admitted that Eastbourne does have the assets of the sea, pier,
Wish Tower (a Martello from Napoleonic times) and a rather
splendid bandstand – not to mention the imposing Beachy Head
from which those seeking peace will occasionally eject themselves. Thus in view of such handy diversions, I was interested
to know what had made the incomers quit that town for our
normally sleepy inland Lewes. In the course of fish paste sand-
wiches, insipid tea and the promise of Agnes Penlow's moderately
decent sponge cake, things would become clear.

It emerged that the husband was a keen angler and had enjoyed
the habit of fishing on the River Ouse. But a healthy regard for
money had made him resentful of the constant drain on his petrol
tank as he sped back and forth to his favourite stretch near Lewes.
Indeed, over the months the lively charms of Eastbourne's assets
had been losing out to the quiet of a riverbank at dawn or twilight,
and increasingly he had yearned to indulge such solace whenever
the need dictated. But his wife too had been beckoned inland
– albeit less by the lure of angling than by history. She had long
been fascinated by the sixteenth century and the marital ventures
of Henry VIII, and in particular the fate of his fourth wife, Anne
of Cleves. In fact, so absorbed had she become by the subject
that she was thinking of writing a short biography or 'even a
novel!', as we were gaily told. She was convinced that whether
biography or fiction, such a project was bound to thrive if its
author dwelled near the house to which the poor (or lucky?) bride
had been banished. As a Lewes resident she could pass or visit
the place whenever she liked. And, indeed, the whole area must
surely echo with footsteps from the Tudor past and thus provide
constant inspiration. 'My wife is haunted by historic emanations,'
Douglas Hamlyn had murmured sombrely – and winked.

'Hah,' Daphne had laughed. 'Better than dreams of dancing
dace and lunging pike!'

We got on to other things: my rural paintings, our hosts'
orangery, the Hamlyns' time in South Africa where Douglas had
been attached to a large insurance firm, and Mr Macmillan's

brilliant put-down of Khrushchev's shoe-brandishing antic at the recent UN Assembly.

This was all plain sailing until Daphne Hamlyn queried my rather unusual surname. 'Oughterard,' she said. 'I don't think I've heard of that before. Is it English?'

I explained that it was Anglicized–Irish and that the original is Uachtar Ard, the name of a rather attractive fishing village in County Galway, and from which our forebears had originated in the seventeenth century. I was about to say a little more about the area when Douglas broke in: 'Oh, so might you by any chance be the sister of the late Reverend Francis Oughterard?'

I nodded.

'Ah, a frightfully nice chap,' he enthused. 'One of the best! I met him occasionally years ago when I was in the sixth form at St Cuthbert's and when we played the local seminary at tennis . . . not that he was a particularly good performer, one must admit, but awfully willing. Such a shame about his early death – but crikey, in what heroic circumstances! I mean, fancy rescuing that poor woman hanging on his church gargoyle. Had it been me, I'd have let her blow in the wind.' He laughed uproariously, while I smiled politely.

'Really, Douglas, what nonsense you talk,' his wife protested. She turned to me. 'Alas, unlike Douglas, I never met your brother, but I know that my cousin near Guildford thought he was charming, "an absolute charmer" she would say, "and a wonderful pianist!" You must miss him very much.'

'Er, what? Oh, oh yes of course I do . . . a great loss,' I said quickly, feeling somewhat bemused. Much though I had been fond of Francis, it had never occurred to me that charm had been his major quality. Decency, and kindness of a nervous sort, most certainly, but hardly *charm* – neither natural nor contrived. But I was also puzzled by the reference to this cousin in Surrey and her extravagant words. Francis had indeed been a good piano player – Bach and Ivor Novello mainly – though public display was not generally his thing, so she must have known him quite well.

I was about to make some conventional response when I felt

a spasm of unease. Was it conceivable that Daphne Hamlyn might be referring to his intolerable pursuer, the doting Mrs Elizabeth Fotherington, my foolish brother's tiresome victim? Could this woman really be the deceased's relative? Somewhat shaken, I replaced my half-bitten sandwich, smiled falsely and tried to think soothing thoughts; thoughts which were instantly banished by her next words.

'Oh *yes*, Cousin Elizabeth thought he was the bees' knees.' She laughed. 'Always on about him. Of course, that was long after his time at the seminary. It was when he had become a fully fledged vicar in that Surrey village. Molesworth, wasn't it?'

'Molehill,' I said flatly.

'Ah yes, that's the name. Douglas and I were in Durban in those days, but her letters often referred to him. "A wonderful pastor" was her phrase. Yes, those were her exact words, "a wonderful pastor".'

Hmm, I thought, that was true enough, I suppose . . . wonderful except in the small matter of erasing a parishioner in a summer wood. Other than that, he could be said to have done a very sound job (smiling blandly, preaching worthy sermons, and dutifully hovering on the sidelines: what some might call exemplary behaviour for an Anglican cleric).

'Such lavish praises!' I laughed, while desperately thinking of how I could change the subject. However, at that point our hostess, who had slipped out to the kitchen, returned bearing the promised cake, and with murmurs of polite appreciation the topic was dropped.

As it happens, the cake was very good and eclipsed the dull fish paste and weak tea, but my pleasure was diluted by the fear of what might be said next. And, indeed, to my dismay it was Charles who resumed the matter. 'But aren't I right in thinking that, like Primrose's poor brother, Elizabeth Fotherington also met an untimely death? Rather horrid, in fact. It was in the papers. I gather she—'

Douglas nodded. 'Alas, that was so. Yes, my wife's cousin was found strangled in a local wood near Molehill, apparently attacked by some drunken reprobate given to spectacular flashing and petty pilfering. As said, we were abroad at the time so I can't recall what happened exactly, but I rather think the chap was put away, or died or something . . . Anyway, I gather the whole case is now closed.'

'Yes, I believe it is,' I said firmly. 'Extraordinary the things that go on!' I sighed and gave Daphne a sympathetic look. There followed a slightly awkward silence, before Charles broke it by saying briskly, 'Ah well, that's life, I fear. We never know what's round the corner, good or bad, delightful or dire.' He turned to Douglas. 'Now, *do* tell us about your splendid companions, the mastiff and poodle. How on earth did you come by that pair?'

Daphne laughed. 'Rather a long story, I'm afraid.'

Fortunately it was – being a saga that allowed me to collect my thoughts, accept another slice of cake, and breathe again.

Once safely back at home – like Charles's drive, the roads are treacherous these days and the council so remiss about potholes – I could review the afternoon; or at least I could once the creatures gave me a chance. The moment I had opened the door, Bouncer hurtled forward to buffet my knees. Maurice of course held back, but then slithered up to have his ears tweaked and to waft his tail around my ankles. Obeisance done, he vanished instantly, leaving the dog to prance and gurgle. I ruffled its ears, made for a fireside gin and settled down.

On the whole, I reflected, I didn't dislike the Hamlyns. Indeed, bright and mannerly, they could be an asset to Lewes society. And with Daphne's interest in the life of Anne of Cleves, she might manage to galvanize the local history society, which lately was becoming rather dull. (I mean to say, who cares whether our forebears ate wheat or rye, slept on straw or linen and suffered from worms or fleas? It's what they did *politically* that is the essential thing!) I would remind the chairman to give her a call or deliver a leaflet. But Douglas too could be useful. Rather like dear Charles, he exudes an air of genial self-confidence and has an agile mind that might cut through the town clerk's tiresome obstacles and get things *done*. None of this humming and hawing

and 'seeing every side of the question' which Colonel Rigby so
laboriously excels in. Yes, I reflected, with luck the Hamlyns
could prove quite a social bonus.

I contemplated my glass, and then groaned. Hmm: a bonus
perhaps, but not without its worry. After all, did I really want a
relation of the wretched Fotherington woman living within a mile
of me? No fear! 'Too close for fun or comfort, sweetie,' as an
old Courtauld beau had been in the habit of saying. I smiled at
the memory and then, returning to the present, scowled. As
Charles had rather tritely remarked at tea, one never knows what's
round the corner – delight or disaster.

As I dwelled on such unknowables, Bouncer padded in with his
mangy rubber ring clamped to his jaws. He lurched forward, and
then with dribbling chops deposited it at my feet. Very occasionally he will do this. Don't ask me why, but I *think* it is a form
of canine empathy. The gift ritual will generally occur when I
am at a low ebb (rarely) or when wrestling with some maddening
conundrum such as how to foil the absurd schemes of the local
council – or, as at this particular moment, how best to handle
the Hamlyns' connection with my late brother's victim. Banishing
the scowl, I politely thanked Bouncer for his offering and with
thespian pleasure inspected the ring. Satisfied, the dog pottered
back to its lair in the kitchen. I edged the gift to one side with
my foot, sat back in the chair, took another sip of gin and
pondered.

THREE

Emily Bartlett to her sister

My dear Hilda,

Thank you for your cheerful letter regarding Mother and her apparently waning interest in whisky and soda. This is indeed good news – but can you rely on it? As you know, our dear parent has always been capricious, and the fact that she has recently been ignoring her usual bedtime tipple is no guarantee that she won't revert with a vengeance – i.e. ditching the soda and trebling the Scotch. Without wishing to dampen your spirits, Hilda, I advise only a cautious *optimism – coupled with extra vigilance. To put it kindly, Mother has a certain ingenuity in getting her own way . . . doubtless you will recall her insatiable appetite for the local scoutmaster, that awful Cuthbert Callow, and the crafty means by which she would outwit us and waylay him! Naturally, I could cite other examples (as I am sure could you), and I mention it merely as a reminder to keep alert and not be lulled by signs of unusual abstinence.*

And talking of alerts, here in Erasmus there is much disarray. I gather a school inspection is looming, a fact that has made our headmaster Mr Winchbrooke even more agitato *than usual. For some reason he thinks this could be the end of us – that the school could actually face closure. Yes, would you believe it? The disbandment of such a prestigious institution! All nonsense, I am sure, and very tiresome for me because as my office is next to his I get the brunt of his alarm. It's bad enough dealing with obtrusive parents, but having my busy schedule interrupted by Mr W's incessant demands for tea and sympathy is really too bad! He seems convinced that the inspectors are out to blackmark the school on account of its being old fashioned and behind the times. And to persuade them otherwise he is intent on devising a smoke screen of modernity – going so far as to suggest that for the duration of their visit I should abandon my usual grey twinset and brogues and instead adopt a shorter skirt, wear scarlet lipstick and totter on stiletto heels. Well, really! Naturally, I affected not to hear such absurdity and busied myself with the typewriter – vigorously.*

However, there is one idea that may be feasible: to replace Primrose Oughterard's pictures of sheep and local churches with those of a more 'challenging' style. Apparently, out will go rustic pastures and in will come blazing geometrics interspersed with images of industrial realism. As Primrose's paintings line the main corridor, their substitutes will be the first things that the inspectors see. Mr Winchbrooke thinks this a grand idea. Well, it may or may not be, but one thing is certain: the artist will not approve. In fact, I rather dread to think of Primrose's face, let alone voice, when she learns of the notion. And if the headmaster thinks that yours truly is the one to tell her, he must think again. So there!

I must sign off now as Mr W is about to dictate a circular to all staff reminding them to treat the inspectors with the utmost deference. Whether the children will do the same remains to be seen.

Your devoted sister,
Emily.

P.S. Remember – do not be fooled by Mother.

FOUR

The Primrose version

I had been up in London all day – shopping for a new hat at Marshall & Snelgrove, lunching with an old school friend (looking singularly old in fact) and then on to a matinee to see Alastair Sim in a revival of *An Inspector Calls*. Such an intriguing play and he was splendid as always. I must say, we are most fortunate in our actors but I fear one cannot always say that of the audience. The two women next to me were both knitting, if you please, and chewing sweets – loudly. However, all in all it had been a most enjoyable little outing, but the train back had been crowded and I was pleased to get home, try on the hat (most successful) and put my feet up with a strong restorative.

Not that they were up for very long, as the telephone rang. 'I say, would you be at home, Miss Oughterard?' a polite voice enquired. 'You see, I've got a bone for old Bouncer. Cook was about to chuck it in the dustbin but I got there first. It's rather a big ham bone actually, but I managed to smuggle it past Matron, and I know that he loves them, so if possible, perhaps I could come and—'

I sighed. Much though I like Dickie Ickington (known generally as Sickie-Dickie) and his fondness for Bouncer, after my sortie up to the gay metropolis I was in no mood for entertaining pre-adolescents from Erasmus House – nor anyone else for that matter. But anything to occupy the dog would be a bonus. 'Of course, Dickie,' I gushed. 'Bouncer will be delighted. But are you allowed out at this time in the evening? I thought you were supposed to be in prep or practising madrigals with the vicar.'

'Well, yes,' he replied, lowering his voice, 'but there's been a bit of a bother, so I am free to come over. Is that OK?'

For a moment I hesitated, and then said it was of course

perfectly all right. I replaced the receiver, went into the kitchen
and told Bouncer that his special friend was about to arrive.
Naturally I didn't mention the pending gift; there would be enough
hullabaloo as it was. I returned to the drawing room, and post-
poning further libation awaited the advent of the ham bone.

Boy and bone appeared within ten minutes. The speed of his
arrival rather surprised me, but he explained that Grandpa (Lord
Justice Ickington) had given him a racing bike for his eleventh
birthday, and that it was absolutely smashing. I couldn't help
wondering whether a racing bike for an eleven-year-old, especially one as diminutive as Dickie, was the wisest of presents
and that 'smashing' might well be a likely result. However, I
said nothing, beamed brightly and ushered him into the kitchen.

After the presentation of the bone and the dog's rapturous
welcome, I asked the donor if he would like some ginger ale and
a biscuit. 'Oh yes please, Miss Oughterard,' the child grinned,
'but Grandpa says that a spot of rum goes awfully well with
ginger ale.' He looked at me winsomely.

'Sorry,' I said sharply, 'I don't keep the stuff, so I fear you
will have to do without. But if you like, I *do* happen to have
some rather good chocolate biscuits.' He did like. And as we
settled by the fireside, I took one while he dealt with the rest.

After a spate of appreciative munching, Dickie leant forward
and said, 'I expect you wonder how I was allowed to get here
at this time in the evening?'

I nodded.

'Well, you see,' he continued, 'there's been a bit of a rumpus.'

'Oh, yes? What kind of rumpus?'

'It's Miss Memling, our assistant matron. She has snuffed it.'

I frowned. 'Really? Snuffed what – or do you mean sniffed?'

For an instant the child looked nonplussed, and then leaning
closer said firmly, 'She is *dead*, Miss Oughterard. Snuffed it a
few hours ago, or at least I think so. There's a fearful shindig
going on and everything has been cancelled, which is why I am
here. Some of the boys are wailing, and all the masters are
running around like headless ducks. So I slipped out while I
could. Mr Winchbrooke is chuntering like a mad bear!'

I stared at Sickie-Dickie, my mind ablaze with bizarre images: Winchbrooke in meltdown mode, staff in mayhem, boys tearful – and strewn somewhere or other an indeterminate corpse, the assistant matron whom I had never met.

'I trust this is true, Dickie,' I said evenly. 'I mean, I know you create awfully good stories, but I hope this is not one of them. Because if it is—'

Indignantly he protested that it was absolutely true, adding, 'Cross my heart and wish to die!' There were accompanying gestures.

I hastily apologized for my scepticism, said it was all very sad and that I trusted the lady had not suffered.

'Shouldn't think so,' he replied airily. 'She was found under the eiderdown clutching an empty gin bottle and wearing a pink rose in her hair . . . Mind you, it was only old grocer's stuff. Grandpa says that when I grow up I should touch nothing less than Gordon's or Tanqueray.' He demolished the penultimate biscuit (while not for the first time I wondered if His Lordship was *quite* the right sort of relative to mentor Sickie-Dickie).

'So, Dickie, are you telling me that this actually happened in her bedroom at the school?' I asked. 'And how awful for whoever found her! I hope it wasn't one of the cleaners; they have enough to contend with as it is.'

'Oh no, Miss Oughterard, it wasn't at the school. It was somewhere else.' The boy sounded vaguely disappointed.

'*Where?*'

He shrugged. 'Don't know. They haven't told us. They just said she had had a mishap and died somewhere. Somebody said it was Brighton.'

When I asked him how he had therefore known about the gin, eiderdown and rose, he said that Hesketh Major had been listening at the staffroom door and had heard every bloody word.

Naturally I rebuked him for the adjective, and suggested that 'single' might have done just as well. He apologized and took the last biscuit.

Not wishing to heighten the drama, I said calmly, 'I expect she had had a tiring day and overdid the necessary remedial. Probably a sudden heart attack. I fear that can happen sometimes.'

Thinking it better not to pursue the crude mechanics of her demise, I then asked him to tell me a little about the woman and, with rose in mind, enquired if she had been a jolly sort.

For a moment he stared at his feet and seemed to brood; and then, looking up, declared that actually she had been a bore of the first water. Hearing this, I was less surprised at his thinking her a bore – a view children often have of their elders – than at its old-fashioned idiom. Doubtless further influence of His Lordship.

'And do you know what?' he continued. 'She didn't know the meaning of petard!'

'What?' I asked, startled.

'*Petard*. She didn't know what it meant because I heard her asking old Pierce, our English master.'

'Er, well,' I replied vaguely, 'perhaps it was just one of those words she hadn't come across. I mean, not everyone—'

'But all grown-ups know what that means. It's what you are hoisted by; a sort of sling thing.'

'No, it's not, Dickie,' I corrected him. 'It's a piece of artillery; like an old-fashioned hand grenade, it explodes.'

'But Shakespeare says that—'

'Yes, but he was using the term "hoisted" as a metaphor for being—' I stopped abruptly. Really, this was hardly the time to be talking of petards and metaphors. A drunken woman employed by Erasmus House had been found dead in bizarre circumstances and the place was in uproar. Come morning I should have to explore! But meanwhile, how to eject Dickie without hurting his feelings? Clearly, our conversation should revert to Bouncer and the splendid gift. Thus, I quickly hustled my visitor back into the kitchen to show him the joyful recipient.

The scene was just as I had envisaged: Bouncer gnawing with foul gusto while watched sourly by Maurice curled at a safe distance on top of the Aga.

At our entry, the dog glanced up briefly, gave a mild wag of its tail and renewed its attack. This delighted Dickie. 'I say, he's really got his gnashers into it now, hasn't he?' he crowed. 'When Cook does some more stew next month I'll try to bring him another one.'

'How nice,' I said hastily. 'Now, I think it's time you peddled back to all that pandemonium before you are missed, don't you? And don't forget to switch on your bicycle lamp. If you come a cropper in a ditch, your grandfather might blame me.' I gave a light laugh.

'Oh *no*, Miss Oughterard,' he replied earnestly. 'Grandpa likes you. He says you know a hawk from a handsaw, whatever that means.'

As I shooed him out, I wasn't quite sure whether to be flattered or worried by the judge's approval. The latter possibly.

I fully realized that things could be awkward for the school. Nevertheless, I had to admit to being intrigued . . . well, wouldn't anyone? Besides, I had my reputation as a trustee and patron to consider. I mean to say, if members of its staff – however drear or lowly – were to be found dead beneath eiderdowns and soused in gin, then surely I should be apprised of the facts and not left to infer them from some whey-faced boy, however eminent his grandfather. Yes, enquiries would be made!

FIVE

The Primrose version

Nicholas Ingaza (my late brother's bane and covert confidant) seems not to understand my quizzical nature and will often accuse me of nosiness. Nonsense, I tell him, curiosity is a most valuable trait, and it is amazing what surprising things (not to say, alarming) casual enquiry will unearth, and that were it not for people like me with a keen interest in local affairs, the world would be a duller and darker place. This of course cuts no ice with Ingaza, who replies grimly that the world would also be considerably quieter and safer. Typical!

Anyway, whatever Ingaza's absurd view, I have to admit to finding Sickie-Dickie's news most intriguing. To put it kindly, Erasmus House is a staid establishment and its ambling regime not noticeably given to drunken horseplay, let alone to deaths of staff members through intemperate excess. As a matter of fact, I had never heard of this Miss Memling and was unaware that the school employed such a thing as an assistant matron. The main incumbent is surely quite enough in the person of Mrs Dragson: a veteran despot fiercely wedded to her duties and an old hand in quelling the boys' wilder antics (while somehow managing to induce in her charges a cringing regard – 'Good Old Dragon' being their usual reference). My young informant had described the headmaster as chuntering like a mad bear. That certainly rang true. Winchbrooke's ration of calm sangfroid is somewhat limited, and I could well envisage the turmoil raging in staffroom and corridors.

But what of its subject, Miss Memling, who, boring though she might have been, had managed to create such tragic upheaval? Had she been driven to drink by serving under the fiery eye of the Good Old Dragon, or had there been something deeper, more complex at work? Frankly, the more I considered the matter, the more my curiosity was stirred – as was my instinct to satisfy it forthwith by approaching the school first thing in the morning.

However, experience and my late brother's blunders have taught me not to be precipitate: there are certain situations which require careful deliberation. Thus, over a leisurely breakfast of blackened bacon and endless coffee, I brooded upon a plan of action. To simply appear at the school and to start asking questions like some pushy journalist would be crude and doubtless unproductive. It was essential that I should have a pretext for being there, something totally unrelated to its current drama and which would not place me in the role of ghoulish spectator. (Naturally, I am no such thing, but people can be *so* quick to criticize!) Armed with a good excuse, I might be able to judge the situation and perhaps get a chance to interrogate Emily Bartlett, the school secretary. We confer from time to time, but she is one of those who means well but is rarely effective. Still, even the least shrewd can occasionally be useful. And who knows, I might encounter Winchbrooke himself and get things from the horse's mouth. Either way, a suitable reason for being there was essential. I mulled it over, and on my third cup of coffee inspiration struck.

It was obvious: I would drop in *en passant* as it were, ostensibly to re-position my paintings which line the main corridor. I have thought for some time that their sequence should be adjusted – i.e. local churches and downland sheep to be displayed before those of a more distant provenance. Also, I am not convinced that they are of the right height for close perusal. Being a decent height myself this presents no problem, but it is amazing how short some people are, and if the pictures were to be lowered by an inch or two their subtleties could be better admired. Yes, this would be an ideal chance to address both missions at once. An excellent idea: a case of two birds etc, etc . . . Or what my father would have called 'a left and a right'. I leapt from the table, tripping over Maurice and making the dog bark. They peered at me reproachfully. 'Tough,' I told them, and ran to collect my coat and brolly.

*   *   *

As I approached the main entrance, the school looked its normal solid self. Well, what did I expect – flames and fireworks? There was nobody about in the grounds, let alone headless ducks (as the staff had been acting, according to Sickie) and all seemed tranquil. Once in the porch, I hovered a few moments before gently pushing the door and slipping in. Here too there was a seemly silence. Presumably the earlier havoc had taken its toll.

I turned into the corridor displaying my paintings . . . and then froze. They were not there, not a single one of them – merely blank spaces which leered at me rudely. Instantly all concern for the dead Miss Memling vanished as my eyes raked the naked walls. I was incensed!

At that moment a child appeared. Not Sickie-Dickie but one of even smaller stature. 'Where are the pictures?' I demanded.

He hesitated, and then mumbled, 'Er, I'm not sure – they have been taken away.'

'Why?' I rasped.

He stared at me blankly, and then with a shrug said nervously, 'Sorry, madam, afraid I don't know and I'm late for my piano lesson.' With that useful information he shot off in the opposite direction. I was left stunned and furious. Clearly, brisk action was required. And without more ado I marched towards Emily Bartlett's office and flung open the door.

As usual she was at her desk typing feverishly . . . Or was it her? The neatly clipped hair was now in tortured curls and the busy fingernails varnished a sickly pink. But as she turned, I recognized the raised eyebrows and pursed mouth.

'Where are my pictures? And what's on your fingernails?' I snapped.

She blinked, and then said, 'I think they look quite pretty actually, and Mr Winchbrooke says they're just the job. As to your paintings – they are in the cellar.'

I glowered. 'Job for what?' I asked. 'And why on *earth* are my paintings in the cellar?' And then, though still reeling from the shock of the empty walls, I recalled my main mission. 'And what's more,' I added, 'what has happened to this Memling woman? As one of the school's trustees it is imperative that I know.'

As quite often, Emily looked pained. She sniffed and, giving a brisk tap to the keybar, said, 'Oh really, Primrose, what a lot of questions, and just when I am so busy!'

There was a brief silence as I adjusted my tone. Stern voice changed to one of coaxing blandishment. This seemed to work, and after I had admired the new hairstyle (crikey!) she became quite fulsome. Thus I learnt all about the impending inspection and Mr Winchbrooke's plans to show the school as being at the forefront of modernity – hence Emily's new nails and awful hair, plus his scheme to 'temporarily' (I would check that) replace my rustic scenes with dubious alternatives.

But as I had hoped, she also told me more of the Memling drama. Apparently, the young woman had been there for only six months, during which time she had made little impact except – as Sickie-Dickie had so clearly stated – by being singularly uninteresting. Quiet, biddable and unassuming, she had drifted around the school like some wraith of Florence Nightingale: looking the part but doing nothing (unless sticking the odd plaster on a muddy knee counts as something). She had been neither liked nor disliked, admired nor feared. 'A nonentity really,' Emily said carelessly, flicking one of the frizzy curls.

So why had she been there at all? I asked. What was her purpose? Emily shrugged but said she thought it was to do with Mrs Dragson's hints of retirement. The deceased had been seen as a possible replacement for when the time came and had been taken on to learn the ropes. The school dentist had made the suggestion – in view of the result, not one of his better ideas – and the headmaster had said he would give it a go.

I was about to ask something further but was interrupted by the simultaneous ringing of two telephones. And while Emily dithered as to which to answer first, and feeling that her usefulness was at an end, I left the office and returned to the main corridor where I lurked and cogitated. As a prelude to my quest, talking with Emily had been a step in the right direction but hardly illuminating. Indeed, if anything, her confirmation of

Memling's dullness made the circumstances of the woman's death all the more strange. Had she bored herself to distraction and thus to the bottle, and then in an access of ennui overdone the dose? It would seem so. But then why on earth that pink rose? Clutching at straws of gaiety? The final pathetic gesture of hope? I stood sombrely, resting my elbows on a windowsill and staring out at the empty quadrangle, visualizing those last inebriated moments under the eiderdown . . .

'Miss Oughterard!' a voice bellowed. 'So glad to see you here. I wanted to explain about your pictures. But we've had a bit of an upset and it's all been very trying! In fact, to tell the truth, it's been damned awful!'

At Winchbrooke's voice the reverie broke. 'That's all right, Headmaster,' I cooed. 'Given the tragic situation, I quite understand and know that the pictures will be back in place the *moment* it is convenient.' This was said with a charming smile and steady eye.

'Oh absolutely, absolutely,' he exclaimed, 'of course, of course! But *they* are coming in a fortnight's time, the government inspectorate, and I've only just got rid of Spikesy. So it's all a bit much!'

'Spikesy?' I enquired, my smile tightening a fraction. 'Do you mean Chief Inspector Spikesy, the nice rational one who replaced the inane MacManus?'

He nodded.

'But why has he been here?' I asked. 'I mean, surely Miss Memling's death was due to—'

'Oh yes, yes, drunk as an owl,' Winchbrooke replied, 'but it's the forensic people – they're not satisfied. They seem to think there was something in the drink – apart from alcohol, I mean. My God, with the inspectors here at any moment and now with the police gearing up, it's all we need! Anyway, dear lady, I fear I must rush off now – Dobbs Minor is having the vapours. I gather Miss Memling gave him some toothache pills and he is now convinced this is a bad omen and will lead to instant death. I must go and calm him down.'

With a swirl of his gown, the headmaster floundered off down the corridor, while I was left mildly dazed. Frankly, the prospect

of being calmed by Winchbrooke was not a happy one, but
presumably the victim would survive.

Back at home I found Bouncer unusually docile, settled in his
basket and giving me only a beady look. Needless to say, the cat
was elsewhere – doubtless harassing some poor mouse in the
garden or the field beyond.
    With things being quiet, and eager to talk over the Memling
business, I decided to telephone Nicholas Ingaza. Naturally I
would be accused of nosiness, but as we hadn't spoken for
some while I was prepared to risk a passing jibe. Occasionally
he can be quite enlivening . . . better to fence with Ingaza than
wilt under Emily's piety or Winchbrooke's explosions.
    I hesitated. Should I dial the art gallery or his home number?
It was nearly midday so the former might be best – but you never
know with Nicholas; like Maurice, his movements are erratic and
he could be anywhere. I began with the home number and was
answered by Eric, his raucous companion.
    'Watcha, Prim,' he bellowed, 'long time no hear! How are
yah, girl?' Fortunately he didn't wait for an answer but went
rollicking on. 'Bet you want His Nibs – well he ain't here.
He's—'
    'At the gallery?' I asked quickly.
    'Nah, in the Smoke fixing a deal. But he'll be back this
evening, catching the six o'clock down from Victoria. I'll tell
him you've phoned. Gladden his heart it will, specially if he's
quids in!' There followed a shattering guffaw, while I laughed
politely.

Evidently 'His Nibs' was indeed quids in, for he returned my call
later that evening sounding almost receptive. 'One's rather tired,'
he drawled smoothly, 'but anything for you, dear Primrose. Now,
how can I help?' (*Dear* Primrose? Yes, drinking obviously.)
    'Oh, nothing in particular,' I said airily, 'but I thought you
might like to know that there's been a little contretemps at the
school here. Quite perplexing really, and it seems that—'
    'Ah,' he cut in, 'you mean the Memling woman, the under-
matron who was found in bed slain by the gin bottle.'

I was astounded, furious. 'How do you know that, Nicholas?'
I seethed. 'You've been up in London, and the whole thing only
happened a couple of days ago. Don't tell me the press has got
hold of it already!'

There was a brief silence followed by a faint giggle. 'Oh dear,
stealing your thunder, am I? So sorry . . . But if you must know,
a little bird told me. You know how it is.'

'A little bird?' I snorted. 'You mean like a racing pigeon, I
suppose.'

'Pacing, not racing. I happened to bump into George Pierce a
short while ago at Brighton railway station. He was patrolling
the platform waiting to meet a friend whose train was late, and
we got talking. Not that he was able to tell me much, but I got
the gist.'

I was puzzled. The name meant nothing to me and I asked
him to enlarge.

'Oh, I thought you might know him. He is one of the beaks
at Erasmus – teaches English or something. He came to the
gallery about a week ago asking if I could loan them some
pictures to replace yours. I gather yours are unfit for purpose.'

'If you mean,' I said coldly, 'that my lyrical landscapes are
unlikely to appeal to the crude tastes of those inspectors, then
technically you are right. Winchbrooke thinks he can impress
them by making a show of so-called modernity. Apparently the
more brash and garish the better.' I paused, before adding, 'I
should have known they might call on your services.'

He let that pass – a further sign he had scored in his London
deal; failure there would have resulted in an instant riposte.
Clearly the mood was mellow: so much so that he suggested we
should meet for a drink when he came over to Lewes to deliver
the new pictures. 'I'll buy you a snifter at the White Hart,' he
said. 'Better that than sitting in your charming drawing room
under the glare of old Scragarse.'

I must explain that Maurice and Ingaza have long shared a
mutual antipathy, and I sometimes wonder if the cat uses an
equivalent term of disparagement. As it happens, the two foes
are not so different, both being thin and dubious, and occasionally disarming. But I doubt that Maurice – unlike Ingaza – is a

tango zealot; though perhaps a sinewy minuet will occasionally grace the midnight rooftops. Who knows what that cat does in its spare time.

Anyway, a drink at the White Hart was fixed for two days hence. I would take Bouncer with me. The dog is beloved of the barman there, and Nicholas is prepared to tolerate his soppy matiness.

SIX

The cat's version

I was just studying a rather bovine mouse and judging when I should make my assault, when Bouncer appeared from behind a bush looking rather smug.

'So where have you been?' I asked.

'I have been talking to Petal,' he replied.

'Talking to Petal? Who is Petal? One of those effete Siamese cats from across the field, I suppose.'

Bouncer hesitated, examining his right paw. And then he said, 'Petal comes from Eastbourne. His people have moved here recently. He is a very big black mastiff. *Very* big.'

'Oh really?' I said sceptically. 'I have never heard of a mastiff with a name like that. It sounds most unsuitable. Are you sure you've got it right? You don't always.'

'Oh yes. He spelt it for me.'

'But spelling isn't your strong suit,' I said benignly. 'I daresay you've got it wrong.'

The dog narrowed its eyes, and then said, 'I have *not* got it wrong, Maurice. His name is Petal: P . . . E . . . T . . . A . . . bloody L. Like those things what flowers are made of. And what's more he has got a special mate called Tarzan.'

'And who is he?' I asked. 'Another mastiff, I suppose. At least the name sounds more fitting.' (Inwardly I was a trifle disturbed. The prospect of a couple of hulking mastiffs roaming about our genteel neighbourhood was not exactly reassuring.)

'Oh no,' the dog replied, 'Tarzan is a titchy little fellow – about your size, I should say, Maurice. He's one of those tiny poodles, all mouth and curls and not much else.'

I blinked. Petal and Tarzan: a gigantic mastiff and a miniature poodle. What a curious alliance. 'I see,' I murmured. 'And have you also spoken to the Tarzan creature?'

Bouncer shook his head but said he had seen him in the distance busy watering a tree. 'Still, I shall soon meet him. Petal has asked me to tea, and the poodle is bound to be there. They belong to the same owners.'

Despite being distinctly nettled by his use of the term 'titchy' as applied to myself, I managed a gracious smile and said that I trusted the tea party would be to his liking.

The dog replied jovially that it was bound to be, especially if there were any cats about. 'Ho! Ho!' he chuckled malignly.

I gave an indifferent swish of my tail. There would be numerous other opportunities to retaliate. And besides, I was currently preoccupied with keeping a surveillance on our mistress. As said earlier, she was beginning to show fresh signs of dangerous activity. I would deal with the dog later.

Thus, before returning to my gatepost at the top of the drive, I jumped briskly on to the windowsill outside her hall and peered in. My vigilance was rewarded, for there was our mistress clamped to the telephone and talking volubly. The fingers of her left hand drummed the table and she wore that familiar frown of indignant protest. Evidently someone was getting a drilling. If merely the town clerk or her so-called friend Emily the school secretary, it would be of no account – par for the course, you might say. But my instinct told me otherwise: the Prim had yet another wretched bee lodged in her bonnet, and one of her closer associates was clearly being apprised of it.

I insinuated my ear through the partially open window. 'And what's more, Charles, as I have always thought,' I heard her say, 'there is something very odd going on there and I intend to investigate . . .'

At that moment she glimpsed me at the window and broke off to make the usual dispersal gestures. I slipped to the ground and continued on my way up the drive. Here, settled on the left gatepost (thankfully re-built after the battering it had received from that appalling mad woman, the target of the Prim's previous foray), I began to cogitate on the absurd whims of humans and of our mistress in particular. My grandfather's sage words come to mind: *Whims are harmless provided they are contained; let loose they can cause unholy havoc.* Unfortunately, our mistress's whims are rarely contained, and the dog and I reap the consequence.

So, I mused, it had been that Charles Penlow person she had been talking to – one of her more balanced associates; there aren't many (and he is certainly better than that shifty Nicholas Ingaza, the Brighton Type, who persists in calling me Scragarse . . . What effrontery to a cat of my calibre!). Perhaps Penlow might be able to exert a calming influence, though I rather doubted this. Once roused and with the bit between her teeth, like the dog, our mistress becomes incorrigible. It had been bad enough with her brother – our previous owner, Francis Oughterard, the vicar – but his imbroglios had been driven by panic, whereas hers develop by cussed obstinacy. I sighed and, extending my paw, tried to bat a passing butterfly. The insect eluded my grasp and flitted away merrily. More frustration; it was too bad! I closed my eyes and turned my mind to reflect on more tangible matters: the consumption of cream and fresh haddock.

SEVEN

The dog's version

Maurice was looking PEE-VISH, but then he often looks like that, so I took no notice and went on with what I was doing: chewing.

'I suppose we shall survive,' he mewed.

'Survive what?' I asked, looking up from my grub.

'Our mistress P.O. – whatever it is she is up to now.'

'Didn't know she was up to anything,' I said. 'Well, nothing except all that painting stuff and those rude words that go with it.' I gave a quick burp and went back to my bowl. But I heard a sigh from the cat. Not a good noise, as it usually means he is about to speak again and interrupt my nosh. I shut my eyes and went on licking the bowl.

I was right of course. The next moment there was a sound of paws hitting the floor as he jumped from the draining board, settled next to me and shoved his face between me and the last bit of meat. 'If you were more alert, Bouncer,' he hissed, 'and less fixated on bones and rabbits, you would know exactly what I was talking about!'

Now, you might think I wouldn't know a word like fixated, but living with Maurice makes you learn a lot of funny words, and I like that one because it's easy to say and remember: FIX-ATE-IT. It means to like something a lot so you gobble it up pronto . . . and I certainly like bones and bunnies. Nothing better! Still, it was a bit rough of Maurice to say that I am not alert. Bouncer is one of the 'lertest dogs EVER! I mean, if it hadn't been for me, that big policeman, MacLoon or Mac something, wouldn't have been rescued last year – or whenever it was. (Yes, I am getting pretty good on *words* but not on *times*. They all seem to muddle together. Oh well, you can't have everything, though the cat thinks it can.)

He went on mewing. And as I was beginning to feel quite full and couldn't remember where I'd left my rubber ring, I thought I might as well listen. I sat back on my haunches and cocked my head on one side. This is a good position because the humans seem to like it (they smile and ruffle my coat), and it's a way of making the cat think I am paying attention. But like I said, this time I really was. Anyway, after one of his shorter miaows Maurice began to jaw.

He said that when that nice boy came to visit P.O. and bring the big bone for me, he had overheard him say something quite interesting about the big school place where she often goes. There had been an IN-CI-DENT. A lady had kicked the bucket in bed and there was a huge RORING IN FUR, or some such. When I asked Maurice why the people were making a noise dressed in fur, he said that the word was f-e-r-o-r-y (or that's how it sounded) and that my ears must be bunged or I hadn't understood. Huh! You bet I hadn't understood. When the cat starts talking foreign, nobody has a clue!

Anyway, he then said that after the Prim had jumped up from the table – making all that din and spilling coffee on my tail – he had decided to follow her when she left the house. He likes doing that, says it's useful stalking practice. 'Smatter fact, the cat is quite good at tracking people, and I told him so once. 'Maurice,' I said, 'for an old cat you're not a bad snooper.' I thought he would be pleased. Huh – like hell he was. He went all hoity-toity and said that he wasn't old and as usual I had got my words wrong, and that he never snooped but just followed his nose and kept a sharp look-out . . . Well, in Bouncer's book that's SNOOPING. But I let it go in case he unsheathed his right claw – he's pretty good at that too. Mind you, I like old Maurice and we play some jolly games together. But you need to be careful and watch your rear. I can tell you, it's not just his eyes that are sharp!

Well, with the mistress out and the cat away, I am going to have a kip in my basket now – a bit of peas and quart, as our old master used to say – and I'll hear what the *snooper* has to say when he gets back.

EIGHT

The Primrose version

As it happened, the following day I was due for my six-month check-up with Herbert Crawley, the dentist who according to Emily had apparently recommended Miss Memling to Winchbrooke. An ideal opportunity to make further discreet enquiry re the deceased.

My visits to Crawley are not exactly the highlights of my social calendar, and normally our conversation – such as it is – confines itself to varieties of toothpaste, runners for the Derby and the exorbitant price of fillings . . . though with mouth agape and deafened by the drill, even these pleasantries are problematic. But with luck something might be gleaned, however small.

When I arrived, it was to be greeted not by some hovering helper, but Crawley himself. He ushered me into the surgery, and after the usual courtesies I expressed surprise at the absence of an assistant and asked if she was on holiday. 'Oh no,' he replied, 'I am currently without any, have been for some time. These days they are either picky or unsuitable. But there's quite a promising applicant being interviewed next week, so I live in hopes. The last one left to go to the Erasmus prep school as a kind of sub-matron.' He paused, and then added, 'Actually it was at my suggestion. I thought she might be better with small boys than with teeth.'

I blinked. 'Er, you mean she wasn't medically qualified?'

'She didn't need to be. Her job was to do the flowers, take the clients' coats, proffer the mouthwash and return their dentures clean and intact. This last she failed to do.'

'Oh dear,' I said sympathetically. 'Why was that?'

'She dropped three lots of teeth – two top pairs and one bottom. All damaged. I can tell you, the clients were none too pleased and I had to claim a hefty amount on my insurance. Besides, she was always spilling the rinse.' Crawley looked pained. 'I had the impression her mind wasn't entirely on the job. She was becoming a liability, so I recommended her to Winchbrooke.' (Evidently the ideal solution.)

'Alas, I gather she has met with a fatal accident,' I murmured. However, as a cue for further intelligence, this failed utterly.

'Yes, I'd heard that,' he said. 'Very sad, but these things happen. Such is life, I fear.' And with that philosophical utterance he turned briskly to his probes, selected the largest and advanced upon my molars.

The session over, and having wished him good luck with the new applicant, I quit the surgery for a café renowned for its cakes. With my freshly spruced teeth this was perhaps a perverse choice, but after the rigours of Crawley's ministrations one invariably feels the need for something sweet and stodgy.

Sipping my coffee and contemplating the cake stand, I also thought of the dropped dentures and spilt mouthwash. It wasn't exactly a major revelation: the woman had merely been clumsy. Well, there are plenty of people like that. Briefly I pictured Francis tripping over the dog, dropping the altar chalice or hitting Pa's thumb with a hammer when they were hanging pictures . . . And yet what musical dexterity! I smiled at the memory. Crawley had said he thought Memling's mind was elsewhere and not on the job. That too was like Francis. Oh yes, there had been quite enough problems to distract my dear foolish brother from matters ecclesiastical! Had this woman, too, harboured some dark and nagging secret? The lavish consumption of gin might suggest so . . .

'Ah, Miss Oughterard,' a voice boomed in my ear, 'we haven't seen you for some time. I trust you are hale?'

I looked up and flashed Mrs Dragson a pearly smile. 'Couldn't be better,' I said. 'As it happens, I've just escaped from the dentist and thankfully all is well.'

'Ah, from Herbert Crawley, I expect,' she replied, settling herself on the chair opposite. 'We have much to thank him for – I don't think!' Seeing my quizzical look, she added, 'I mean about the Memling woman. If he hadn't been so eager to foist her on to Mr Winchbrooke, there wouldn't have been all this drama!' She summoned the waitress and ordered a tomato sandwich, and then, eyeing my cream concoction, said severely, 'Hmm, that won't do the gnashers any good – still, I suppose it keeps old Crawley in work.'

I gave a faint smile and quickly steered her back to the topic of the school's 'drama'. 'Yes,' I said, 'I hear your assistant has died in unfortunate circumstances. It must be awful for you!'

'Rather more awful for her, I imagine,' she replied dryly. 'She wasn't the most riveting of people; still, she didn't deserve that sort of end. Most unpleasant. I suppose she had something on her mind, couldn't cope and took to the bottle – not that she ever indicated there was anything wrong. In fact, she never indicated anything very much, except that she missed the Cape.'

'You mean South Africa? Is that where she came from?'

Mrs Dragson nodded. 'Yes, somewhere in the Durban area, I believe. She would have done better getting a job looking after the wallabies out in the open, far healthier than in cloistered Erasmus with our young scoundrels.'

About to make further inroads into my disparaged cream bun, I hesitated. 'But aren't wallabies Australian?' I queried.

'What? Oh well, springboks then. Either way she should have stayed in the fresh air with the sun and wind. Somebody like that needs a more bracing environment. And what our little wretches need are love and firm handling. Frankly I don't think either was her particular forte: little feeling and no discipline. Still, as I always say, *nil nisi bonum* and all that . . .' She took a bite of the meagre sandwich and then promptly doctored her tea with three lumps of sugar. Hating sweet tea, I instinctively flinched.

'So do you think it was suicide or just a catastrophic mistake?'

Mrs Dragson shrugged. 'Either, I suppose. It's still being investigated.'

At that moment the bell tinkled as another customer entered looking rather breathless. It was Bertha Twigg, the school's beefy gym mistress. 'Hmm, here comes trouble,' my companion muttered, and adopting a genial tone hailed the other to come and join us.

'Ah,' exclaimed Bertha to Mrs Dragson as she plonked herself down. 'Glad I've found you. I've got a message.'

'Really? Who from? And why aren't you in the gym dealing with Fox Minor? It's time for his remedials. He ought to be on the wall bars by now.'

'Yes, but he was late and the headmaster has delivered a *directive* and told me to look for you.' She broke off and, turning to me, said, 'So sorry, Miss Oughterard, I know talking shop is such a bore but this is rather urgent.'

I smiled politely and toyed with the remains of my cake.

'Yes, a directive,' Bertha continued to the other. 'We are all required to assemble in the chapel this evening and say prayers for poor Miss Memling. The senior boys must attend, and he said that you must ensure they are properly attired but that it is essential that those with coughs or colds be excused. He doesn't want any noisy interruptions.'

'But it's my day off,' Dragson protested.

'Not now it isn't,' Bertha replied jovially. 'And what's more, the new chaplain has said he intends to preach a short sermon on the evils of drink. That should be jolly!'

'Well, it won't endear him to Winchbrooke,' Mrs Dragson observed acidly. 'The quickest way to receive his cards, I imagine.'

The two women started to discuss school matters and, glancing at the clock, I saw that it was nearly lunchtime and that Bouncer would be getting restless. Thus, feigning an urgent appointment, I left.

As I walked to the car I pondered what the morning's encounters had revealed of the dead woman. It didn't amount to much: clumsy and inept, ill suited to bossing small boys and apparently not exhibiting much emotional warmth – other than an attachment to South Africa whence she had come. So if she was so fond of that country why on earth leave it? By all accounts Durban was a pretty sophisticated city and would surely have provided as many opportunities for advancement as here. Still, in view of Sickie-Dickie's earlier comments, plus those of Crawley and Dragson, she wasn't the most dynamic of individuals so perhaps professional advancement was not a priority. In which case, what was? Presumably there must have been something. Such brooding was cut short by an awful thought: it was early closing day and I had forgotten to buy fresh dog food for Bouncer. Horror! Summoning all energy, I spurted to the grocer's and arrived just in time to catch Mr Todds closing the blind. I knocked on the glass and made frantic gestures, and he opened the door.

'Forgotten something, have we?' he enquired gloomily.

'Yes,' I gasped, 'nourishment for my poor dog!'

'Nothing poor about Bouncer,' he grumbled. 'A ravening hound, if you ask me.' He brightened. 'I suppose he'll be wanting his favourite, the expensive type?'

I nodded and he disappeared inside. A ridiculous sum of cash was then exchanged for a heavy consignment of 'Dogs' Special Din-Dins' with which I staggered to the car boot.

As I let in the clutch and started to move off, I caught sight of Douglas and Daphne Hamlyn staring into the window of the fishing tackle shop. They were accompanied by a mountain of a mastiff in a pink harness. I was tempted to stop and have a friendly word but, eager to feed my own ravening hound, pushed on.

Driving at just under break-neck speed, I recalled the recent tea party at Podmore Place and made a mental note to ask Charles Penlow to persuade Douglas to join the town council. But in thinking of that afternoon, I also recalled something else. Hadn't the Hamlyns, like Miss Memling, also come from South Africa or lived there for a time? . . . Oh yes, of course they had, for it was to them that Daphne's cousin, Mrs Fotherington, kept sending those letters praising my brother's virtues; and it was why the couple, then so far from England, had been vague about the published details of her death. It was a trivial coincidence. But it made me smile, thinking that if any more springboks were to assemble in Lewes our little town could be 'twinned' with Durban. That would give the council something to crow about!

NINE

The Primrose version

The morning's painting had not been a success. It was one of those days: sheep morose, fields dull, the church two-dimensional and the solitary cow clearly dead. I stared reproachfully at the canvas and cursed. Ah well, perhaps my rendezvous with Nicholas Ingaza would lighten things – or enrage me so much that I would return galvanized for battle and produce a masterpiece.

With that happy thought I discarded my brushes, strode from the studio, nearly tripped on the stairs and rounded up Bouncer. 'We are going out for a little drink,' I said. 'Promise me you'll be on your best behaviour, otherwise no bone this evening.' He seemed to get the message and looked suitably compliant. I fetched his lead and my handbag, while Maurice watched disdainfully from the sidelines, no doubt pleased that he would have the house to himself for a while.

I drove into Lewes, found a space in the small central car park and, having hauled the dog from the back seat, walked down to the White Hart. We were bang on time – well, almost – but no sign of Ingaza. The bartender, besotted of Bouncer, greeted us cheerfully and asked if I would like something while we waited. Normally I would have said yes, but peeved by my feeble showing in the studio that morning and in no mood to sub my own drink, I politely declined and said I could wait. This I did for several minutes, when, just as I was about to succumb to the alcohol imperative, the door opened and Ingaza slipped in.

'So sorry, Primrose,' he oozed, 'had to see a man about a dog – well, a transaction, actually.'

'You don't say,' I replied dryly.

'Oh, but I *do* say. You see it was all rather productive, so much so that I'll buy you a double Sidecar.' He beamed while thin fingers reached for his wallet. I have to admit to being taken aback by such largesse, especially before lunchtime. He must have made a mint!

The first sip entirely changed my mood and I asked him affably if the exchange of pictures at the school had gone all right. He said it appeared so. Stripped of my own landscapes, the walls were in the process of being cleaned and freshly distempered in preparation for the supposedly 'relevant' replacements which he had left with Emily Bartlett in Winchbrooke's office.

'Actually, I don't think she liked me awfully,' he said. 'Can't think why.'

I appraised the slick pinstripe, spiv tie, sleeked greying hair and lazy eyes. 'Some women might,' I said, 'but not Emily.'

'Ah well,' he said smoothly 'can't have 'em all.'

Taking another large sip of my Sidecar, I giggled and said, 'Actually Nicholas, I doubt if you've had any.'

He took it very well, and with a wink and a leer said, 'My dear, so right, so right!'

We got on to other matters: Bouncer at first, whom he tolerated. 'Now that's a normal animal,' he observed, tossing a couple of crisps in the dog's direction, 'not like that godawful cat of yours!'

'Mine?' I queried. 'Well, in a way he is of course. But you will recall that both Maurice and Bouncer were orphaned by Francis; they're his memorabilia, one might say.'

For an instant the sharp veneer softened. 'Yes,' he murmured, 'you're right again . . . his funny old memorabilia.' There was silence as we sat brooding and toyed with our cocktails.

And then, looking up and changing the subject, he asked why I was so interested in the unfortunate Memling affair.

'It's her death of course,' I said, 'it was so odd.'

He shrugged and said that a lot of people died in Lewes and not always explicably, especially those ladies of a certain age. He gave a grin and winked.

'If, as I suspect, you are referring to me, Nicholas, you can think again,' I said indignantly. 'I'm as fit as a flea. Besides, I'm only two years older than you!'

'My dear girl, of course I wasn't thinking of you,' he laughed, 'just all the other old bats. Here, let me get you a top-up.' He went to the bar and returned with replenishments, at the sight of which my annoyance strangely vanished.

'You see,' I explained, 'the thing about Memling was that she was young – well, youngish, about thirty or thereabouts; and as you so kindly informed me when we last spoke on the phone, she snuffed it in the Majestic, not normally an hotel patronized by the plain and insignificant. And why on earth she should have been drinking so heavily, I cannot imagine!' I took another appreciative sip of my Sidecar, while he produced a pack of his customary Sobranies, offered me one and took one himself.

'I met her,' he said casually.

'*Met her?* You never told me that!' I exclaimed.

'Well, the last time we met I had only just got back from London. I was tired and you were in one of your assertive moods – not the time for lengthy reminiscence.'

I let that pass, and said that, as I was now in my meekest mood, would he kindly enlarge.

Apparently she had wandered into his gallery about a month previously, mooched around a bit and then hovered by a poster promoting a talk on fifteenth-century Netherlands art which a pal of his was due to give in a few days' time.

'I saw her studying it and thought she might be a potential punter. So I went up and said that for five bob, including coffee and illustrated brochure, it was excellent value and asked if I should add her to our list? She replied that if she gave me her name I wouldn't believe her. Naturally I evinced polite interest, and she said that she shared her surname with one of the artists – the superb Hans Memling whose *Angel with a Sword* was on our poster!' Ingaza chuckled and flicked his cigarette ash. 'I asked if he was an ancestor but she said she had no idea. I was surprised at that, and said that if I were in her shoes I'd have been making it my mission to find out. Could be money in it, I joked.' (Joke, was it? I suspected he had been deadly serious.)

'Anyway,' he continued, 'she seemed hesitant about the talk, saying she was very busy, and that as to a mission about tracing ancestry, she was currently engaged on a rather more pressing one. I didn't bother to enquire what it was as I had just seen one of my more useful clients come through the door and wanted to catch his eye . . . and frankly wasn't especially interested in any case. But I gave her a brochure for the talk, and said if she changed her mind we could probably squeeze her in.' Ingaza paused before adding, 'Can't say she was the most inspiring person I've ever met – and I rather agree with you, not your ordinary sort of toper. Cocoa and plain water would have been more to her taste, I imagine.'

'*Exactly*, Nicholas,' I broke in. 'It's all the more strange that she should have died in the midst of gin! There's some mystery here and I certainly intend finding out.'

He closed his eyes and groaned. 'No, Primrose, the hand of *anno domini* is upon us, give it a rest. It was bad enough coping with the Topping thing and the Beachy Head business, not to mention your investigation of that dead swimmer last year. For God's sake, don't stir up anything else. My nerves won't stand it and I shall have to calm them in Tangier again.'

'Huh!' I countered. 'Any excuse to return there. Besides, I am certainly not in the grip of *anno domini*. Never felt so good. Positive, that's me!'

'Don't we know it,' he said grimly.

Despite the difference of opinion, we parted affably and I wished him well with his new tango partner (the dreaded Mona having called it a day).

'Oh yes,' he preened, 'another gold cup, I fancy!'

As I left the pub, I glimpsed Sergeant Wilding on the other side of the road pushing what looked like a brand-new bicycle. It was about time too. The previous one had been fit for a museum or rubbish dump.

I have always got on well with Wilding, whose stolid manner and earthy humour I rather enjoy. I wondered if he could shed any light on the Memling business. Winchbrooke had said the police had been at the school making routine enquiries, a procedural requirement in cases of unexplained death. But it was worth checking all the same. Thus, I crossed the road and in my most genial tone congratulated Wilding on his new acquisition.

'It was the inspector's idea,' he explained. 'He said the old one wasn't doing the image of the police force any good. Blow the force, I told him; it wasn't doing my backside any good – the saddle was knackered. His Nibs laughed and said that a first-rate copper with a knackered saddle, let alone anything else, was most unbecoming and he would see to it straightaway.' Wilding gave an appreciative nod. 'On the ball, is our Mr Speakeasy. Not like that pompous idiot, the last one we had . . .'

With those words he eased himself on to the now solid saddle, and was about to move off when I said quickly, 'And how *is* Mr Spikesy these days? Very busy as usual I daresay, though I imagine that when he was at the school the other day it was just a routine visit . . . all very sad of course and so disturbing for the staff.'

'Routine? Yes, yes, it was. But there's been what you might call a fresh development – not that it's my place to comment, of course.' And then with a slow grin, he added, 'Fishing, are we, Miss Oughterard?'

'Perish the thought!' I said indignantly. 'Would I do that?'

'No, of course you wouldn't,' he replied. And so saying, and with a wink and a chuckle, he trundled away.

I watched as he went. Wretched man, he certainly knew how to tantalize!

Back at home, I felt it my duty to go up to the studio. I had a fresh scene in mind and really ought to get started. But too often duty defers to curiosity. Thus, instead of the studio, I opted for the terrace, where, sitting in the sun and nursing a black coffee, I reviewed what I had so far learnt of Aida Memling. It wasn't much, but a picture was gradually forming.

She originally came from South Africa, and according to various reports – including those of Sickie-Dickie, Mrs Dragson, the dentist, Nicholas Ingaza and Emily Barrett – had not been the most vivacious of people, indeed Emily having called her a nonentity (not that one can always rely on dear Emily's judgement, though in this case it did seem to echo the general view). She had not been obviously disposed to drink, let alone to drunken bouts of the kind suggested by her state at the Majestic. And while she had discharged her duties at Erasmus correctly, there had been no obvious sign of matronly zeal.

So far, the one positive clue as to what stirred this woman had been Ingaza's reference to some unspecified *mission*, apparently a matter so important that it eclipsed any urge to trace her possible link with the artist Hans Memling. So, surely, something must have been going on behind that staid exterior. What *was* it that had been directing or taxing her mind?

My thoughts moved from the woman herself to Sergeant Wilding's cryptic remark that there had been a fresh development, and about which he had been so maddeningly discreet. If that were indeed the case, it could surely imply that there really was something more sinister than had first appeared. And if so, then my instinctive hunch had been correct: that her death was distinctly fishy. I turned to Bouncer snoozing at my feet. 'You see,' I said triumphantly, 'your mistress knows a thing or two.' He didn't seem overly impressed, merely opening one sleepy eye and promptly shutting it again. I poured more coffee and basked in the sun and my own satisfaction.

Some while later, just as I was beginning to think of Maurice's supper, the cat appeared from behind the chinchilla cage. Whether he had been sitting there all the time, I don't know; more likely roaming about on one of his field trips. Either way, as always, he was punctual for his evening meal.

But instead of making a beeline for the kitchen, this time he seemed content to loiter in the sun, going so far as to jump on my lap and purr. Goodness, what had I done for such an honour? For a moment the purring ceased as he stretched a languid paw to toy with my sleeve. And then, closing his eyes, the sound softly continued. Had he been human, I would have said he was in a mood of mellow and kindly patronage. But there is nothing human about Maurice!

TEN

The cat's version

Hmm . . . not the most restful of mornings. Bouncer has learnt a new word: *brouhaha* (last year it had been *hullaballoo*). He has done nothing but bellow it all over the garden, terrifying the chinchillas and disturbing me. It is not normally a term in my vocabulary – *shindig*, *furore* and *palaver* being my preferences – and I rather gather that his instructor was Petal, the giant mastiff with whom he had tea the other day. I suppose it is too much to expect a creature of that size to teach him something soft and sibilant, and all I can say is that if he goes on like this, our mistress will descend from her studio and hurl the paint brushes. She has done it before, and has a surprisingly good aim. The last time it happened the dog's backside stayed a startling vermillion for days on end. The vet had to use the clippers.

But Bouncer's derrière aside, the dramatic death of one of the school's staff is becoming more mysterious. When listening to the conversation between the Prim and the bearer of the dog's ham bone, I had assumed that the corpse he referred to had been found in the school itself. But evidently not. During my afternoon prowl, I had decided to drop in on Lola, the school's moderately alert white Angora. She is a vain creature and takes inordinate pride in her ridiculously lush fur coat. However, she is also a handy informant (naturally, one likes to keep abreast of things), and she told me that the dead woman had been found not in her bedroom at the school, but 'elsewhere'. Naturally, I enquired exactly *where* elsewhere. But she merely purred and said wouldn't I like to know. Well of course I wanted to know! But if she imagined I would rise to that kind of tease she could think again – and I doubt if she knew anyway. Thus, with an indulgent smile I gave a nonchalant flick of my tail and strolled into the long grass as if looking for mice. (In such situations it doesn't do to hurry, or they will think they have scored.)

However, on my way home frustration turned to yet further surprise, for scampering across my path was the poodle creature called Tarzan, the small sidekick of Bouncer's new mastiff friend. On seeing me it froze and then yelped, 'Oh Christ!'

This startled me somewhat. During my life I have been called a variety of names – some seemly, some disgraceful (among the latter being the Brighton Type's 'Scragarse') – but never have I been assigned Messiah status. Admittedly, last year I was awarded my CFE – Companion of the Feline Empire; nevertheless, I did feel that this current term was a trifle excessive. I gazed in silence at Tarzan wondering how best to correct the impression.

Tarzan gazed back, little ears flattened and nose a-quiver. I was just about to say modestly, 'Actually, my name is Maurice,' when it squeaked, 'I think your name is Maurice, sir. Bouncer has told me of you.'

Sir? I thought. Well, that's a rarity! I emitted one of my more dulcet mews. Other than its twitching nose, the poodle remained motionless and continued to stare uneasily. As he appeared to know who I was, clearly that initial utterance had not been a case of mistaken identity but simply an oath of shock – no doubt a nervous response to meeting a cat of my status (rather than a commonplace tabby, such as Tiddles down the road). I mewed again and asked casually what Bouncer had been saying of me.

'Oh, he said you were nice, very nice,' Tarzan said quickly. He paused, and then added, 'In fact, sir, he said you were the best cat he had ever known and that it would be an honour for me to meet you!'

Again, I was somewhat taken aback. Such effusive praise coming from Bouncer was not entirely in character. Had he really said those things? I was sceptical. But who knows, perhaps the dog was at last beginning to appreciate my finer points. If so, it was certainly about time. Anyway, I decided to tarry a little longer with the newcomer. After all, he seemed perfectly couth and courteous – which is more than can be said for many canines of my acquaintance.

'I gather you and Petal are new to this area,' I said. 'I trust you find it to your liking.'

The poodle nodded and said that he liked it better than the coast where they had been before. 'We were always being taken for walks on the beach. I didn't like those big waves, they were horrid. And however hard I barked and snapped they wouldn't go away. Beastly things!'

Having only once encountered the sea, I was inclined to agree with his view. 'But what about your friend?' I enquired. 'Did he dislike the waves too?'

'Petal? Oh no, he loved them. Petal paddled. He tried to swim once, but there were complaints from the humans because they said he frightened the children; he's a bit big, you see.'

Yes, I could imagine the scene: small toddlers, like kittens, cavorting in the shallows, their gentle play suddenly broken by some hulking hound launching itself upon the waters in a tidal wave of raucous delight! Shuddering inwardly, I smiled and asked if the creature missed the seaside.

Tarzan said that he did rather and would sometimes get a bit mopey. 'And even when I dance on my hind legs and do tricks for him, he doesn't laugh as much as he used to. But when Bouncer came to tea he cheered up no end! They had big noisy games and I turned somersaults in the flowerbeds.'

'But what about your owners?' I further enquired. 'Didn't they object? Many humans make a fuss about that sort of thing, especially if one of the players is an unknown intruder.'

'Oh no. They weren't there. You see, it was one of those days when they disappear to that big place – London, I think it's called. In fact, that's what they have done today . . . which is why I have been able to slip out and explore this nice wood – *and*, sir, meet you!' The poodle beamed and executed a quick pirouette.

Clearly, in the course of our conversation it had lost its initial fear and was now fully at ease . . . although, I was pleased to note, still showing a proper respect. Thus, smiling benignly, I waved a gracious paw and murmured that I had some pressing business to attend to (i.e. my supper). Tarzan took the hint, and with cheerful squeaks scampered off, presumably to continue his woodland reconnaissance.

I continued on my way feeling considerably better than when I had been affronted by Lola. At least Tarzan took me seriously. Naturally, vanity is not one of my traits, but being a cat of some distinction – my recent decoration (Companion of the Feline Empire) testifying to that – I do think that some deference is due. This I had certainly received from the poodle. Whether its friend will echo that courtesy remains to be seen. Anyway, with lifted spirits, I returned homeward in genial mood.

When I slipped through the garden hedge, I saw our mistress sprawled in a deck chair on the terrace. For once she seemed peaceful – not rushing around, as is often the case, or jabbering down the telephone. So, temporarily shelving the idea of haddock, I thought I would linger a little and bid her good evening. I sprung onto her lap and teased the sleeve of her dress and then, nicely settled, closed my eyes. She had seemed a trifle surprised by my attention – unlike the dog, one is not given to excessive display – but for ten minutes we enjoyed a companionable silence.

ELEVEN

Erasmus House

A	s was to be expected, Mr Winchbrooke was not in a happy frame of mind. The last few days had been frightful, and once everything was resolved and life back to normal – as it surely would be – he had a good mind to retire. Robinson at Worthing had done it, and on very feeble grounds; whereas he was years older and had far more to cope with. Far more! He bit his thumb and scowled.

She had *said* she was going to Frinton to visit a sick friend, and he had wished her well. Instead of which she had turned up in a bedroom at the Brighton Majestic, conspicuously drunk and dead. Extraordinary. On the other hand, it could have been worse: she might have expired within the precincts of the school itself. At least they had been spared that! He shut his eyes and gave thanks for small mercies.

Opening them again, he thought of another small mercy. He had feared that Primrose Oughterard would kick up a fuss about the replacement of her pictures, but she had been surprisingly docile. The new lot were now in place, all ready for the arrival (and approval) of the inspectorate. Fortunately a number of days would elapse before those jolly fellows descended. But meanwhile he had to parry the persistence of the local press, answer damn-fool questions from the police (how on earth should *he* know who her relatives were?), and deal with agitated phone calls from parents worried that their precious offspring might be disturbed. Disturbed? Like hell! *Delighted* would be more accurate. Podcraft of the fourth form (son of the popular journalist) had already produced a stupid article on the event, though fortunately confiscated by the English master – not so much on account of the content as its grammar, which was execrable.

And now, on top of everything else, there was yet further

horror: the school boiler had burst that morning and the mainte-
nance men unable to fix it for at least two days. With a groan
he dwelt gloomily on shattered pipes and icy bath water, glared
at the overflowing in-tray and slumped in his chair to await the
next excitement.

It came in the form of his secretary, Emily Bartlett. She marched
into the office and placed a sheet of typed foolscap on his desk.
'What's that?' he asked.

'It's your speech for this evening,' she said briskly. 'I've
checked the punctuation, deleted a few words and rearranged the
last paragraph. But it's all there and you should have no trouble
with it.'

He stared at her, bemused. What on earth was she talking
about? 'Your speech, Headmaster,' she reminded him, 'the one
you are giving to the senior boys this evening about our sad loss:
your preliminary address before the chaplain's sermon on the
dangers of drink.'

Oh Christ, of course, the assembly at six o'clock! He cleared
his throat, smiled falsely and gave fulsome thanks for the scrupulous editing. When she had left, he took a red pencil and
carefully reinstated the doctored parts. Then, opening his desk
drawer, he withdrew a flask of brandy.

In fact, despite the headmaster's gloom, the evening's assembly
passed off moderately well. The boys had been orderly (except
for Podcraft who was sniggering and had to be sent out), the
masters suitably grave – or at least looked so – and his own
address had hit just the right note between shocked concern and
kindly reassurance.

Earlier in the day he had taken the precaution of speaking
firmly to the chaplain, suggesting he tone down his proposed
'evils of drink' theme. After all, the school was training the
children for the *world*, not for entry into some prissy puritan
seminary! Besides, he had reasoned (to himself as much as to
the chaplain), too much emphasis on alcohol might have the
opposite effect – far from deterring, it might induce undue curiosity. The less said about her drinking habits – or anyone else's

– the better. 'Stick to God and prayer,' he had advised. Aware of which side his bread was buttered on, the chaplain had duly complied, deleted the colourful bits about the snares of gin and replaced them with words on the restorative value of prayer and the dangers of smoking. ('If God had wanted us to smoke,' he had inserted jovially, 'he would have made us all chimneys!')

Naturally, in his own tribute to the deceased, Winchbrooke could not altogether ignore the alcohol factor, but he avoided it as best he could. Thus, he had glossed over the actual amount she had imbibed (a full seventy-five-per-cent litre bottle, plus probably earlier draughts) and played up her dodgy heart. 'Remember, boys, even a small amount of alcohol when coupled with a weak heart can go a long way – and alas, that was the case with poor Miss Memling. Most of you will know' – most did not – 'the Latin phrase *multum in parvo*. Normally that is used to mean something positive, but it can also be the opposite: i.e. much bad is sometimes contained in little matter. In other words, even trivial actions can have tragic results.' He had paused to let that sink in, though was disappointed by the blank faces.

Nevertheless, pleased with his little homily and with the subject of drink safely out of the way, he pushed on quickly to sing her praises. In preparing his speech, this part had been the most difficult to concoct. But after some thought he had come up with three traits which, at a stretch, she could have been said to exhibit: a decorous sense of duty, a self-effacing modesty and a quiet deportment. 'Qualities which we should all try to emulate,' he had declared. This last injunction had been followed by a grim stare at Briscoe's sardonically raised eyebrow. The deputy head had been sitting poker-faced in the front row and it was his first sign of animation.

A few sentences later, and having warned his audience of the dangers of rumour, gossip and the crude embellishment of questionable facts, Winchbrooke reached his peroration – a stern reminder of the arrival of Her Majesty's inspectors the following week and the need for every boy to give of his most loyal best. 'The future of our school depends on *you*!' the headmaster barked. A rousing version of 'Fight the Good Fight' (to the accompaniment of drum and trumpet) had then been lustily sung – an outpouring which made the chaplain's sermon on the avoidance of cigarettes and the benison of peaceful prayer seem a trifle bland.

Afterwards, as they adjourned to the dining room (the headmaster having escaped to the welcome of wife and accommodating whisky), Briscoe was heard to murmur to Mrs Dragson, 'Anyone would think that Memling's consumption of alcohol had been utterly minimal and those few drops merely for medicinal purposes!'

'And why the Majestic?' she had whispered. 'We thought she was off to Frinton.'

Others had overheard and joined in. 'Perhaps she had a lover,' the new geography master suggested helpfully, 'and wanted to impress him. Ladies will sometimes do that.'

'Is that your experience?' Briscoe had asked coldly.

The geography master blinked and said vaguely that he wasn't quite sure.

'In which case,' the deputy head dryly observed, 'perhaps you should confine your research to maps and isobars and not enter into the realms of speculative psychology.'

The geography master said nothing, but inwardly wished he could devise a means of killing the speaker without being found out.

The next day Mr Winchbrooke felt considerably relieved. Yes, he told himself, the evening had gone well and his words seemingly appreciated. The lady had been given her due and, as directed, the chaplain had made no mention of the drink issue and had preached a passable sermon. Some of the boys had actually appeared interested. So, with a bit of luck he could now temporarily shelve the Memling thing and concentrate on essentials: plans and ploys for the coming inspection.

Thus it was with some annoyance that when the telephone rang he heard Inspector Spikesy's voice requesting more information. Really, what now! They had already given the police one interview, not to mention saying generously that if no relative came forward to claim the body once it was released, the school would cooperate with the local council in arranging a civic burial. For goodness' sake, he silently fumed, what more was expected? As it happened, quite a bit more.

'There's been a development,' the chief inspector said, 'and I'd be glad if you could be available to answer a few more questions. We'll be with you in a couple of hours if that's convenient.'

It wasn't remotely convenient but the headmaster reluctantly agreed. 'So what's the development?' he enquired.

'Poison – or it amounts to that. Methaqualone. It was in the drink. Combined with booze and a weak heart, it's invariably fatal. No wonder she died. Could even have been murder.'

Winchbrooke gazed up at the ceiling and mentally began to compose his letter of resignation.

TWELVE

The Primrose version

I had called in at the chemist to pick up some more antiseptic (essential for gardening mishaps), when I bumped into Douglas Hamlyn waiting to be served. He said how much they had enjoyed our meeting at the Penlows' and that Daphne was going to telephone to invite me for a drink. Naturally I said that I should be delighted, especially as, having glimpsed them with Petal the other day, I was dying to meet the dog. 'He looked very handsome in his pink harness!' I added. Douglas laughed and explained that they had deliberately chosen that colour as it reassured people, especially children, who would occasionally be alarmed by his gargantuan size. 'You see, he is really as soft as soap, and with not a vice in the world,' he said.

I smiled, thinking of the anarchic Bouncer.

He turned to give his order at the counter – the usual things such as razor blades, plasters and so on, but also, I couldn't help noting, sleeping pills and a packet of migraine tablets. This last caught my attention, as in my younger days I too had suffered from this type of headache and knew how wretched it could be. I wondered if they were for him or for Daphne, and was about to ask, but stopped. It was too early in our acquaintance for such enquiry. From somewhere above I heard my mother's reproving voice: *Think before you speak, Primrose, or people may think you are being familiar. And we wouldn't want that, would we?* No, we wouldn't.

Douglas must have told his wife of our encounter immediately he got home, for that afternoon she telephoned to ask if I would be free that evening which, as it happened, I was. She suggested I might like to bring Bouncer, but I thought it best to leave him be. He had already exercised his lungs on baiting the chinchillas, playing tag with squirrels and harassing an escaped sheep; quite

enough alarms and excursions for one day without being faced
with the social stimulus of other canines!

Needham Court basked peacefully in the evening sun. I mention
this because the last time I was there it had been the dead of
night and in somewhat tense, indeed furtive, circumstances. Now,
in daylight and under new ownership, I saw it from a more
congenial angle. And whereas before I had been creeping about
in some nervousness, now I could approach boldly and with the
prospect of a cheery welcome.

This I certainly had, not only from the new owners but also
their two dogs who – unlike the Penlows' dour Duster – seemed
delighted to greet me. The poodle pranced and the mastiff
(divested of its pink harness) slowly wagged a friendly tail. Later,
as we sat on the terrace sipping martinis, it came to sit beside
me and thrust its jowly face against my knee. Whether this was
done out of politeness or because it caught a whiff of Bouncer
upon me, I wasn't sure. Either way, I didn't object.

I asked if Douglas was getting as much fishing as he had
hoped. He nodded enthusiastically, saying it couldn't be better
and he had joined the local angling club. 'But you know, what
I really enjoy as much as the sport itself is being able to wander
along the river bank at dusk listening to the fish jumping and
the hoot of an early owl. I'll take a rod with me, but quite often
I am happy to sit and do nothing, just savouring the night air. I
suppose it's what you might call communing with nature.' He
smiled.

'Yes,' Daphne cut in, 'communing with nature and then coming
home with midge bites and damp trousers and demanding a
second supper!'

We laughed and I asked about her interest in Anne of Cleves,
mentioned at the Penlows', and if she was really thinking of
writing a novel on the rejected bride. She said that the idea was
certainly getting a grip and that, as hoped, moving to Lewes had
triggered fresh insight – but whether she could deal with an actual
novel, she wasn't too sure. Perhaps a short story or a couple of
articles.

'Huh,' Douglas snorted. 'Daphne will write a novel all right, you'll see. Very inventive is my wife, and she's a persistent eager beaver. Once she has decided on something she won't let it go. Plenty of grit there!'

Hmm, I thought, someone after my own heart. Not like dear weedy Emily.

And thinking of Emily, my mind switched to the Erasmus House business. I was just about to ask if they knew about it when Douglas exclaimed, 'It must be ghastly for the prep school and the curious death of that matron. I wouldn't want to be in the headmaster's shoes, would you? There's bound to be some sort of enquiry going on. I gather it has quite a sound reputation and the current chap has a steady pair of hands.' Personally, I thought that a bit of an exaggeration, but being a trustee and as the school housed a number of my pictures (albeit temporarily confiscated!), I did owe Winchbrooke some loyalty, and so said nothing but nodded vaguely.

Daphne was less vague, for with a snort of laughter she cried, 'Steady hands? I doubt it; he practically pranged my car this morning, missed the wing mirror by inches, and never a word of apology. He was with another man, and when they got out he was clutching him with one hand and gesticulating violently with the other. It was too early to have been drinking but he did look distinctly wild!' She started to pour me another martini but was interrupted by the ringing of the telephone and, slipping from the room, left Douglas to complete the task.

While she was gone, we discussed the two dogs whom they had rescued from an Eastbourne animal sanctuary. 'Actually,' he said, 'it was the tiny poodle that caught our eye, but it refused to be separated from Petal and kicked up an awful fuss. So as we were soon to move to this large place, we took the mastiff as well. Apart from a mammoth appetite, he's no trouble at all.'

We touched on other things: their time in Durban, which apparently he had much enjoyed, but all the same was glad to be back in 'the old country' which he had started to miss. Knowing that the Memling woman was also said to be from that part, I asked if the name meant anything to him. He said he had heard of such a family but couldn't entirely place them. He frowned, trying to recollect . . . But being more concerned with Sussex than with South Africa, I changed the subject and took the opportunity to say he might like to put himself forward for the town council, or better still the county; but he didn't seem terribly keen, so I didn't pursue it. And at that moment Daphne returned.

'That was Rufus,' she announced, 'jawing as usual.' Turning to me, she apologized for the interruption, explaining that he was her brother who lived in London and was an actor, and like many thespians took himself a mite seriously. I asked if I would know him.

'Shouldn't think so,' Douglas said. 'Rufus rests a lot.'

'O come now, Doug, that's a bit unfair,' Daphne protested. 'It's these theatrical agents; they can be so lazy, and I keep telling him to get someone else. Besides, he may not be Laurence Olivier, but he's been in two good productions recently and the critics were quite generous.'

Her husband had bent to pick up Tarzan who promptly started to lick his face, so his reply was muffled, though it sounded a little like, 'So that makes a change.' But one couldn't be sure.

Declining a third martini (invariably less enticing than the first) I said that I really must be going as my own less than biddable creatures would be tearing the house down. And so after kindly farewells and valedictory noises from Tarzan and Petal, I left Needham Court and made my way across its manicured lawn and out through the wicket gate into the lane. Here, like Douglas on his riverbank, I paused to sniff the evening air and to gaze at the now shadowy outline of the distant downs. There was no hurry: failing an almighty scrap, the house would be intact and the animals curled peacefully in their respective lairs: Bouncer in his basket and Maurice – unless on mouse patrol – in the cupboard under the stairs.

Thus, walking slowly, I reflected on my genial hosts and made a mental note to reciprocate at some point. They seemed a well-suited pair: the older husband being the quieter of the two and the perhaps more staid, and the wife brisk and vivacious – what one might call a good team. My earlier fears that they might re-open the subject of the dead Mrs Fotherington had proved groundless. Still, it doesn't do to be complacent (as Francis had been only too aware) and one would need to be careful. I had a momentary image of Pa forever bellowing Baden-Powell's dictum: *Be prepared!* As children, of course, we never were, hence the incessant falls from trees and bicycles.

Back in the present, my thoughts turned to Daphne's actor brother and I wondered if Rufus was part of his stage name. I can't say it meant anything to me, so perhaps professionally he used another . . . though given Douglas's somewhat negative comments, that might not mean anything either. Still, as Daphne had rightly said, not everyone can be an Olivier.

However, it was not the brother that interested me as much as her description of Winchbrooke and his 'wild' behaviour and erratic driving that morning. Admittedly the headmaster is not the most docile of people and can certainly get ruffled, but venting his spleen in quite such a public way was surely unusual. I wondered who he had been with – the doubtless nervous passenger and recipient of his vehement outburst. Presumably a member of staff, probably his deputy Thomas Briscoe. Yes, it was bound to have been some school matter . . .

A screech owl hooted. Its shrill cry cracked the silence and gave me a jolt. But it gave me something else: a sudden thought. Of course, it was obvious! Winchbrooke's agitation that morning was surely connected with the Memling affair and the 'fresh development' about which Sergeant Wilding had been so coy. Yes, that must be it. Some fact concerning the dead woman had come to light, a fact so worrying as to put the headmaster into a flat spin!

Consumed with curiosity, I quickened my pace from stroll to stride, keen to get home to relax over a coffee and ponder tactics, i.e. devising the best means of discovering more. For more there certainly was!

THIRTEEN

The Primrose version

S urprisingly, that night I slept extremely well and awoke at dawn with renewed resolution to pursue my quest. Clearly, the only way to discover what was going on was to approach the school again. A member of staff had died in bizarre circumstances, and this time I would use no pretext for my visit. After all, I argued, I was a long-serving trustee, and that being the case there were things I should most certainly know about! Thus armed, I drove to the school and parked boldly in front of the headmaster's window.

But when I entered, to my surprise and rather as before, there was nobody about – this time not even a solitary child on its way to a music lesson or anywhere else. Goodness, I thought, given the circumstances, had all the parents descended to sweep their offspring away? Surely not. But then in the distance I heard the sound of a vacuum cleaner and, following my ears, I encountered one of the cleaners shunting the machine around and smoking a fag. Raising my voice, I asked her where everybody was.

'Well, they're all gorn, aren't they? Most of them at any rate,' she said.

'Gone? Gone where?'

She switched off the hoover and, flicking ash on to the floor, explained that the English master had organized a big outing to Stratford-upon-Avon to see some play or other and a number of staff had gone too. 'His Lordship is here and one or two others – and that snooty secretary of course – but most of the rest is gorn. A good job too. We can 'ave a bit of peace and quiet.' So saying, she dug in her overall for a fresh cigarette and, switching the machine to full throttle, continued her hoovering.

I too went at full throttle – to Emily's office. But there was no sign of her, though I did catch the drone of voices from

Winchbrooke's study immediately adjacent. I was tempted to march straight in but I suppose it wouldn't have been the most subtle of moves. Instead, I went along to the staffroom where I found Emily and Bertha Twigg sipping tea.

'Hello!' Bertha cried cheerily and offered to fetch another cup (politely declined). Emily, evidently thinking she was being clever, tittered and asked if I had come to check on the safety of my banished pictures.

I ignored this, but, glancing at her fingernails, said helpfully that if she wanted to impress the inspectors when they came she had better wear a different brand of polish. 'It's amazing how quickly cheap varnish chips.' I smiled, looking pointedly at her forefinger.

She pouted and tossed her head.

These little pleasantries over, we got down to serious matters – Miss Memling and the fresh development. I was about to make polite enquiry but I didn't need to, for without prompting, Bertha Twigg had told me all. 'We had fun yesterday,' she said gaily. 'The police were here and took away some stuff from Miss M's room – papers and a notebook. And do you know what,' she added, round eyed, 'they think someone may have slipped her a MICKEY FINN!'

Even as I absorbed this astonishing news, I couldn't help being amused that Bertha should be familiar with that particular term or take such relish in using it. Perhaps in addition to her craze for physical jerks and the gym's vaulting horse she was a secret devotee of the American crime writers Hammett and Spillane. If so, as an addiction it was several steps up from Emily's crochet and jigsaw puzzles.

I asked what sort of Mickey Finn it had been. Bertha looked vague, but Emily said firmly, 'One of the constables said it was metha-something. It's a kind of sedative.'

Such technical knowledge from Emily also surprised me, and I asked how she knew.

'Oh, I think Mother told us once . . . She used to know lots of things; doesn't now, of course, except how to be difficult.' Emily gave a martyred sigh and studied her index finger with its chipped nail polish.

'It's all very curious, isn't it!' Bertha exclaimed happily. 'I mean, it's not every day that one works at a school where a murder has been committed!'

'It was *not* at the school,' Emily said severely. 'It was at that expensive hotel in Brighton. Nothing to do with us at all. Besides, we certainly do *not* know that it was murder! Nothing has been announced officially. For goodness' sake, Bertha, be careful what you say. Loose talk can be dangerous, as Mr Winchbrooke so rightly reminded us the other evening. We do have our reputation to consider. Personally, I find the whole thing distasteful and embarrassing.'

Bertha looked suitably chastened. And I have to admit that, priggish though she often is, Emily did have a point. Miss Memling's peculiar fate was not something Erasmus House or any school would wish to advertise. Years later of course it might become a plus, but at the present time it was a definite minus!

Having ascertained the essentials, I left them to it and returned to my car. Passing Winchbrooke's study, I could still hear a rumble of voices: presumably the headmaster and senior staff discussing what to do next – either about the police interruption or the approaching inspection. Both probably. No, not a nice position for Winchbrooke, and I felt a degree of sympathy – for his wife too, who would doubtless be bearing the brunt of it all.

But the new revelation had certainly spurred me on, and I was determined to get to the bottom of the thing. Despite what Ingaza keeps saying, I am *not* nosey, but simply one who is intellectually stimulated and who takes her civic duties seriously. When convenient, of course.

As I left the building to go to my car, I sensed a movement to my right. 'Psst!' a voice hissed. I stopped abruptly, unused to being so accosted. A small figure appeared from behind a clump of bushes.

'What on earth are you doing, Dickie?' I exclaimed. 'I thought all the boys were supposed to be away in Stratford seeing a play. And why all this cloak and dagger?'

'Well, you see, Miss Oughterard,' Sickie-Dickie whispered, 'I was given detention and gated. Daddy is upset because he knows a lot about Shakespeare and this Macbeth person and says I've missed a treat. But Grandpa said it served me right for being caught.'

'Caught at what?' I asked.

He lowered his voice conspiratorially. 'For sneaking into her room when I shouldn't.'

'Whose room? Mrs Dragson's I suppose. But if you must push in uninvited what else can you expect? Still, being gated does sound rather an extreme punishment for—'

'*No*, not hers, Miss Memling's! The Dragon's been jolly nice and given me some toffees.'

I was intrigued. 'So what were you doing there? And in any case how did you get in – wasn't the door locked?'

He explained that it should have been, but the janitor had been in such a hurry for his lunch that he had left the key in place. 'Old Perks is a bit absent-minded these days, and my pal Sparks saw it dangling in the lock and dared me to go into the room and see what was what.'

'And what *was* what?'

Dickie shrugged. 'Nothing. It was just boring.'

'In what way?'

He replied that it was dull, with nothing interesting. 'Just her white starched apron slung over a chair, and a dressing table with ladies' things on it – a jar of hand cream, hair curlers and all that stuff. There were some dead flowers in the wastepaper basket, a bit smelly I thought, and with some crumpled paper from that nice Mr Ingaza's art gallery in Brighton.'

Ingaza's gallery? This rang a tinkling bell. Casually, I asked him what sort of paper, and he said it had looked like brochures to do with paintings. He had been about to snaffle one to prove to Sparks he had been in her room when he noticed a small unframed picture of an angel sellotaped to the wall high above the dressing table, and which he thought might have come from one of the brochures. 'It had whopping wings and seemed to be holding a sword. I am quite good at drawing angels,' he said modestly, 'so I thought I would take a closer look . . . but that was my, my, er – *downfall*, Miss Oughterard!' he whispered dramatically.

'Goodness gracious, Dickie, whatever do you mean?' I exclaimed.

He said that to get a closer view he had scrambled on to the dressing table, and in so doing clumsily overturned its folding looking-glass and sent the whole thing crashing to the floor. 'There was a fearful noise and glass everywhere. And then the door opened and in came Mr Briscoe.' Dickie sighed and shook his head. 'So I knew I'd had it.'

'Hmm,' I said dryly, 'what one might call a classic case of breaking and entry.'

'Or entry and breaking.' He giggled.

I smiled, asked if he would like some more toffees to supplement Mrs Dragson's and reached under the dashboard.

'Oh yes, please, Miss Oughterard,' he said gleefully. 'I was hoping you might have some!'

As I drove off, I warned him not to tell his grandfather of my gift as I shouldn't like to come up before him on a charge of giving succour to gated criminals. 'Oh, he would be very lenient, Miss Oughterard. Like I said before, he *likes* you – it's the others who have to watch out!'

Driving home, I pondered two things: what would the good judge, Sir Richard Ickington, have thought of my criminal brother; and why had Miss Memling been so attached to the *Angel with a Sword* that she had felt the need to tear out a photo of the painting and, rather like a schoolgirl, stick it on her bedroom wall?

FOURTEEN

Emily Bartlett to her sister

My dear Hilda,

Since my last letter, here at Erasmus the most extraordinary – and unsavoury – events have occurred. Oh, nothing to do with the inspection (yet to come) but in connection with that assistant matron I may have mentioned. She has been found dead!

Now, you may think that such a thing is unfortunate but unremarkable. But I can tell you, Hilda, the whole business has been distinctly strange and shocking. (Naturally, I would have called you, but since you tell me that Mother's unusual burst of activity has sabotaged everything in sight, including the telephone cord, I feel that a letter may reach you more speedily, and I shall rush to the Post Office the moment this is finished.)

Anyway, as said, matters here are most disturbing and I have been inundated with extra work which is extremely tiresome. You see, the lady in question was discovered expired at Brighton's Majestic (not the most retiring of places) clasping of all things an empty bottle of gin! To have been found like that in the hotel bar would have been bad enough, but this was in one of its bedrooms if you please! And now something worse has emerged: the autopsy shows that in addition to the gin she had been imbibing some frightful drug, and it was this in combination with the alcohol that did its worst. As said, it is all very unsavoury. And frankly I think it should be a lesson to Mr Winchbrooke to be more particular as to whom he employs in future. I mean to say, this kind of thing puts the school in a most embarrassing position – not to mention those of us who are connected with it and work so tirelessly to preserve its good name. Incidentally,

Hilda, on <u>no</u> account tell Mother of any of this – she will either suffer a heart attack or explode with mirth and have a distasteful accident. Neither will be helpful.

And talking of not being helpful: Primrose Oughterard was here this morning, lurking around and trying to wheedle more information out of Bertha Twigg and myself. Foolishly, Bertha told her about the matter of the drug. I say foolishly, because if I know Primrose she will put two and two together, make six and declare the matter sinister. It is not in the least sinister, merely shocking and sordid.

Of course, things are not helped by the prospect of the inspection. Mr Winchbrooke is churned up enough as it is, but as you can imagine, these recent events have not exactly soothed his worry. The local police have been here asking questions about the deceased and her habits, but since she was new and rather uncommunicative there wasn't really much that anyone could say. I believe one or two of her belongings were removed, but whether this is significant I wouldn't know. It may just be a required procedure. Anyway, I gather it is the Brighton police who are leading enquiries, and these will doubtless be largely directed at the Majestic where the grisly event occurred. Thus I like to think that we at Erasmus will be left in peace to deal with the coming inspection!

To ensure top marks, Mr Winchbrooke is eager to present the school as being at the forefront of modernity. Thus, in addition to his earlier sartorial advice, he has now suggested that I should get a curlier perm and apply nail varnish. I have to say, Hilda, at first I was reluctant to do this – recalling Mother's appalling scarlet in the old days. But having selected a subtle shade of pink, I think it rather suits me: what one might describe as understated yet distinctive. Needless to say, dear Primrose has already made disparaging remarks, but then she would, wouldn't she!

Oh, and talking of Primrose, I happened to be in Brighton yesterday and saw her and the awful hound outside the Ingaza Art Gallery in close conversation with its dubious owner. I say 'dubious' because although in a spivish way he always looks very smart (too smart, Mother would say), I am not entirely convinced of his probity: a sharp operator, if you know what I mean – though doubtless P. would declare him a paragon of virtue!

Ah well, a busy bee as always, I must sign off now – but do get that telephone fixed and try to divert Mother from further rampage.

Your devoted sister,
Emily

FIFTEEN

The dog's version

'She's definitely going bananas,' I said to Maurice, 'because when—'

'Do not say that!' he hissed.

'What? That she's going ban—'

'Be quiet!' he hissed again and poked me with his claw.

I flattened my ears and backed away. What was wrong with the rotter? We had spent a fine time earlier shouting at the chinchillas, Boris and Karloff, and rocking their cage – or at least, it's me that rocks; Maurice springs on to the roof and dangles his tail in front of their wire. It sends Boris mad! So what the hell was bugging the cat? Maybe he couldn't stand the idea of the Prim getting all het up again and spinning around like that top Tarzan was playing with the other day. When she gets like that the cat complains and says it disturbs his *mee-using*, whatever that's s'posed to mean.

'Ah,' I growled in a matey way, 'I expect you are worried that the Prim is going to have one of her turns. Is that it?'

'No, Bouncer, that is not it,' he said in his most cattish voice. 'It is your use of that word. I have told you before not to use it.'

'Uhm, I'm not quite sure what you mean,' I began, a bit puzzled.

'B-A-N-A-N-A-S!' he screeched. 'You know they make me ill!'

I shut my eyes tight till the sound died down. And then it came back to me: a long time ago when the cat had lived with that lady what the vicar killed, he had stolen some of her lunch and was then sick for days afterwards. The vet said it was the banana and that he was LERGIC to it. I think that means it churns him up no end. Anyway, I do vaguely remember that he told me once never to use the word . . . but if I listened to everything His Nibs tells me I would go bananas myself. Ho! Ho!

'I am SORRY!' I barked at my very loudest (anything to keep the peace), and noticed that this time it was Maurice who shut his eyes. When he opened them, he seemed to look surprised and a bit NON COMPOST, as F.O. the vicar used to say. Most likely this was because the cat is not used to me pologizing . . . not like that little Tarzan chap who does it all the time. Doesn't mean it, of course. For instance, the other day when we were playing in that big garden belonging to his people, I was just about to bite the ball when the little tyke nicked it from right under my nose and yelped, 'Oh, so sorry, Bouncer, so very sorry!' and raced off at top speed and turned a double somersault. Mind you, the cat is rather taken with the poodle's 'good manners' and says he is 'the couthest canine' he has ever known. (Not sure what that means, but I think it's a kind of good mark – which coming from the cat is quite something.)

Anyway, back to our mistress. As I was trying to tell Maurice, when she came home from that big school place she looked very thoughtful – in fact nearly forgot to give me my grub and I had to keep reminding her by making big burping noises. And then after she had at last filled my bowl she went into the study – the place where all the books are – and sat for a LONG time at her desk. She wasn't doing anything, just sitting. Not even reading the paper. I nudged my head round the door a couple of times, but she didn't notice. Too busy *mee-using*, as Maurice would say.

But then there was suddenly a crash from the study like a chair being kicked over, and the next moment she was pounding up the stairs to the painting place, muttering something about angels. Well, I just hope she isn't thinking of getting me any more of those Angel Choows – sweets for dogs. I hate 'em. And if she tries shoving them at me again, I'll make sure that I'm sick like the cat and his bananas. And I know just where to do it: in the middle of the hall mat. Even she is bound to notice it there.

She is still upstairs now, sloshing paint all over the shop I expect. So I think I'll go for a gentle potter and speak politely (or not) to the sheep.

SIXTEEN

The Primrose version

Oddly enough, my unexpected encounter with Dickie Ickington had been surprisingly fruitful, his breaking-and-entry saga being most illuminating. Well, perhaps 'illuminating' is a trifle exaggerated, but it certainly set me thinking. It opened up a fresh angle to the Memling affair and one that I would certainly look into. In fact, by the time I reached home my thoughts were whirling all over the place; so much so that were it not for Bouncer's reproachful burps (always a hungry sign), I should have forgotten to feed the wretch. That job done and, skipping lunch, I sat in the study and, as Pa would say, reflected furiously.

However, such intense cerebral activity was rather wearing, and I decided that a little artistic endeavour was called for. I hadn't been up to the studio for some days and it was high time I got going again. Although Wealden churches and Sussex sheep are my speciality (and the punters seem to like them), I have recently enlarged my repertoire to include those 'blunt, bow-headed, whale-backed Downs' so beloved of Kipling, and I was eager to pursue them further.

But immersed though I was in the new subject, my mind kept returning to the conversation with Dickie and the idea it had sparked. But I really needed to chew this over with somebody – somebody intelligent like Charles Penlow, for example. But I knew the Penlows were currently adrift somewhere in Dorset overseeing cats and grandchildren and wouldn't be back for ages. It occurred to me to try the Hamlyns: Daphne was bright and imaginative and Douglas, like Charles, was no fool; he would consider my theory seriously. Still, did I know them well enough for such a speculative discussion? Not really. And in any case, as newcomers to the area they would probably have little knowledge of the school or its staff – let alone an obscure under-matron. The Balfours at Firle are old friends and might be appropriate, but Freddie isn't of the sharpest – and delightful though Melinda is, she would simply shriek with laughter about the whole thing.

No, there was only one person I could talk to, who I knew well enough and who, though irritating, might show useful insight: Nicholas Ingaza. At our previous meeting in the White Hart, apart from revealing he had briefly met the woman, he had taken little interest in her demise and typically urged me to cease further enquiry. But that of course was before the autopsy findings, i.e. that in addition to the copious alcohol consumption and weak heart, Aida Memling had also been heavily doped. Surely that made the case appear more intriguing, even to Ingaza's jaundiced eye!

It so happened that the following day I was due to go into Brighton to pick up some fresh painting materials from the art shop in King Street. Ingaza's gallery was only a short walk from there and thus I could drop in 'on passing', as it were. If necessary, I had a good excuse which would appeal to his ego: to congratulate him on yet another triumph in the Sussex annual tango competition. Evidently Mona's replacement had stepped up to the mark.

Bouncer likes the seaside, so I had decided to take him with me. And as we made our way to the gallery, I planned my strategy: begin with fulsome congratulations on the tango success, then once he was sufficiently flattered gently reintroduce the topic of Memling's death in the hope of getting him even moderately responsive. Finally, go in for the kill: present him with my dazzling theory and see what he makes of that! A plausible programme, but knowing Ingaza he could skuttle the whole thing. Still, it was worth a try and, yanking the dog's lead, I entered the gallery.

For once there was hardly anyone there, and he was sitting at his desk in the corner reading *The Racing Times*.

'So who's the demon of the dance hall?' I gushed.

He put down the paper and grinned. 'Not bad, not bad at all. It's amazing what one learnt at Merton all those years ago; it wasn't just Classics they taught us. My tutor and I used to practise in the evenings. His sliding foot was superb.'

'Hmm,' I said, 'and did his foot slide along the tiles at the Jermyn Street baths as well?'

'Goodness me, Primrose, your mind is disgraceful! Enough of such sentimental nostalgia.' He gave a slow wink. 'Now, what do you want?' (I must explain that once upon a time Ingaza had been caught in an 'incident' at those Turkish baths and as a result had been detained for three weeks at Her Majesty's Pleasure, a sojourn which he had found not uncongenial and in some ways as instructive as his time at Oxford.)

I told him that what I wanted was to repay his recent generous hospitality at Lewes by giving him good coffee and decent cake at the café next door. It was an offer which he graciously accepted.

We settled at a window table and talked a little more about the Tango Cup which, having been won for the third time, he now owned *in perpetuo*. It was a trophy which clearly delighted him. 'But mind you,' he said grimly, 'I shall have to watch Eric. If I put it on the mantelpiece the sod will use it for an ashtray or shove his darts in it!'

Then with coffee and cake delivered, I made my opening gambit. 'Have you read the local paper?' I asked brightly. 'I mean your big Brighton edition, not our little Lewes one.'

'Yes,' he said shortly. 'Eric gets it every evening.'

'So I daresay you will have read the article on Memling and the Majestic.'

He gave a perfunctory nod. 'Hmm. It's quite well written. I think they've got a new chap on the job. The last one was just a hack. No style at all.'

'Oh, really, Nicholas,' I protested, 'it's not the style that matters but the content, i.e. the *facts*.'

He shrugged. 'Well yes, I agree, there are a few of those, but they don't add up to much. We know that she reserved a room under the name of Joy Johnson. But for what it's worth, we now know that there was an empty box of chocolates on the floor, a toothmug on the bedside table from which she had also been drinking, and that though covered with the eiderdown she was fully clothed. It also says that, other than her own, no fingerprints have been found apart from the maid's, and that the door was unlocked . . . And that's it. Not exactly shattering information, is it? On the face of it suicide would seem the obvious answer.' He sipped his coffee, fiddled with a piece of cake, and then scanned the room vaguely.

I had the impression that he was trying to avoid my eye. Thus I gave a brisk tap on the table and, leaning forward, said, 'And is that what you really think, Nicholas, that it was suicide?'

Reluctantly he met my gaze. 'My views are of no consequence and neither are yours. But since you are unlikely to take yes for an answer, I must admit that it sounds a bit odd.'

'Why?' I asked eagerly.

'Well, one could argue that if she had been drinking on her own she would hardly have dosed herself with that drug, unless of course she really was intent on suicide and wanted to be sure . . . On the other hand, if it was a serious intention to end her life and the drinking was deliberately calculated, what was the rose doing? To shove that in your hair when your mind is set on perfecting the mechanics of self-extinction seems a bit unlikely: a peculiarly frivolous touch "not congruent with the circumstances" as a judge might say. No, I think there had been a companion with whom she was, or had been, carousing. It was he or she who had slipped her the dope, either directly into the bottle or into the toothmug. The paper says she had been swilling from both.'

'So you think that somebody, having shared in the general gaiety, had waited until she was on the way out, or possibly stayed till the end, and then sneaked away?'

He nodded. 'Yes, something like that. Mind you, they would be taking a risk, but in a large popular hotel like the Majestic there must be masses of comings and goings; and dressed unobtrusively – or in disguise even – her companion could have passed without being noticed.

'Disguise? You make it sound like something out of *Boys' Own.*'

'I don't mean a false beard; something more subtle than that. Assuming it was a male, he could have started out in a dinner jacket, common enough at the Majestic, and then perhaps worn a mac or duffle coat when leaving by a side entrance.'

'OK. So he took her out on the tiles, plied her with drink, compliments and chocolates, and then went back to her room for more drinkies, laced the stuff with dope, ensured that she was totally and fatally sloshed, and then scarpered.'

'Yes,' he said, 'something along those lines.'

I could certainly visualize such a scene, but frowned as I thought of a flaw. 'But what about the apparent lack of additional fingerprints – on the chocolate box for example? If they were having such riotous fun there must have been some traces.'

'The assassin would have been careful to handle as little as possible and once she was out for the count wiped all the essentials. And even if some clear ones did emerge, unless the person has been previously fingerprinted there won't be any records.'

'So you are suggesting that she had some fancy man, or someone who was keen to give her that impression,' I said. 'It's a nice idea, but it doesn't *sound* like the lady. Everyone, including you, says she was a bit dull and strait-laced.'

'Ah, but still waters run deep: a façade of probity and principle. A bit like you, dear girl. Except that in your case the waters are not so much deep as merely damn choppy or occasionally tempestuous.' He lit a cigarette and gave a lopsided grin.

I was about to erupt, but with his epithet in mind, said coolly that if he was going to be rude he could at least give me a cigarette. He hesitated and said that he only had two left.

'Then I'll have one of them,' I snapped. I took the Sobranie, and for half a minute or so we smoked in silence.

And then I said, 'All right, Nicholas, that may have been the method but what about the damned motive? Why should someone want that rather dreary woman out of the way?'

He paused, blowing a smoke ring, and then asked why should anyone have wanted the sprightly Mrs Elizabeth Fotherington out of the way.

'But that was entirely different,' I said defensively of Francis. 'She was driving him mad. She pursued him wherever he went! All he wanted was peace and quiet.'

'Exactly, Primrose,' Ingaza said, suddenly serious, 'she was a threat; and whatever her personality or reasons, Francis couldn't stand the strain. In his case, his nerve broke and he blundered; whereas if my surmise is more or less right, this current disposal has been carefully engineered. Still, I suspect the situation is not so dissimilar: there was a pursuit, or in this particular case maybe a persecution of sorts. Poor old Francis hadn't a clue what to do – and then, without realizing, he had done it! The whole thing took him by surprise. But this person knew exactly what they were doing. But in both cases, whether dull and dreary or vapidly bright, the victim was some sort of bar to the other's freedom. So much so that they were extinguished. With Francis it was a moment of madness; with this one it was calculated.'

'And what do you think we should do about it?' I asked encouragingly.

Ingaza stared at me. '*Do? Us?* My dear Primrose, if you imagine for one moment that I am getting involved in your bloodhound activities, then you can think again! Just because I have made some rather obvious deductions doesn't mean that I am about to play Sherlock Holmes. I never knew the woman, and neither did you. So I suggest that—'

'But you did know her,' I cut in. 'You told me about her visit to the gallery and that you gave her one of your Memling brochures.'

He raised his eyes to the ceiling. 'That is hardly knowing her,' he said impatiently. 'We spoke for less than ten minutes . . . although now I come to think of it, she did apparently return that afternoon and ask my assistant for two more. The boy said she had wanted them to give to friends. Actually, at the time I was a bit annoyed and told him so. Those things are not exactly cheap, you know, which is why we don't commission them to be doled out like Smarties to the hoi polloi.' He gave a disdainful sniff, stubbed out his cigarette and stood up to go.

'They weren't for friends,' I said.

'What?'

'The brochures; she didn't give them to any friends.'

'Really? Oh well, I expect . . .' He broke off, frowned and resumed his seat. 'So how do you know that?'

'Ways and means,' I said carelessly. 'As a matter of fact, they were found discarded in her wastepaper basket – that is to say, all except one of their front covers which had been torn off and sellotaped to her bedroom wall.

His first reaction was of indignation. Really! Instead of passing them on to friends as she had implied, his precious brochures had been indifferently cast aside. What cheek! However, after a couple of choice oaths he simmered down. 'Huh!' he muttered. 'At least she had the good taste to appreciate the angel picture – the original is very fine. So it must have held something to catch her fancy, something that stirred that rather grey mind.'

'Oh yes,' I said, 'there was something that stirred it all right, but I doubt if it was the technical mastery.'

Ingaza looked puzzled. 'Oh? Perhaps you could be a little less oblique, dear girl. I'm not sure that I—'

'You say it must have held something to catch her fancy. What the angel *holds*, Nicholas, as I am sure you recall, is a blooming great sword! Memling's painting is of an *avenging* angel, one of those that was supposed to go around smiting wrongdoers and administering holy justice. According to the Bible, those angels had righteous missions: to slay the wicked. Memling's angel has a beautiful face and a pair of beautiful wings, but it also holds a lethal weapon.'

If I thought that my words would produce a fascinated reaction, I was wrong. Ingaza merely took out his handkerchief and blew his nose loudly. He put it away, murmuring that he was sure he was getting a summer cold, and then bent to pat the dog. I couldn't care less about his summer cold, and why he should want to pat Bouncer (by that time asleep under the table) I had no idea. I suspected these actions were simply delaying tactics to avoid further engagement with the topic. Well, he could think again! I pressed on.

'And after all, Nicholas,' I continued, 'you yourself have just said she was likely to have been killed because she was a threat to someone. And also, if I remember correctly, when you described your encounter with her in the gallery you said she had mentioned having some *mission* – one more serious than tracing her possible Memling ancestry. Don't you see, it all adds up: her mission was *revenge*. She wasn't just an inadvertent threat; she was deliberately out to get someone who had wronged her in the past – but someone who was able to catch her first and clip those wings for good!'

This time there could be no delaying tactics. A look of defeated resignation passed over Ingaza's face. 'All right, Primrose, I see your point. It's a neat little scenario, but with no real substance. Don't addle your mind with it. Plan a holiday – I am told the Maldives are most pleasant at this time of year.'

I ignored his thoughtful suggestion but admitted that my thesis had no firm evidence. 'Although,' I added casually, 'I expect that seeing the angel poster so beautifully displayed in your gallery and then being offered a brochure with its facsimile on the front cover probably fired her mind, sort of rekindled the missionary zeal. Maybe if she hadn't seen those tangible bits of paper, she might have dropped the revenge idea: grown bored or felt it foolhardy and impracticable. In fact,' I added slyly, 'given the way things have turned out, some might see the day she visited your gallery as having been the worst day of her life: a day of fatal reckoning, as it were . . .'

'Just go to the Maldives,' he said tightly, 'and send me the bill.'

SEVENTEEN

The Primrose version

I left the café both piqued and pleased. Typically, Ingaza was being difficult, but on the other hand he had certainly presented a plausible picture of Miss Memling's last hours. The scene made sense and I was sure he was right about her being a threat somewhere – though he hadn't sounded entirely enamoured of my avenging angel suggestion. Still, in the same way that thoughts stimulate words, words stimulate thought. And our conversation had certainly got my mind buzzing and made me even more curious about the whole affair.

On our way back to the car I took Bouncer the long way round to give him exercise and to let him sniff the ozone. Walking along the seafront we passed the imposing Majestic and I wondered how it was dealing with the recent publicity and the inevitable police enquiries. Presumably it wasn't every day that its management had to cope with guests thoughtless enough to expire on its premises, particularly in so graphic a way.

I was tempted to slip in for a drink and make discreet enquiries, but thought better of it. They might not allow dogs, and in any case its employees had probably been issued with strict orders not to engage in gossip with guests, let alone anyone who had just dropped in for a casual lunchtime drink, with or without dog. No. Without handy contacts among the staff it would be pointless to even try.

But as we continued to the car an idea struck me. *I* might not have any contacts, but I knew someone who did: Eric, Ingaza's chummy companion. The day porter was one of his mates at the darts club and I knew they were quite close. Unlike Ingaza, Eric was by nature garrulous and might be able to supply the odd detail beyond those reported in the paper. Yes, I might be able to wheedle something out of him – albeit at a cost. The cost of my eardrums. I had once asked Ingaza whether shouting was his friend's normal mode of speech, and if so it must be very wearing. Oh no, he had replied, he only does it at darts matches and on the telephone, particularly the telephone, otherwise the dear chap is quite bearable.

Thus the next day, and picking a time when I guessed Ingaza would be at the gallery, I braced myself to parley with Eric.

'Wotcha Prim,' he yelled (his usual salutation). 'How goes it then?'

I hesitated, not sure whether he was referring to my health or my current pursuit. But assuming the former I thanked him for his kind enquiry and said that I felt very fit.

There came a throaty chortle from the other end. 'So I've heard. Fit enough to rattle old Nick yesterday. Most unsettled he was when he came back last night, kept muttering about you being a blooming bloodhound and he was damned if he was going to get involved. You've been a naughty girl, haven't you; been on at him about that dead matron that was found at the Majestic and who came to his shop that time.' He sucked in his breath, the noise whistling against my ears, and said, 'His Nibs is a delicate flower and doesn't like being got at. Gets all shirty. Still, after a couple of snifters and another polishing session with his tango cup, he was all right again. Mind you, I think you've given 'im something to think about, because after supper he rummaged in his desk to find one of those Memling brochures and kept staring at that picture of the angel with its sword. And then he muttered, "Christ, I think she may have something." Well, I don't suppose he was talking about the angel, was he, so he must have meant you. Like I said, you've touched a nerve there, Prim!'

This was followed by a bellow of laughter, which made me wince. But I also felt pleased to think that Ingaza might be taking my suggestion seriously. Bolstered by Eric's mirth, I decided to speak frankly. 'Actually,' I said, 'speaking as a nosey bloodhound, I don't suppose you happen to have heard anything further from the Majestic . . . I mean beyond what was in the papers? For example, had anyone actually seen the lady that evening, and if so could she have had an escort?'

This was met with another throaty chuckle. 'Cor, His Lordship is right, you don't give up, do you! Still, I like a gal with a bit of go in her. And I like your pictures too – best sheep in Sussex they are!'

'And do those charming compliments,' I replied sweetly, 'mean you are going to indulge me with some little titbit that will keep the bloodhound quiet?'

For a few moments the line went quiet. And then he said, loud and clear, 'She had thick ankles.'

At first I thought I must have misheard, but with that vocal power it seemed unlikely. So what in God's name was he talking about? Or was I just being strung along? More of that nonsense and I would put the phone down!

'I am not sure that I follow you,' I said politely.

'Like I said, she had thick ankles which didn't look right in her high heels. Leastways, that's what Fred told me. It was about eleven o'clock and he was just going off day duty and waiting for the night porter when he saw this couple come in through the swing doors. The bird was pretty far gone, giggling and stumbling and clutching the bloke's arm. They had obviously been out on the town and not dining in the hotel. She was wearing a stole over a blue evening frock like what the victim was found in, and her hair was pinned up, though half of it had come undone. He said she had got too much lipstick on which smeared her mouth and made her look silly – he's very pernickety is Fred. Anyway, they went up the main staircase in the direction of the bedrooms.'

'What about the man?' I asked quickly. 'What was he like?'

'I asked Fred that but he was a bit vague. Dinner jacket, average height, maybe early middle age; nothing special, a lot of the guests there look like that. Besides, it was the woman he noticed – her lipstick and ankles.'

'But the man was certainly her escort?'

'Oh yes, she couldn't have got up the stairs otherwise.'

I asked him if the police were aware that she had definitely been with a male companion. He said that if they did, the information wouldn't have come from Fred. 'He's a bit shy of the coppers if you know what I mean – they're not best friends.' Another laugh blasted the line. (As it happens, I did recall Ingaza once saying that Eric's mate had had the odd brush or two with the law, so presumably Fred was content to keep a low profile. After all, unless under special interrogation, why open your mouth?)

Doubtful that I would gain any more useful 'titbits' from Eric, I thanked him for his invaluable time and help, and making excuses said that I must fly as I had to clean out the chinchillas' cage.

'Ah well, no peace for the wicked,' he chuckled. 'But tell you what, Prim, we must meet up one day, have a – wotcha call it – a *rendezvous*. Get His Lordship to bring you down to the darts club one evening and we'll push the boat out, have a good old natter and set the world to rights. See yer!'

I replaced the receiver, and despite having gained further intelligence and although it was only midday, felt suddenly worn out. Talking with Eric on the telephone was one thing, but the prospect of meeting him in person to push the boat and set the world to rights was utterly exhausting. I returned to the drawing room, slumped on to the sofa and stared fixedly at the picture of Pa glaring from above the mantelpiece. 'Well,' it seemed to say, 'if you must embark on these paperchases, what the hell can you expect? You're bound to feel tired, especially at your age!'

'Absolute nonsense,' I murmured, and promptly went to sleep.

I was awoken about an hour later by Bouncer's cold nose. He wanted his food. This I duly supplied. And sitting in the kitchen watching its fast disappearance I pondered Eric's report.

Unless Fred was a born liar, it would seem that Aida Memling alias Joy Johnson had most definitely been with a man that night, a man who had accompanied her to the bedroom. And given what Ingaza had surmised, that companion must surely have contributed to her death. So far so good . . . But why was such action necessary? My revenge thesis was all very well, but revenge for *what*? And even more perplexing, what had she been intending to do about it? Blow the gaff on some deadly secret? Or perhaps confront the wrongdoer(s) and demand money for silence. Even threaten physical violence? But whatever her intention, a woman on her own like that must have had a nerve – something which, according to what had been said of her retiring personality, was surprising. But as it is always being said, still waters run deep . . . And after all, who would have expected my dear brother to behave as he did!

I stared at the dog who, cocking his head on one side, looked as bemused as I was.

EIGHTEEN

The Primrose version

Naturally, absorbed though I was with the Memling mystery, I had no intention of forgetting my social commitments: the vicar's tea party (for example) and the WEA's annual painting jamboree (frightful). But the one most occupying my mind was to ask the Hamlyns over in return for their recent hospitality. I had glimpsed Daphne the previous day in Lewes, hauling the Petal creature to the vet's, and this immediately jogged my mind. Yes, I would invite them for cocktails the following week. The garden was looking at its best and I had just taken delivery of a new (and expensive) carpet for the drawing room, both of which I was eager to show off.

But it occurred to me that such a display would be wasted on only two people, and that in any case things might be jollier if I invited one or two others along as well. But who? The Penlows were away, and I knew for a fact that Freddie Balfour had a streaming cold. Freddie can be amusing, but less so with adenoids. There was always the vicar of course, but then there always was. Hmm . . .

Having thought for a bit I came up with the answer: the Winchbrookes. She was always good value and he, no doubt burdened by the prospect of the school inspection, could probably do with a diversion. Besides, if I timed it right, I might just be able to ascertain a little more of the Memling business.

Thus I immediately telephoned both sets, and rather to my surprise each was available on the suggested date. Daphne said they would be delighted and that she was dying to meet 'your remarkable cat'. I said that there was nothing remarkable about Maurice except that he was difficult. I almost suggested she bring Petal and Tarzan, but it occurred to me that if either Bouncer or the headmaster were in truculent mood that might not be a good idea.

Agnes Winchbrooke was also very amenable. 'Wonderful,' she breathed, 'just what he needs – something gay and convivial to take his mind off the inspection, not to mention this other ghastly business! And how nice to meet some newcomers to Lewes. Do they have children, I wonder?' If she was fishing for potential pupils at Erasmus, she had lost a catch. As far as I knew the Hamlyns had no children and certainly not of that young age.

The day of the soirée dawned and I was busy brushing cat fur from the cushions, polishing the decanters and ensuring there was enough whisky for Winchbrooke, plenty of gin, plus Dubonnet à la the Queen Mother, and a large assortment of H&P's crackers. I wasn't going to play around making fiddly canapés out of these but put out some Stilton. If no one else liked it, I did. At six o'clock I opened the French windows to the evening sun, shoved Bouncer into the kitchen (Maurice was on the prowl) and awaited the troops.

The Winchbrookes were the first to arrive, both looking and sounding on good form, she in a blue velvet sheath (a trifle tight for the portly figure) and he sporting a bow tie. A keen gardener, his wife was immediately drawn to the open window to gaze at the voluptuous roses on the terrace now at their August peak, while Winchbrooke's gaze was drawn to the whisky decanter.

With drinks in hand, we engaged in preliminary chit-chat, my ear alert for the ring of the bell. And then, having made fulsome comments on the roses, Mrs Winchbrooke urged her husband to admire them too. As he dutifully moved towards the terrace, she whispered to me, 'He's a bit on edge these days as you may guess, so when your other guests arrive try to steer them away from the subject of *you know what*! They are bound to ask questions.'

I muttered that I would do my best, and at the sound of the doorbell went to let them in. 'We are *so* sorry to be late,' exclaimed Daphne Hamlyn, 'but at the last minute we lost Tarzan. Couldn't see the little pest anywhere! But it's not really like him to go off on his own. We looked all over the place, and do you know where we eventually found him – in the back seat of the car, just sitting there quietly. So we brought him with us. He's there now.'

I laughed and said that they must of course bring him in, but drinks first. 'After that treasure hunt you could do with a fortifier. And come and meet the Winchbrookes; they're one ahead of you.'

Introductions were made, garden admired and all was merry and convivial. I noticed that Winchbrooke's consumption of whisky and soda was swift, but in this respect Douglas Hamlyn wasn't far behind. The ladies stuck to Gin and French while I, busy passing the biscuits and keeping the conversation suitably wide, filled my glass sparingly with anything to hand.

However, with general topics initially exhausted, there was a lull, at which point Daphne turned to Winchbrooke, and with a broad smile said, 'Well, Headmaster, your school's been having a pretty bad time, hasn't it? I imagine it's not every day a member of your staff gets scuppered in a snazzy hotel. Presumably not too good for business. Must be quite a facer!' I saw her husband wince and close his eyes, while Winchbrooke regarded her impassively. 'You could say that,' he murmured, 'but we in education have a great deal to put up with, sudden death being just one of the problems. And as far as I am aware business proceeds as normal.'

Considering his short fuse, I was impressed with the response, while at the same time deciding that should Daphne want any more martini, I would omit the gin and substitute water.

There was a slightly awkward pause, and I grabbed the moment. 'I say,' I cried, 'we've forgotten poor little Tarzan. He must be rescued! Do bring him in, Douglas; I am sure he will be very good.'

Douglas responded with alacrity (and relief?) and went out to the car. A minute later he returned with the poodle in his arms. He set it down on the floor, where it trotted around, busily sniffing at this and that before darting on to the terrace – not I think to admire the roses, but to scamper up and down waving its short tail and making little squeaks.

'He does that when he's looking for something,' Douglas said. 'It's generally his ball.'

I said that he was probably after food and called him in to have some biscuits. These he ate daintily, albeit leaving a discreet circle of cracker crumbs on the new Tientsin rug.

At that moment Maurice wandered in, and I feared he might resent the new guest and vent his spleen. I saw his back beginning to arch, but then it seemed to relax and instead of a screech of indignation he emitted a soft mew. Cat and canine circled each other, actually touched noses, and together withdrew into the hall. Never had I seen Maurice being so courteous, let alone with a strange dog, and I told the Hamlyns that Tarzan must have magical powers.

'Probably a practising hypnotist.' Winchbrooke laughed, seemingly recovered from Daphne's crude gaffe.

Douglas laughed too and said that actually he was just a soapy little sod.

Fortunately this little interlude seemed to restore calm to what might have become choppy waters and we got on to the topic of animals and their oddities, Daphne saying that they had once known a pet giraffe in South Africa who every morning would wake its owners by tapping on their bedroom window – five times without fail.

After further anecdotes and chit-chat, things started to wind down and the Hamlyns said they must be getting back to Petal who had not quite recovered from his session with the vet (toenails and teeth). 'Besides,' Douglas said, 'the idiot frets if he's left for long without his curly friend.'

In the hall we found the curly friend fast asleep, Maurice evidently having lost interest and wandered off. I waved them goodbye and returned to the drawing room to find Winchbrooke finishing his whisky and Mrs Winchbrooke standing at the bookcase inspecting my small collection of gardening books. I went over and offered to lend her one. As she made her choice, she gave me a nudge and said quietly, 'Well, that was a near miss. Thank God for dogs!'

With the two of them now on their own, it would seem the ideal opportunity to enquire further about the Memling case – *not*, of course, in Daphne's brazen way, but more tactfully. But how? In a minute they would be on their way, Mrs Winchbrooke already looking vaguely for her handbag. What could I do to detain them, to seize the moment while there was still the chance? Smiling sweetly, I wracked my brain . . .

As it happened, I didn't have to do anything. Bouncer saw to that. Although I had shut him in the kitchen, he must have sneaked out by the side door which I may have carelessly left ajar. For there he suddenly was, like a *canis ex machina* poised at the French windows all ready to bound in and greet the departing guests.

'Oh, Bouncer!' cried Mrs Winchbrooke. 'How lovely to see you!' She put down her handbag and went forward to pat his head and ruffle the shaggy fur. Ever the showman, the dog trotted into the room, rolled on its back and waved its front paws in the air. I had forgotten how fond the lady was of dogs and could see that her attention was entirely taken with this performance. She crouched down to tickle his tummy. Winchbrooke too was grinning, and I quickly offered him another drop of whisky. He hesitated, and then said jovially, 'Oh well, since you press me, just one for the road perhaps. The coppers are coming again tomorrow and I shall need strength for them!'

'Oh dear,' I said sympathetically, 'are they being tiresome? It must be a rotten strain. Is it Mr Spikesy? He's generally quite civilized.'

'Yes, he's pretty decent, though he's been called away and someone else is handling it. Not that there's much to handle at our end. It's the Majestic that's taking the brunt. Pretty bad for business, I should think.'

'That's not what I have heard,' Mrs Winchbrooke said, resuming her seat. 'I am told they are doing a roaring trade since it happened.'

'Hmm. So bully for them,' her husband observed dryly. 'Despite what I told your' – he paused fractionally – 'lively guest, our own situation could well be affected. I've already had one parent babbling about taking his boy away. It's like dominoes: one falls and the rest go down.'

'Nonsense,' I said briskly, 'Erasmus is a fine school with an excellent reputation. It can hardly be held responsible for what some foolish person does in her own spare time. And after all, I am sure you have been most helpful to the police in their enquiries.' This was sincerely meant, but it was also a soother

for my next remark. 'And did they take anything from her room?'
I asked casually.

'Hardly anything as far as we could make out,' said Mrs
Winchbrooke. 'They found a folder at the bottom of her wardrobe
but that was empty except for a couple of things, though they
didn't make much sense. One was a picture of an angel torn from
some book or other, and the other was a typed letter postmarked
from Penge. I say letter, but it was just a couple of lines with
no signature or salutation. Spikesy showed it to us and asked if
we knew anything about it or had she mentioned it at all.'

The reference to the angel brought me up sharp, but I was
intrigued by the other item; and again, as lightly as possible, I
asked what it had said.

She frowned, trying to recall. 'Something like, "Silly-Billy!
Tides turn, you know." A bit odd really, because that was all that
was written, except for a reference to Shakespeare's *Hamlet*. Not
a quotation, just an act and scene number. Can't remember which.'

'Act Three, scene three or maybe four,' interposed Winchbrooke.
'But frankly I wasn't very interested in anonymous scraps of
paper. With Her Majesty's Inspectorate imminent I've got far too
many other things to deal with.' He cleared his throat and leered,
'Not least the task of seeing that the exchange of one set of our
paintings for another has been efficiently handled.'

He thought he was being funny. I did not. However, I smiled
politely, while resolving that he should taste not one more drop
of the Oughterard whisky.

After they had gone and having cleared the debris, I sat and
cogitated.

I thought first of the angel photograph and wondered if it
matched the Memling one stuck to her wall above the dressing
table as reported by Dickie. If so, it too might have been torn
from one of Ingaza's brochures. Apparently she had had three
of them, one from him and the two later cadged from the assistant.
Such angelic obsession would certainly tie in with my revenge
theory.

But even more intriguing was the cryptic and anonymous note
with the Shakespeare reference. What on earth had it meant? It

sounded archly reproving, and not the kind of crude threat normally associated with anonymous letters. But maybe it wasn't intended to be hostile; maybe it was part of a sort of pen-pal game like a crossword in which obscure clues would be exchanged weekly or monthly. Apparently its provenance was Penge, not somewhere that has ever aroused my curiosity – unless you count the notorious murder of 1877. One of the innumerable London suburbs, I believe it has a reputation for gentrified order and hardcore dullness . . . perhaps an appropriate place for Miss Memling to have had a puzzle-addicted friend.

Still, crossword or not, significant or worthless, I would still have to rummage in Shakespeare. I wondered what the police were making of it – not much, I imagine. But the message must have meant something, and on principle I was damn well going to find out! I went into the study and, standing on tiptoes, hauled down the Collected Works. But faced with the small print and *Hamlet*'s long Act III, and knowing that I should have to scrutinize virtually every line, I stayed my hand. After all, tomorrow would be another day . . .

NINETEEN

The cat's version

'She is off her chump,' Bouncer said, between chews of that disgusting bone.

I flicked my tail and replied that of course she was, but this was a matter we had long commented upon, but perhaps he had forgotten.

'I have not forgotten,' he retorted indistinctly, 'but what I mean is that she is even more off her chump than before.' He rattled his bowl.

I considered this observation, and then remarked that on the whole it was probably better to have owners who were deranged than those who were, by human standards, moderately sane.

Food finished, he looked up. 'Wotcha mean?'

'I mean, Bouncer, that though well beyond sanity, our previous owners – the bank manager who absconded with the money, and then F.O. the vicar who erased my boring mistress – were considerably more interesting than many of the owners of some of our colleagues. Take the master of Tiddles, the cat down the road, for example: he does nothing but smoke a pipe and do the crossword – *all* day! And then there are Duster's people in that huge house – both very nice, of course, but being of the few humans who are totally balanced, they don't do much to amuse poor old D who always looks the epitome of grey sobriety.'

Bouncer burped and said, 'Looks like what?'

'The epitome of – oh, never mind,' I said hastily. 'And as for that enormous piece of white fluff at the school, Lola, the reason she is such a gossip is that she has to invent her own excitement to compensate for the Winch people who do everything to keep that establishment afloat and very little to entertain *her*.'

'Hmm,' he snorted, 'but she's got some entertainment now. I

mean, all that killing stuff the Prim is busy with is quite interesting, I should think.'

'Yes, but that is not generated by her *owners* – or at least as far as we know – and therefore doesn't count. No, the essential thing is to have owners who are not only the source of food, warmth and the rest of life's comforts, but who – tiresome though that sometimes is – are fundamentally raving lunatics.'

The dog was silent for a moment considering my words. And then, cocking his head on one side, said: 'Ah, so they sort of make a C-A-B-A-R-E-T for us. Is that it?'

'Exactly, Bouncer!' I beamed. 'My goodness, your vocabulary enlarges day by day!'

'What?'

'For a dog, you know a lot of words,' I explained.

He was obviously pleased with that, for he wagged his tail, gave a quick scratch and then made a scrupulous inspection of his nether regions.

Reconnaissance complete, he lifted his head and said, 'So what about the owners of Petal and Tarzan, are they lunatics?'

I shook my head. 'I shouldn't think so – unless you count being too dense to find Tarzan when he hid yesterday. They were going to leave him at home when they came here, but he wanted to see us . . . well, me mainly, so he jumped in the car. And they took ages, calling his name all over the place and he thought they would never get here.'

Bouncer seemed puzzled. 'But what made him want to see you, Maurice?'

'Well,' I said modestly, 'I think he regards me as a sort of mentor, an example of style and distinction.'

The dog looked dazed. 'Oh yes?' he muttered.

'Yes. But mind you, it doesn't do to permit one's protégés too much latitude in case they take you for granted. So after a few kind words in the hall, I told him I had a mouse to catch and had to be on my way.'

'Ah,' he said, 'so that's why you weren't there to see my C-A-B-A-R-E-T with the Winch lady. I was jolly good and she really liked it! Old Bouncer knows how to pull the crowd all right.'

I was about to say that fortunately I had been spared that particular spectacle but thought better of it. It might have been ill advised. Like our mistress, the dog can be temperamental and make sudden movements unforeseen.

TWENTY

The Primrose version

I t was the first Sunday of the month, and as a regular practice Bishop Troughton from Chichester comes to St Michael's to preach his monthly sermon. Our local rector is a worthy if unremarkable cleric and his sermons are not a patch on Troughton's, who invariably has something useful to say and whose voice is sufficiently clear to make his message intelligible. Such professionalism should be supported, and thus I go when I can. So, despite being keen to pursue the Shakespeare quotation, I decided to postpone my prep till after lunch.

As usual on such dates, the church was full, and being a little late I was lucky to get a decent seat. However, I squeezed in at the back which suits me quite well as it means one gets a full view of the nave, the many wall sculptures and the remarkable St Swithin window. The other windows depicting St Augustine and Thomas à Becket are also engaging.

In addition to these features, I also had a view of Emily Bartlett and Bertha Twigg. They were sitting halfway down next to the aisle. Bertha wore her usual church headgear, a beret of indeterminate hue, while Emily's hat struck me as being rather curiously shaped. However, there is no accounting for tastes – and it may have been the latest fashion, though I rather doubted this.

With the procession moving at stately pace towards the chancel steps, the service soon got under way. And after a spate of incense spraying, hearty hymn singing and mumbled prayers, Troughton took to the pulpit to deliver his sermon. As usual, it was interesting and articulate, and initially my attention was fully absorbed. His theme was the precariousness of fortune and the dangers of complacency. 'Beware the lizard that lieth lurking in the grass,' he resoundingly quoted from the fifteenth-century poet John Skelton. I nodded inwardly, thinking of Francis and the way that his later life had become so dominated by these tiresome lizards, or snakes as we now term them.

But then he said something which diverted me from both sermon and pulpit: something about how you never knew when the tide was going to turn. The point fitted his theme but the words gave me a jolt. *The turning of the tide* – a common enough phrase, but which echoed the one used in the cryptogram I would pour over that afternoon! It was an unsettling moment for, much as I tried, I could not return my mind to the good bishop's oratory. And once more I started to dwell on that curious message.

Thus, service over, I was eager to return home and study the Shakespeare, but was waylaid by Bertha Twigg who zoomed up and asked if I would join them for a coffee. I hesitated and asked where she was thinking of, since most places would surely be closed. 'Ah, but there's that new place at the bottom of Cleves Lane . . .' she said. 'They are Italian and do super ices and keep open all week. Most enterprising for Lewes; the owners probably come from London. We might go there.' Actually, I was itching to get away, but it being Sunday and the spirit of Christian charity upon me, I said I would join them. (After all, one could always dredge up an excuse for a quick exit.)

Waiting for the coffee, with Bertha avid for ice cream, we chatted about the bishop's sermon, the choir's tuneful singing and the sexton's streaming cold. I also falsely admired Emily's hat. 'It was my aunt's,' she told us. 'Everyone admires it.' I was unconvinced of that, but naturally said nothing.

When our coffee arrived (rather good), she turned to me and said, 'As a matter of fact, Primrose, I've been meaning to ask your advice.'

'Oh yes?' I said, not especially interested.

'Yes, it's about something I found in a book Miss Memling lent me.'

Suddenly I was all ears, and I enquired what sort of book.

'It is on the flowers of South Africa,' she said. 'She knew I was a keen horticulturalist and thought I would enjoy it.'

Frankly, I had seen little evidence of Emily's horticultural zeal; her principal interest seemed to be potted marigolds and garden gnomes. But I was curious as to why she should want my advice on the book. 'So what about it?' I asked.

'Well, as I said, she lent it to me. But quite honestly, what with the auditors and the coming inspection, I have been *so* busy lately that I haven't had a chance to open it. Not a minute to spare! And then of course there's been all the problems of young Blenkinsop and Mr Winchbrooke's dental appointment and . . .'

I was rapidly losing interest in her saga of busyness and was about to turn to Bertha when I heard her say, 'And so last week when I was tidying my *inundated* desk, I came across her book and this piece of paper fell out.'

'What piece of paper?'

'Well, I have it here actually, because I was going to show it to the headmaster tomorrow in case he thought the police might be interested. Although I shouldn't think so for one minute – it's all in pencil and virtually illegible with lots of crossings out; a sort of rough copy of a reply to a letter, I imagine. Still, one does try to be helpful, doesn't one?' She turned to Bertha. 'Wouldn't you agree?'

'Oh absolutely,' the other mumbled, spooning ice cream into her mouth.

'And you say you have it with you?' I said casually.

Emily opened her handbag and laid a crumpled piece of paper on the table.

I picked it up and gave it an idle scan, then studied it more closely. Emily was right: it was obviously a hastily drafted reply to what had presumably been some sort of request for information. Picking my way among its scrawled adjustments and deletions, I made out the following:

Dear Sir,

As indicated, I am most interested in your proposal and would be very willing to supply you with copious details for your article. The more known about such tragic situations the better. Invariably they arise from an incident which pushes the victim over the edge and sets them on the road to ruin. It is right and proper that this particular case be examined and the originator exposed. I can certainly meet you to discuss matters further and would be able to give a full—

There were more heavy crossings out, and at this point the writer gave up. Bored? Summoned by the school bell? Or had a fresh response been started? But more to the point was whether a fair copy had ever been made, and if so, had it been sent?

'So do you think I should show it to the police tomorrow?' Emily asked earnestly.

I told her that it couldn't do any harm and that in such investigations even the most seemingly irrelevant items could sometimes have a bearing. I quickly re-read the thing before passing it back.

'And did she get many letters?' I asked.

'Not that I remember – in fact I don't recall any at all. You see, that's another little job Mr Winchbrooke foists upon me: checking the staff mail and putting it into their pigeonholes. I mean, you might have thought he could get an underling to do that.' Emily sniffed and pursed her lips.

'But there aren't any underlings,' Bertha said, not unreasonably.

'No. And therefore it is high time I was given an assistant!'

'You'd do better to ask for more pay,' I said. 'Funding an assistant would cost the school more money than a pay rise. Besides, you could then put hard cash in your pocket.'

Emily regarded me with sudden interest. 'Well, yes, I suppose I could—'

'You could always give in your notice,' Bertha said helpfully.

Emily looked pained. 'Certainly not! I have been at the school for years; they would be lost without me!'

I can't say I was overly concerned with Emily Bartlett's professional dilemmas and managed to steer the conversation back to Miss Memling. 'But if she didn't receive any letters,' I said, 'it seems rather odd that she should have been composing what seems to have been a reply.'

I think Emily thought I was querying her memory, for she looked piqued and said curtly that perhaps it had been written earlier on, before the matron had even come to the school. I was prepared to agree but was forestalled by a splutter from Bertha.

'Huh!' she exclaimed. 'There *are* such things as telephones, you know. There was nothing to stop her being called on one of those – as I was made only too aware.'

I was puzzled and asked in what way she had been so aware.

'It was about a month ago, and I had been practising some pretty tricky horse somersaults in the gym. But it was all going so well that I had quite forgotten I was supposed to be phoning my brother at five o'clock that evening. Pogo is a bit pernickety and gets awfully shirty if you keep him waiting. So when I realized that it was already a quarter past I dashed off to the phone box in the hall. But there was somebody in there gabbling away like mad. I paced about outside thinking they would finish at any moment. Huh! They did not, and I was kept waiting endlessly.'

'You mean it was . . .?'

'Yes, of course I do. It was Aida Memling. Jabber, jabber, jabber!'

I was a little surprised at this, as I had understood Miss Memling to have been a rather tacit type, and said as much to Bertha.

'Well, not then, she wasn't,' she snorted. 'She was in there for ages, and when she finally came out she was all pink in the face and smiling.'

'Did she say anything?'

Bertha shrugged. 'I wasn't really listening as I wanted to get on the blower and speak to Pogo. But I think she said something about an interview and how she was going to be a star turn. Not that I can see that woman being a star turn at anything except for keeping people waiting outside phone boxes!' With an indignant sniff, Bertha bent to demolish her ice cream.

'So what's the system?' I asked Emily.

'Well, we don't encourage incoming calls for staff, but occasionally a member will get one, and if I am on duty I'll transfer it to the general phone box in the hall and let the recipient know.'

'And did you do that for this one?'

She sighed impatiently and said she really couldn't remember. 'I am busy enough as it is being secretary to the headmaster and his deputy and dealing with *their* calls, without having to act as a telephonist for lesser members of staff. Frankly I can't see the need for that general phone box. If people want to make or receive calls, they should go into Lewes. There's a perfectly good one at the top of the High Street, not to mention the two booths in the post office.' She glared and I could see I had touched a nerve there and didn't pursue the matter.

Instead, I said charmingly that I thought she was doing a grand job and that the next time I saw the headmaster I would make hints about her pay rise. (I would too. Winchbrooke needs the occasional shove from a trustee!) This seemed to do the trick and she calmed down and graced me with – I think – a grateful smile.

With this new information about Memling buzzing in my head, I gathered my gloves and handbag, and with lavish smiles made for the door. So eager was I to get home that I nearly ran down the Dragon, Mrs Dragson, evidently taking a constitutional before lunch. I gave a gay wave which, I noticed, was not reciprocated.

TWENTY-ONE

The Primrose version

Once home and after hurling food at the dog, I made a cheese sandwich and went into the study to commence my trawl through *Hamlet* Act III. Winchbrooke had said he thought the reference had been for either scene three or four. So what was I looking for? Presumably something to do with tides turning. Impatiently I scoured both sections. Not a word, of course. I tried again, this time going through the whole damned act. Nothing.

I cast my mind back to the bishop's sermon that morning. What was it exactly he had been saying about tides? That they could turn for good and turn for bad, and that sometimes the tide we were being borne upon so safely would suddenly reverse and take us to our destruction: i.e. just when we thought our projects were sound, they could backfire and blow us sky high. In other words, he had warned, our plans could rebound upon us and sometimes spectacularly. But with God's grace etc, etc . . . Hmm, so maybe the Shakespeare reference had not contained the word 'tide' at all, but was simply to do with the irony of self-ruin.

I applied myself once more, but was startled by a petulant miaow from Maurice. So absorbed had I been that his entrance had passed unnoticed – an oversight with which he was evidently displeased. He was crouched on the floor behind me, staring fixedly at my desk. I knew exactly what was about to happen, and before I could shoo him away he had taken a flying leap and landed on the open Shakespeare.

'Oh really, Maurice, must you!' I exclaimed, and tried to push him off. He sat his ground and with a loud mew started to tweak at my jumper with his paw. 'Don't!' I said. 'It's new.' Naturally, the injunction was ignored. But I managed to thrust him aside, and with interruption accomplished and a swish of his tail, he leapt back on to the floor and curled up on the rug.

Peace and silence regained, I continued with my task. And then halfway through scene four where Hamlet talks with his mother after stabbing Polonius, I came upon a passage which could certainly be relevant: 'For 'tis the sport to have the engineer / Hoist with his own petard . . . But I will delve one yard below their mines / And blow them at the moon.' I brooded. Might this indeed be the bit?

And then with a start, I knew that it was. I had a sudden vision of Dickie Ickington on the night he had come with the ham bone for Bouncer, and his scornful allusion to Miss Memling not knowing what a petard was and her having to ask the English master. I could hear the little voice: *And do you know, Miss Oughterard, she didn't even know what a petard was* . . . At the time there had been more pressing topics to pursue than semantic niceties. But at this current moment the word resounded in my mind with an almighty clang. If Miss Memling had wanted to know its meaning, in all likelihood it was because she had only just encountered the word. And where might she have found it? By searching for the Shakespearean reference just as I was doing now. And why should she have done that? Because she had been the recipient of that enigmatic note found carefully filed at the bottom of her wardrobe.

I let out a yelp of triumph, which woke Maurice and sent him scudding out of the room. Yes, it was obvious: the words Silly-Billy in the note may have sounded kindly, but the message had been not merely a reproof, but a threat – a threat to stop whatever she was doing or suffer the consequences: i.e. to be hoisted by her own petard and be blown to kingdom come. Well, the lady may not have gone sky high exactly, but she had certainly been annihilated all right.

And what had been the cause of this event? Surely her relent-less mission of retribution, to wreak vengeance on those who had trespassed. But now the tide (or the worm) had turned, and the persecutor herself destroyed. So, had the anonymous note from Penge been in retaliation to her own insistent threats or warnings? Had that quiet and colourless woman employed to administer plasters and cough medicine to small boys been on a ruthless pestering campaign to create maximum angst among those she deemed her enemies? It might seem so. I thought again of Emily Barrett's description of her: a nonentity, she had said. But perhaps even nonentities can be dangerous . . . in fact, given their unremarkable image, doubly so.

Pleased with my efforts, I returned to the kitchen for another sandwich. Bouncer saw me and gave a reproachful yelp. I slung him a crust of bread and then, taking the sandwich and some coffee, went back to the study. There was more to consider: the draft letter that Emily had produced and Bertha's complaint about the telephone call.

The scribbled words on Emily's piece of paper would certainly seem to suggest she had been in contact with somebody, and since the missive had begun with 'Dear Sir' it was obviously a man, who – according to Bertha – may have telephoned to seek help with an article he was writing. And judging from the eager tone of the reply, its topic had clearly evoked a reaction . . . so much so that not only had she been ready to cooperate but even to agree to a meeting. Tantalizingly, at this point the words had become indecipherable and petered out. Still, it was something to set the old brainbox going!

I thought back over Eric's account of his pal Fred having seen a couple ascending the stairs at the Majestic. The latter's description of the lady had certainly sounded not unlike what I had heard of Aida Memling (albeit in these circumstances tight). So was her companion (and probably the killer) the same person who had contacted her at Erasmus and whom she was ready to meet and supply with 'copious' details? But who was he, for goodness' sake? Some journalist on to a good story and keen to exploit it for all its worth to make his name? Quite possibly. But in which case, why kill the source of his facts? Surely she would be more useful alive than dead. If he had been a canny professional, he could have used her for further research on the subject (whatever that was) or to re-confirm the details she had given him.

But supposing he wasn't canny; supposing he had over-wined

and dined her, and unaware of the dicky heart had slipped her the drug hoping it would make her even more garrulous and malleable . . . and then, realizing his ghastly mistake, had scarpered.

Hmm, I brooded, such lethal blunders do occur (and again my panicked brother came to mind). But then I saw the irony and couldn't help smiling. Assuming that the 'petard' note had been serious, and its writer really intent on putting an end to things, then 'Chummy' at the Majestic had conveniently relieved them of the burden. There would be no more pestering from that particular source; the job was already done!

I shoved back my chair and, glancing at the window, noticed the suddenly beaming sunshine. Time for a walk. I whistled to Bouncer, and together we bounded forth, me to admire the Downs and he to gawp at the sheep.

TWENTY-TWO

Emily Bartlett to her sister

My dear Hilda,

How good to get your letter and to hear of your success in the knitting and crochet competition. Personally, I should love to engage in such things, but, alas, my time here at Erasmus House does not permit such charming pursuits. It's busy, busy, busy all day long! And keeping Mr Winchbrooke on his toes is an uphill task – especially that now we are to face the school inspectors at any minute. The prospect is not helped by the dreadful Memling business – and of which you were rather dismissive when I first told you. <u>No</u>, Hilda, drunken deaths are not 'two a-penny' as you so casually remarked – least of all in Lewes, a most salubrious little town, and among members of an educational establishment such as ours. And as said, the discovery that the lady had also imbibed some awful dope gives the whole thing a distinctly sinister air.

Mind you, disagreeable though this is, some of the masters are already taking bets as to whether she died naturally (if you can call a vast ingestion of gin and drugs natural) or whether it was <u>death by an unknown hand</u>, i.e. murder!! This is a topic which seems to excite members of staff far more that the coming inspection. At the moment, according to Grieves, the new geography master (who, between you and me, I don't think will last long), the odds are even. But frankly, if the staff continue to occupy themselves in this way rather than in preparing – or inventing – their teaching agendas, classroom records and lesson synopses for the inspectors' perusal, then I very much doubt if we shall triumph with the flying colours that Mr W. keeps chirping about. Still, who am I, a mere lowly secretary, to pass comment?

You ask after my slightly difficult friend Primrose Oughterard. Well, as you know, <u>she</u> is always ready to pass comment – and on anything at all. But I have to say that recently she has been unusually helpful in declaring that in her role as one of the school's trustees she will lobby the headmaster to increase my salary. I call that most thoughtful, and it just goes to show that under that sometimes quite <u>impossible</u> exterior there are good intentions. And on the assumption, Hilda, that she succeeds in her lobbying and that I do indeed become the happy recipient of increased funds, we must celebrate by a week at the seaside – <u>not</u> Blackpool, as you once suggested, but somewhere seemly like Hove or Torquay. Or, to be adventurous, even Le Touquet! You may remember the parents once taking us there as children, and you being sick all the way. And back. (Naturally, should we ever embark on such a voyage again, I trust you would come equipped with the necessary pills.)

And talking of pills, I do hope Mother is behaving. How kind of the local vicar to invite her and other elderlies to the annual parish luncheon. She is bound to enjoy it, though I trust they supply suitably large table napkins. But a word of caution: I do not advise she be encouraged to reminisce about her past youth. Some might regard that as a colourful interlude, but I can assure you it would not go well with the church authorities.

Your devoted sister,
Emily

TWENTY-THREE

The Primrose version

I had bought a rather succulent pork chop and was just trying to decide if I should fry or roast it, and whether to have potatoes or turnips – or both – when this pressing concern was interrupted by the telephone.

It was Winchbrooke, asking if I would be free to attend the interment of the unfortunate Miss Memling in Brighton's municipal cemetery. 'You see,' he explained, 'we have now had the coroner's report and the police verdict, and together they conclude that it was death by misadventure. It was the mix of gin and drugs on a weak heart that did it. The body is to be released, and despite enquiries no one has come forward to claim it. So that being the case, and as earlier planned, Erasmus is cooperating with the local authorities to witness the – er – well' – he cleared his throat – 'the disposal . . . So if you could help represent the school, we should be most obliged. Naturally a few of the staff will be there, but I feel that the presence of a trustee or two would also be appropriate.'

The prospect did not exactly gladden my heart, but I am all in favour of citizens doing their civic duty, and so somewhat reluctantly agreed to his suggestion.

Of course, at the back of my mind was the question of the verdict: 'death by misadventure'. This would surely mean that no one else was implicated. A rather strange conclusion, considering what the Majestic's porter had observed. But as Eric had told me, the man was of a 'retiring' nature and had evidently kept his head down. However, though slightly surprised, I was hardly going to pursue the point with the headmaster, and certainly not on the telephone. Besides, the verdict would obviously please him and he would be unlikely to welcome any scepticism from me.

After assuring him that I would do my best to be present, I went upstairs to sort out suitable attire. Never having encountered the lady, I felt that my usual funeral black would be overdone, and instead opted for a coat of mid-grey with matching hat. That settled, I rushed down to the kitchen to deal with the abandoned chop and pour a good glass of wine. I say 'rushed', for that evening the television was showing an early Sherlock Holmes film with the delectable Basil Rathbone. I don't watch much television, but this was not to be missed. The gentleman deserved a second glass . . .

It was a fitting day for a burial: damp, grey and listless. The municipal cemetery with its serried ranks of headstones seemed to stretch endlessly, its anonymous vista unbroken by trees or shrubs, or indeed any living thing – except for those few of us gathered to watch, soberly and uncomfortably, the lowering of the coffin into its gaping hole.

I say uncomfortably, not just on account of the dank weather, but because so little was known of the deceased. Miss Memling in death seemed as indeterminate as she had been in life. And while some heads were respectfully bowed, the responses were dutiful rather than instinctive. Unlike with many burials, there were neither tears nor wistful smiles; no sympathetic handshakes or mutterings of condolence. Only an awkward respect – respect for the dead in general, and not for any particular person. I was glad when it was over.

Formalities finished, I wandered back to the car park with the other attendees. We were rather a subdued bunch; subdued by the now drizzling rain, but also, I think, by the raw brevity of the thing. One moment she was there, the next dismissed for ever.

There weren't many of us: Bracken the deputy mayor of Lewes, the Winchbrookes, the town clerk (any excuse for an hour off!), Thomas Briscoe with a couple of senior masters, another Erasmus trustee whose name I always forget, Emily Bartlett and, rather surprisingly, Bertha Twigg. I shouldn't have thought that such sombre events were Bertha's 'scene', and certainly not those of so stark and stiff a nature. A full church service with spectacle

and music, and followed by a whopping bunfight, would surely
be more to her liking. As a change from hurling herself over the
wooden horse and swinging perilously from the high ropes, this
meagre ritual must have seemed a bit of a let-down . . . No, I
am being unduly flippant. Bertha is a kind-hearted girl, and
despite her indignation over the telephone incident, she may have
been the only one of the assembled 'mourners' to have felt
anything at all.

Actually, what surprised me even more than Bertha's presence
was Mrs Dragson's absence. You would have thought that as
mentor to Aida Memling, and the one most likely to have known
her best (as far as that went), she would have been there, if only
for form's sake. Still, we can't always meet social requirements;
perhaps she had an appointment with the dentist or an urgent
summons from the tax man.

Back at the cemetery car park the group quickly disbanded
and drove off in their various directions. I had been going to say
a few words to the headmaster, but Winchbrooke was obviously
in a hurry to get away and wore the look of a man both impatient
and relieved. With the assistant matron now safely beneath
ground, he could attend to more urgent matters. So along with
most of the Erasmus contingent, he and his wife returned to the
school, while I gave Bertha a lift into the centre of Lewes for
some shopping.

On the way there, I enquired casually about Mrs Dragson.
'You don't suppose she forgot about it, do you? Or perhaps she
was having a quick shut-eye after lunch, and when she woke up
it was too late – though it's not like her to be caught napping!'
I laughed.

Bertha also laughed, and said that she thought she had been
doing something much more interesting than napping.

'Oh really? What sort of thing?'

'Well,' Bertha said, lowering her voice despite there being no
one else in the car, 'between you and me, I think she had an
assignation.'

'An assignation? Whatever do you mean?'

Bertha gave a stifled giggle. 'I mean I think she has a fancy
man!'

I was taken aback. Mrs Dragson was a widow of several years, and being resilient, assured and independent, seemed entirely content with that status. Was she really seeing some man, 'fancy' or otherwise? She was a stickler for correct protocol, and he would need to be a pretty special beau to stop her fulfilling a professional duty, and particularly one lasting less than an hour.

'I should think that's hardly likely,' I remarked. 'And apart from anything else, she's not exactly in the prime of youth, is she?'

'Ah well,' Bertha replied sagely, 'that sort of thing can hit at any age.'

That too took me aback. Clearly this rather lumpish gymnast knew more of life than one would have guessed.

'Er, yes,' I agreed, 'of course. But what makes you think she has been seeing someone?'

'There have been *sightings*,' Bertha replied enigmatically.

Naturally, my instinct was to ask what sort of sightings and by whom, but experience has taught me that sometimes an assumed indifference can be more useful than obvious curiosity. Thus for a couple of minutes we drove on in silence. But at the outskirts of the town, just where the A27 verges off into the Lewes Road, Bertha cleared her throat and said, 'Of course, I could be wrong about the *other* commitment. She may just have preferred to stay away and not play the hypocrite.'

'Why hypocrite?' I asked, braking to avoid a rabbit.

'The Dragon didn't like her. As the senior matron she had to be patient and helpful, of course, but I think that was a *front*, a veneer to gloss over her real feelings.'

'Goodness, Bertha, you sound as if you've been reading Raymond Chandler or Freud!' I exclaimed. 'Why should she have disliked Miss Memling?'

'Because she thought she was nasty.'

'*Nasty?* Whatever do you mean?'

'She thought she was some sort of threat.'

'Really? What sort of threat?'

Bertha said she didn't know but thought it was something to do with hatred. She paused, trying to remember, and then said,

'Yes, that's it, Mrs D said that she was someone who cherished a hatred and had an unforgiving heart.'

'Good Lord,' I exclaimed, turning my head to look at her, 'that's a pretty big indictment, isn't it? Are you sure?'

'Oh yes. The Dragon doesn't mince her words, you know.'

Hmm. Evidently not. When I asked why Mrs Dragson would have taken that view, she said she had no idea but supposed that she had seen something there not quite nice. (As shorthand for Mrs Dragson's actual words, *not quite nice* seemed a bit of an understatement.) Bertha added that the Dragon was a pretty good judge of character and could tell her arse from her elbow. I have to admit to being surprised by the expression. Evidently these days gym mistresses are more aware of such distinctions and are rather more eloquent than when I was at school.

I asked why she should think Mrs Dragson a good judge of character.

'Well, it was last term and a new chap had come to take over the senior boys' science classes. None of us liked him because he was so vain and always thought he knew best. But right from the very first day, Mrs D had taken against him: she said that there was something very wrong there and that he wouldn't last out the term. And do you know, she was dead right. After a few weeks he started to have sudden fits of temper and would throw the board rubber around and swear appallingly. The boys didn't know whether to admire or hate him – the latter mostly. In fact, he made two kids cry and there was an awful scene. Mrs Dragson was furious, and I remember her storming into the staffroom declaring that she was going to report him to the headmaster, and that if he continued firing off like that he would damn well get hoisted by his own petard. And he was too! Winchbrooke blew him to smithereens and he was sacked the next day. I believe he's in a sanatorium now.'

I was silent, absorbing her words as I carefully overtook a wandering lorry. The picture of the young man's derangement was disturbing, of course, but far more startling was what, according to Bertha, Mrs Dragson had angrily predicted: that he would be hoisted by his own petard. Had she really used that expression?

It is often observed that if you are confronted by a hitherto unfamiliar word or phrase, in the next few days you will encounter it all over the place. I knew the idiom, of course (as did Sickie-Dickie, albeit not its proper meaning), but in my experience it is not all that widely used or publicly known. It is not, for example, like Hamlet's 'To be or not to be' or Churchill's 'We shall fight on the beaches'. An interesting coincidence therefore that the senior matron at Erasmus House had been heard using the Shakespearean term and that the now dead junior matron should have apparently been sent a textual reference to the self-same quote. Coincidences are rife, of course, and it would be foolish to set much store on this particular one . . . Wouldn't it?

Brooding on this, I forgot to press Bertha for more details of the Dragon's alleged 'fancy man'. But such gossip could wait for another time. Besides, by now we were nearing the town centre and my passenger's mind was clearly fixed on things of greater moment than the words and behaviour of a middle-aged school matron: the acquisition of a 'super-duper' new tracksuit with blazing stripe from thigh to ankle, and which apparently was going to 'slay 'em in the aisles!' Crikey.

TWENTY-FOUR

The Primrose version

The day had been rather wearisome. I had been up in London – an outing I normally enjoy, but this time my purpose had been prosaic: to sort out some affairs with my solicitor and to harangue the art suppliers for sending the wrong paints and brushes. It was the second time they had muddled the order, and since the girl on the telephone had been hopeless, I had decided to confront them in person. This worked: abject apologies from the top man and a twenty per cent discount off my next order. Quite right too!

I had expected to squeeze in a little shopping at Dickins & Jones, but somehow the rigours of the day had taken their toll, and I was more than ready to quit the 'gay metropolis' for the quieter airs of Sussex. However, I had no intention of ending my trip without the prospect of at least some enjoyment: I would try my chances for the Brighton Belle. The style and comfort of one of its Pullman cars would make a pleasant welcome at the end of a somewhat tiresome day. Thus, I took a taxi to Victoria, rushed to the booking office and just in time managed to procure a seat. Breathless but relieved, I then proceeded in seemly fashion to the waiting train.

As I made my way among the crowds, I happened to glance to my right and saw a familiar figure – but a figure not in her usual brogues and navy coat and skirt; instead, she was wearing a rather smart fur jacket and high (or highish) heels. Despite the difference in attire, I immediately recognized the straight back and brisk walk of Mrs Dragson. She was making for a different platform from mine and was probably intending to catch a standard train to Brighton or perhaps to Lewes itself. But then she stopped and waved to somebody in the crowd and I saw someone wave back – a man in a trilby hat, perhaps a friend she had suddenly recognized or who had been seeing her off. Before hurrying on, she turned her head to glance at the clock, and I was surprised to see she was wearing lipstick. And so was I, of course, but I hadn't noticed it on the Dragon before – evidently another item of the off-duty mufti.

I wondered idly what she had been doing – a business appointment, lunch with friends, a matinée? But then another thought struck me and I smiled: maybe it had been an 'assignation' of the kind Bertha had so slyly hinted at! But there was no time for such prurient speculation, for ahead of me I could see the guard beginning to pace about and, hastily grabbing a paper from the newsboy, I leapt aboard the Belle.

Collapsed in my seat, I ordered a dry martini from the steward, selected Oeufs Benedicte from the menu, and under the glow of the pink table lamp I settled down to scan the *Evening Standard*.

I flipped through the pages, though there was little of real interest. But as I was about to put it aside, my eye was caught by a small advertisement for Brighton's Majestic, which included a photograph of its imposing façade. The hotel described itself as being an establishment of traditional values and the epitome of style and elegance . . . not adjectives I would personally apply. Nor was I quite sure what was meant by 'traditional values' . . . drink, dalliance and death? I thought of Miss Memling and suspected that the promotion was an attempt to throw a glossy veil over its recent embarrassment.

A firm believer in living for the moment, I banished such speculation and applied myself in earnest to the poached eggs and dry martini (both impeccable), and for a good twenty minutes was totally absorbed in such welcome necessities . . . But with the last of London rapidly receding, and with coffee and a cigarette, I sat back to muse on matters nearer home. I thought again of Mrs Dragson – not to speculate about any private life she might have, but to brood on what Bertha had said in the car about her dislike of her assistant whom she had apparently considered a 'threat'. Indeed, her words had been startlingly graphic: one who had *cherished a hatred* and was possessed of *an unforgiving heart*. Well, those are not terms to be used lightly, and not by one as steady as Mrs Dragson.

Had those actually been her words? Or had Bertha, in her rather melodramatic way, been exaggerating? But if Bertha was right, and Mrs Dragson had really felt such antipathy towards the dead woman, perhaps that was the reason for her not attending the burial. Nothing to do with prior commitments – of any kind – but simply reluctance to display a respect which she could not feel. Quite possibly. But if that were the case, *why* might she have felt that?

I had asked Bertha the same question, but all she could say was that Mrs Dragson was a shrewd judge of character. Well, so she might be, but that doesn't get one very far. Among the staff there was the general view that the woman had been dull and uncommunicative (except when on the telephone to the unknown caller!), but evidently Mrs Dragson had seen beyond that impression to something else, and something not very agreeable. After all, in their respective roles the two women would have been in fairly close contact. Had this proximity enabled the senior one to gain a sharper insight? I thought of my own theory: that Aida Memling had cast herself in the role of avenging angel pursuing a mission of righteous punishment. Had Mrs Dragson sensed a concealed belligerence, glimpsed a vindictive side to this 'non-entity'? It was interesting that my perhaps theatrical analogy of an avenging angel should chime so closely with another's perspective – and this a perspective of one who had actually known the woman. I took another cigarette, lowered the table lamp's pink shade and pondered.

By now, the Belle was nearing its namesake. It had been a most civilized journey and I was almost sorry that it had ended so soon. I would most definitely use the train again when travelling back from London. No other would do!

I disembarked, waved goodbye to the steward, picked up the car and made for home. I did, however, remember to stop off to collect Bouncer from Mr Richardson, our friendly vet, who on occasions will agree to play host for the day. He doesn't own a dog himself but keeps goats. Surprisingly Bouncer is very attached to these and will sit for long periods just staring at them in silence. Richardson says he thinks the goats must enjoy the scrutiny because they become spectacularly skittish.

*   *   *

The next morning, while attending to the chore of cleaning the cat's litterbox, I was also ruminating on my new art project and planning to spend a session in the studio getting the measure of Chanctonbury Ring and the surrounding Downs – until I was forestalled by an apologetic phone call from the library gently reminding me that my annual subscription was a fortnight overdue and asking if I would be interested in renewing it. Well, of course I would be interested, and was annoyed to think that I had been so remiss. As a general rule I am pretty punctilious in such matters. It doesn't do to get a reputation for being 'careless'; one loses face – a condition no Oughterard can accept. Of course, dear Francis was decidedly careless, but at least he died with his reputation intact – and given those theatrical circumstances, one might even say enhanced.

Thus, I dropped everything (which wasn't much unless you count the cat's litter) and dutifully went into the town to pay my dues. As I was approaching the library, I bumped into Daphne Hamlyn coming out. She was laden with books. 'Goodness,' I remarked, 'you're going to be busy.'

'Ah well,' she exclaimed eagerly, 'I've caught the history bug. These are all to do with the Tudors and Henry's various wives, especially Anne of Cleves. Our coming here to Lewes has really set me going and I'm completely bitten! And as I think I told you, I'm hooked on the idea of eventually writing something on the subject. It's really got hold of me and I've joined the History Society. The chairman has been terribly supportive and said I should give a talk to the members next year. What excitement! I've already thought of a possible title: "Anne and Henry: an ill-matched couple". What do you think?'

I can't say that I was overly impressed, but she was clearly madly enthusiastic so I made the appropriate responses, and then asked if Douglas had also caught the bug.

'Huh!' She laughed. 'The only bugs he has caught are the ones on the riverbank. Now that we've moved here from Eastbourne he can't keep away from the place; always there! So, you see, in our different ways we are both obsessives – he with his rod and gaff and passion for the open air, and me with these!' She gestured to the books.

At that moment, a voice said, 'I say, may I help you with those? I can carry them to your car if you like.' A boy wearing an Erasmus cap and blazer stood there. Behind him hovered another boy, smaller and also in school uniform: Sickie-Dickie.

Daphne looked startled, and then beamed and said he could indeed carry them and how nice it was to be approached by one so gallant. Together they went out to the car park and I was left with Dickie. 'What a surprise,' I said. 'Aren't you normally in lessons?'

He explained that a few of them had been allowed into town that morning as a special reward for being good (!!) and that they were being supervised by Mr Pierce, their English master, who had told them to bugger off and return his library book.

'That's nice,' I said vaguely. 'And is that your friend? He seems very polite.'

Dickie nodded. 'That's old Sparks – he likes doing things like that. And in any case, we are having to practise for the arrival of the inspectors. Mr Pierce said we've got to charm the blighters out of the trees. When I asked him why would the inspectors be in the trees, he told me to be quiet or I'd get a clip round the ear.'

I thought it best to ignore that, and instead asked breezily what the boys had been up to recently. 'The last time we met, Dickie, you were being gated because you had been caught in poor Miss Memling's room. I trust there hasn't been any more breaking and entry!'

'Oh, no fear, Miss Oughterard! We are doing something much more fun now. We're *sleuthing*. You see, old Sparks wants to be a detective when he grows up, so he's getting in training and I'm helping him.'

'Very sensible – but, er, who are your targets?'

'Anyone who looks suspicious. There's a lot of people like that.'

'Including me?'

'Oh *no*, Miss Oughterard, you are above all suspicion – and besides, following you would be *dangerous*.' He gave a cheeky grin.

'You bet it would,' I said grimly.

Just then Sparks returned looking pleased with his gallantry. 'One down, two to go,' he said to Dickie. He took a notebook from his pocket and made an entry.

I must have looked puzzled, for Dickie explained that in preparing for the inspection they had been instructed to practise being courteous and to perform three helpful deeds each day which were to be logged and then checked by a member of staff. He added that this was all very well, but the task cut into their sleuthing activities and they had enough stuff to do as it was.

I agreed that it must be most frustrating and suggested that they narrow their scope and restrict it to just one suspect.

And with that helpful advice, I was about to hurry off to renew my subscription, but was stopped by Dickie, who said, 'Oh yes, we've thought of that and we've got a special person in mind.' Catching my arm, he asked eagerly, 'Do you want to know who?'

I hesitated, feeling embarrassed. Would it be wise to be party to these childish games? After all, their target might be somebody like the headmaster or the vicar, and naturally I should be obliged to wag an admonishing finger. It would be better if I knew nothing . . . Too late.

'It's the Dragon,' he whispered.

That startled me. The lady having so recently been in my thoughts, I couldn't help but be intrigued. 'Oh really?' I said casually. 'And why on earth should you select her from the many?'

'She's been meeting someone,' Sparks said.

'How *remarkable*,' I replied sardonically. 'I expect you've also met one or two people in your time – hence our encounter just now.'

'Yes, but not after lights-out and in the school tool shed.'

I have to admit that did rather take me aback, and I was momentarily nonplussed.

'You see,' Dickie broke in, 'it was about nine o'clock and I had got up to have a sla— to spend a penny, and when I looked out of the window, I saw her walking across the garden as if she was going to the shed. I was a bit puzzled by that, because there's nothing in it except the lawn mower and old Wilks' things, so I told Sparkie and we decided to sneak out and sort of sniff the air. It would make good sleuthing practice. We got out by the side door which isn't locked till later, crept over the lawn and looked through the window. It was a bit cobwebby, but we could see them there all right because the man had a torch.'

'What man?'

'The *chap* she was with.' He sniggered. 'Sparks thought they were up to something – you know, necking and all that. But they weren't' – [well, that was a relief!] – 'they were just sitting there jawing – on and on, and I got a bit bored. But Sparks said he was going to try to listen at the door because it wasn't shut properly.'

'Oh yes? You do know that listeners hear no good of themselves,' I said severely.

'But they weren't talking about *us*,' Sparks said, 'but somebody else. The man said, "So that's fixed all right, no more trouble there, though it's a shame it had to be done like that. Not the tidiest of methods."'

I shrugged but asked what had happened then. He said rather lamely that as it was getting jolly cold and the duty master would soon be locking the side door, they had crept back to the dorm. 'But still,' he added brightly, 'as a tracking exercise it worked pretty well, don't you think?'

'Oh indeed,' I agreed, 'but if you don't run off now, Mr Pierce will track you to this very spot and demand to know why you've been so long in returning his library book.'

'Oh no,' Dickie said, looking at his watch, 'it'll be a good ten minutes before he comes out of the pub. Come on, Sparkie, there's just time to get an ice cream!' And, doffing their caps to me, they scampered off.

TWENTY-FIVE

Emily Bartlett to her sister

My dear Hilda,

 Well, I won't say that peace reigns here – it rarely does. But at least one disturbance is dying down: the business of Miss Memling's demise in what I can only describe as those distasteful circumstances. (Naturally, Hilda, one doesn't wish to sound a prig, but I do feel that the manner of the matron's passing is almost as shocking as the death itself. Most unsettling and unsavoury!) Anyway, the vital thing, you will be pleased to know, is that the official verdict has been 'death by misadventure'. This is a great weight off Mr Winchbrooke's mind – and, I may say, off yours truly's. At last one can put the whole sorry affair behind one and look to the future.

 Mind you, not all are so relieved. As said in my last letter, several of the masters had been laying bets on the outcome, and those of a more suspicious (or hopeful) mind are out of pocket and looking rather glum – in particular Grieves, the new geography master, who, being wet behind the ears, was distinctly reckless in his financial outlay. Ah well, youth will learn . . . not, it would seem, that Mother ever learnt very much in her early life, except perhaps how to be difficult; an art she has been assiduously perfecting ever since.

 Anyway, on to lighter things: Miss Memling's interment in the Brighton public cemetery. Mr Winchbrooke was most insistent I should attend, saying that in my role as his essential clerical aide it was only fitting that I should be there to represent the school along with the others. I think his decision to include me in that select little band to have been most gracious – and trust he will recall the compliment when he is approached by Primrose regarding my pay rise (fingers crossed!). And talking of Primrose, she was also present, looking, I have to say, rather elegant in a dark grey suit and matching hat. When she tries (not often) she can appear quite imposing – I suppose it's the long legs and assertive nose, features apparently shared by her late brother.

When we were returning from the graveside, I said to her what a relief the verdict had been. She replied darkly that just because something was a verdict didn't mean it was correct, and that very often the term 'misadventure' was used when the authorities hadn't a clue and didn't know what else to say. You know, Hilda, when we were at school we were told that those of an artistic bent were the least cynical – or at least that is what Miss Pinksome was always declaring. Well, it is certainly not an observation that can ever be made of Primrose Oughterard!

I had fully expected Mrs Dragson to be there, but when in the previous week I reminded her of its time and date, she said dismissively that she wouldn't be going as she had other things to do – or it might even have been 'better' things. But either way, considering they had worked so closely together in the dispensary and she had been Miss Memling's overseer, such an attitude struck me as not being entirely comme il faut, *as our friends across the channel would say! I shot her a distinctly cold glance (presumably the one that dear Mother says makes me look like a frozen parsnip), but she didn't seem to notice, or if she did there was no reaction.*

I will let you know how things go with that little salary matter (but let us hope it is not so little!). Primrose can be fiendishly persistent, so I like to think she will prevail with Mr Winchbrooke. It would be tactful of me to invite her to tea, my only fear being that she will bring the barbarous dog. However, if it results in our enjoying a sprightly trip to Torquay or Le Touquet, the experience will have been worth it!

From your devoted sister,
Emily

TWENTY-SIX

The Primrose version

I have to admit to being both intrigued and suspicious about what Sickie-Dickie and his pal Sparks had told me. If what they were saying was really true about Mrs Dragson meeting an unknown man in the toolshed after dark, then it was, to say the least, surprising. She has always struck me as a sensible and dignified woman and not one given to such questionable charades.

On the other hand, the little beasts could have been stringing me along and lying for all they were worth. If I found that to be the case, then I should complain to Judge Ickington immediately and tell him of his grandson's absurd imagination, not to mention disgraceful cheek. I would also make it clear that I was unlikely to chat with the boy in the future, and that I trusted that His Lordship would instruct him in the dangers of calumny. Huh! Primrose Oughterard was not to be taken for a ride – least of all by small boys, however well connected!

But the more I brooded, the less I believed the pair to be so irresponsible. I had known Dickie for several years. We had always got on well, and I had never had any reason to doubt his basic honesty. And his idolization of Bouncer was surely reassuring. (Children indifferent to cats and dogs have always struck me as questionable.) I had met his friend Sparks only once before, but he too seemed a polite enough boy and not one to make up outlandish lies, even if he was mad on playing Sherlock Holmes. Would he really have invented overhearing that snippet of conversation in the toolshed – about something having been fixed but in an unfortunate way? They were hardly the most riveting words. If the two little scallywags had been intent on concocting an elaborate hoax to make me (or their subject) look a fool then surely they could have done better than that.

So on the assumption they had been telling the truth, what

then had been going on with the normally sensible Mrs Dragson? Why on earth should such a respectable lady have been conducting a nocturnal rendezvous with a man in a shed in the grounds of Erasmus House?

Yet even as I pondered this oddity, I heard my mother's impatient voice: *Remember, Primrose, curiosity killed the cat, and it'll be the death of you too! Stop lurking at keyholes and get on with your homework. You've plenty to do!* I winced at the memory, and dutifully mounted the stairs to the studio to continue my assault on the South Downs.

It was a good move, for I soon became thoroughly engrossed. The new brushes and paints were doing sterling work (it's amazing how a good discount can stimulate the muse) and I worked with deep concentration, my mind set exclusively on trying to capture the form and spirit of those ancient whale-backs. The sun had gone down, and the evening dusk was stealthily gathering. Time to stop and to enjoy a well-earned snifter.

I stopped all right, but the snifter was delayed. For as I descended the stairs, I could hear sounds from below of the dog scrabbling and the cat mewing peevishly. The creatures were getting restive and evidently wanting their supper. Too bad; they could wait. The artist's needs were greater than theirs. But as I reached the bottom of the staircase into the hall, I saw that it wasn't the kitchen they were clamouring to get into but the porch. Bouncer was pawing the door with insistent growls, so presumably they had heard something or someone outside. The evening rag was already on the mat and would have arrived much earlier, so it wasn't the paper boy. But something had definitely disturbed them.

I opened the front door and Bouncer bounded ahead yelping and barking. The cat too had streaked past me, tail high and emitting one of its more ear-splitting screeches. Tentatively I followed and then stopped abruptly. Something lay in my way. I peered through the gathering dusk, and with a start realized it was the body of a man: face downwards and moaning. The two animals had also stopped and were silently staring – the dog's hind legs quivering, the cat's tail twitching.

I gazed down nervously. The moaning increased, and with a

heave the recumbent figure turned over and looked up at me. It
was Douglas Hamlyn.

'Ah,' he said, 'sorry about this.'

Despite the gloom, I discerned a hipflask at his side. 'You
mean being drunk,' I replied briskly.

'Exactly . . .' He sighed. There was a slight pause, and then
he added, 'Well not fearfully drunk, just mildly.'

'I see,' I said, 'mild enough to fall flat on your face in the
middle of my drive. Next time let me know when you are going
to do it properly and I'll take cover. Meanwhile you had better
have some strong coffee. Can you get up or do you need a hoist?'

'I'll manage,' he murmured, and having groped for the
discarded hipflask, laboriously got to his feet. Whereupon, as if
in encouragement or applause, Bouncer promptly stood on his
hind legs and gave him a friendly nudge. Douglas staggered but
remained upright.

I leant him my arm and the three of us made our stumbling
way back to the house – or rather the humans stumbled, the dog
just trotted. Maurice had already vanished.

Once inside, and after availing himself of the downstairs loo and
I had produced ink-black coffee, our guest relaxed and achieved
an air of semi-sobriety. Naturally he was full of apologies, but I
was more interested in why he should have been in that condition
in the first place and why on earth he had chosen my drive for
the grand finale.

He explained that he had been grappling with a few problems
recently and that with Daphne being away up in London visiting
her brother, had felt that a stiff drink and brisk walk might do
him good and with luck ensure a good night's rest. But unfortunately, having had a couple of whiskies before setting out,
downing a refill en route had made him a trifle befogged; so
much so that on his way home he had taken a wrong turn down
my drive, tripped and fallen his length.

'And I am afraid that, having hit the ground, I found it quite
pleasant to lie there for a while communing with the ants and
beetles – that is, until I was disturbed by your two inquisitive
friends.' He smiled and added, 'I am sure it is a state you are

not familiar with, Miss Oughterard.' (Oh no? I recalled my time
at the Courtauld.) He started to apologize again, but graciously
I waved this aside and instead said that since he had evidently
been kept awake by his problems (and I recalled the chemist's
sleeping pills), would he like to tell me about them.

There was a long silence during which I offered him a cigarette. Drawing on it heavily, he replied, 'Well, no, if you don't
mind, I wouldn't really. And in any case it's a rather long story.'
Under his breath I heard him mutter, 'Too bloody long.' There
was another pause while he continued to puff and inhale. I noticed
the shaking fingers. Drink? Nerves?

And then with a sigh, and looking at me steadily, he said,
'Actually, perhaps I will tell you some of it. It's a bit tricky, you
see, and, er, what you might call domestic – or at least partly.
Can I count on your discretion?'

'Absolutely! Now, what is it?'

He hesitated, and then extinguishing the cigarette and taking
a deep breath, he began. 'It all stems from those two women
when we were in South Africa, but Eunice was the worst. She
was rather awful and it all went wrong – terribly wrong. Yes, the
problem was Eunice Mary Mel—' To my dismay he broke off,
clasping his head in his hands.

It was an uncomfortable sight and I felt sorry for him for I
could see his shoulders beginning to shake. There was a brief
silence. And then, collecting himself, he cleared his throat and
started again. 'You see, there's been a spot of bother recently
and my wife seems to think that we should . . .'

Alas, I heard no more; for at that moment we were interrupted.
An interruption of excruciating noise and commotion. In the hall
Maurice and Bouncer were engaged in fisticuffs. That is to say,
they were having one of their serious set-tos.

Normally their disputes are relatively mild, voiced by low
growls and indignant miaows, but very occasionally things will
erupt into full-on fury of hellish proportion. This was just such
a time. With a bloodcurdling shriek the cat shot into the room
followed by the dog roaring like the Hound of the Baskervilles.
For a few seconds they rampaged wildly. Then, like a feline
Nijinsky Maurice made a flying leap to the top of a bookcase,

from where he hissed abuse at the bellowing dog, whose antics to reach him toppled the flower vase and dislodged a number of books.

It was my turn now and, seizing the poker, I brandished it fiercely and managed to shoo them out through the open French windows. Unperturbed, they continued the battle on the flagstones. But I wasn't having that. The garden tap was close by, and with its attached hose at full throttle, I quickly put an end to the mayhem.

Sodden and silent, they slunk into the bushes, and rather breathlessly I went back to the drawing room. Here I found our visitor even paler than on arrival and making feeble efforts to straighten the cushions and gather the spilt flowers and fallen books. Well, I thought, at least that will have sobered him up! It had, and amid mutual apologies, he hastily took his leave.

Needless to say, I was simply furious with the animals; not so much because of the fracas itself – embarrassing though that had been – but because with a bit more probing I might have learnt what had been bugging the man. Certainly he had been reluctant to explain, but when under the influence it is amazing what can seep from normally tight held lips. *In vino veritas*, as I had discovered in my student days. And as I have to keep telling Ingaza, I am certainly no nosey parker, but I could have been *helpful* and given sound advice, something I like to think I am quite good at doing. Wretched creatures!

Later, with animals fed and subdued, and me with by now an even more necessary restorative in hand, I sat and mused on the events.

Yes, obviously Douglas had been tight, but the inebriation had shown an aspect of his character hitherto unseen: vulnerability. Gone was the air of quiet but genial self-assurance, and in its place one saw uncertainty, strain and confusion. Alcohol in some will induce a boringly bovine stupor, in others cackling mirth or rampant aggression. In this man, behind the typically slurring speech and unsteady gait there was clearly a nagging and helpless worry. He said the problem was a long story – 'too bloody long,' he had murmured. But he had also implied that the trouble was partly domestic, something he was evidently unable to cope with (and feared?). Was Daphne threatening divorce; were they perhaps about to split? If so, this was hardly an unusual cause of anxiety . . . and yet, it would seem, not something shared by Daphne, who, when last seen at the library, had seemed in the peak of high spirits and clearly intent on pursuing the subject of her talk to the History Society: the marital problems of a couple occupying a different era and a different rank. Few things change, it would seem, whatever the period or social context.

On that rather philosophical and sleepy note, I was about to rouse myself to go upstairs to bed, but my eye was caught by something in the corner of the sofa: Douglas's silver hipflask. Really, why couldn't visitors, drunk or sober, remember to take their belongings with them! Would he sheepishly enquire after it the following day, or should I take the initiative and telephone a tactful reminder? But then, of course, he might not welcome such a reminder, preferring to put the whole incident behind him, and if that meant losing the thing then so be it. Oh well, I thought, a petty enough question and not one worth losing sleep over. I left the thing on the sofa, feeling too tired even to pick it up. Its fate could be dealt with in the morning.

When morning came, I still felt rather tired but managed to drag myself downstairs to give the cat its milk. But with nothing particularly scheduled, I then returned to bed with coffee and the newspaper. The previous evening's drama had faded somewhat and seemed almost inconsequential – one of those embarrassing social upsets which we all encounter at some time or other. A little later, and feeling much restored, I dressed and went into the drawing room to retrieve Douglas's hipflask from the sofa.

It wasn't there. Not on the sofa nor anywhere else; not a single sign of it in the whole damn room . . . I began to think that I must be unhinged, that I had reached the age of hallucination and memory loss. No, of course not; what nonsense! I must have picked it up after all and left it in another room. I looked around the hall, the study, the kitchen. Nothing.

Was it possible that Douglas had returned and sneaked into the house to retrieve it? Surely not. Besides, the doors were locked for the night. Weren't they? Front and side door, yes. But the French windows? I rushed to check, and then cursed. The bolt was still pulled back, so somebody could have gained entry and taken the thing from the sofa only a few feet away and then slipped out again. It was just feasible, I supposed, but unlikely. When he left, Douglas hadn't looked fit for anything very much – and besides, what bad manners!

So perhaps, after all, my original assumption had been correct: I had imagined the whole episode and was losing my marbles. I seem to recall that Pa went a bit peculiar towards the end. Was his daughter following suit? If so, whom should I telephone first – my executor or the doctor?

TWENTY-SEVEN

The cat's version

J ust occasionally one has to hand it to the dog – not often, of course, but just now and then when his absurd pranks do provide a risible diversion from my pursuit of sparrows and recalcitrant mice.

One such time was when we were living with F.O. the vicar, and Bouncer had commandeered the interior of our master's piano stool as a secret larder for his disgusting bones. And they weren't just thrown in higgledy-piggledy but neatly arranged in careful order according to size and age. (For a dog of such unkempt appearance and crude manners, Bouncer can be very fastidious where food is concerned.) Eventually, of course, the humans discovered the hidey-hole and the balloon went up – but not before such novel usage had afforded me the greatest amusement.

That example brings me to his current exploit: the appropriation of an object that one of P.O.'s visitors had foolishly left behind – the same visitor who had the bad manners to prostrate himself across our drive the other evening. It was a tiresome incident as I had just curled up for a quiet doze before embarking on my nightly rounds when Bouncer pricked up his ears and started to make the most irritating noises. He scrabbled about and kept insisting that there was something peculiar outside. I told him that the only peculiar thing outside was the cage housing the chinchillas, Boris and Karloff, and would he kindly be quiet. Naturally he ignored my protests and said that his sixth sense was working overtime. I am generally sceptical of this sixth sense, but occasionally it doesn't hurt to indulge the dog, and so I joined him in the hall to alert P.O. She came crashing down the stairs grumbling and cursing and let us out to investigate.

Rather to my surprise, Bouncer had been perfectly right. For as soon as I sniffed the open air my fur stood on end, and I knew something was amiss. Cautiously the three of us proceeded to explore the drive. But within a few yards we had encountered the man sprawled across our path, moaning and spluttering. When he turned over I recognized him immediately, for he had been among the guests invited to the house some days earlier. He was in a state of what humans term *stupefied inebriation*, but perfectly docile and clearly in no condition to be of trouble to us or our mistress. That being the case, I rather lost interest and wandered off in search of more lively engagements, leaving Bouncer and P.O. to cope with the inebriate.

I will draw a veil over the next two hours for there was an unsavoury episode concerning the dog and myself – Bouncer's fault, of course. We had one of our major altercations (fortunately rare) which for a short period causes universal havoc and much spit and noise. It resulted in P.O. going berserk and resorting to the garden hosepipe. But as said, I prefer not to dwell on the incident. It was a contretemps unbecoming to a cat of my station. *However*, at least it brought the intruder to his senses, for he eventually slunk back up the drive.

By the morning, refreshed from our exertions, Bouncer and I had achieved an amiable rapprochement – so amiable, in fact, that he was eager to tell me of his latest stunt: an absurd piece of tomfoolery!

While I was sipping my breakfast milk, he sidled up and shoved his head next to my ear. 'I say, Maurice,' he snuffled, 'you'll never guess what I've done.'

I replied that it was bound to be something indelicate and that such topics were not appropriate at breakfast.

'Oh, this won't put you off your milk,' he said. 'It's jolly good!'

I sighed and, pushing the saucer to one side with my paw, told him that I was all ears.

'I've nabbed his whatsit,' he chortled.

'You've done *what*?'

'His whatsit – that thing he left on the sofa. I've got it in my basket, under the rug.'

I regarded him blankly. 'What thing on the sofa and when did you take it?'

He explained that he had woken at dawn and, noticing that the kitchen door had been left open, thought he would have a little potter before going back to sleep. He went into the big room where the man and P.O. had been talking (and which our quarrel had mildly disturbed), in search of his toy rubber ring – invariably mislaid. While sniffing around he noticed an alien object lying on the sofa, and on investigation saw it was something the man had been holding when being helped into the house.

'And you see, Maurice,' he continued, 'I was fed up not finding my old ring because I like carrying things in my mouth and thought that this would do PRO TEM', (a term recently learnt from me and which he declaims loudly at every opportunity). 'So I grabbed it between my teeth and carried it all the way back to my basket. I expect there'll be one hell of a hullabaloo when they find it's not there,' he chuckled. 'But it's safe and secret with old Bouncer! Do you want to see it?'

Well, after that saga what could I say? 'Of course, Bouncer,' I mewed. 'Show me immediately.'

Having provided my morning milk, our mistress had conveniently returned to bed, so I knew it would be safe to admire his trophy undisturbed. I cannot say that I am enamoured of the dog's basket, but, gritting my teeth, I peered into it as he tossed the rug aside. It was an object familiar to me, having seen such a thing several times in the hands of my late master, F.O. the vicar. He would drink from it when particularly agitated by the police, the bishop or the Mothers' Union.

Its lid was dangling from a metal cord and, although empty, some of the dregs had spilt on to the bedding. Personally, I found this distasteful. For a cat of my sensibilities, the smell of gnawed bones and damp dog hair combined with this acrid liquid was distinctly disagreeable and I backed away. But Bouncer, being less discerning, was sniffing it with snorts of approval. 'Cor,' he growled, 'this is a bit of all right!'

I winced. And, having murmured something about having to see a man about a mouse, I withdrew to my shelter under the stairs.

TWENTY-EIGHT

The Primrose version

Perturbed though I was about the hipflask, I had no intention of allowing it to ruin my day. There was surely some logical explanation which in the fullness of time would be revealed.

Thus taking myself firmly in hand, I concentrated on other matters: driving into the local garage for the car's monthly wash and then on to Brighton to meet Ingaza. He had telephoned earlier, keen to discuss an extension he was having built for the art gallery. For months he had been tussling with the authorities to grant planning permission, and which – no doubt wearied by his tireless offensive of grease and guile – they had finally allowed. Hence the victor had felt a small celebration was called for at the Old Schooner (a hostelry much preferred to the flashy Majestic). I wondered whether to take Bouncer, but hearing gentle snores coming from his basket in the kitchen I thought better of it. Let sleeping dogs lie!

As I waited at the garage for the car to be sluiced and polished, I noticed Inspector Spikesy. He was sitting on a bench in the sun, evidently also waiting to collect a vehicle. Winchbrooke had said something about his having been away on some other business and his place taken by a locum. Therefore, apart from his initial visit to the school during the Memling crisis, he would probably have had little to do with the case. Still, something further might be gleaned, and it was worth a try. I was sceptical of the 'misadventure' verdict and still most intrigued by the peculiar circumstances. In any case, I like Spikesy and our conversations are always congenial.

We exchanged waves and I went over to chat. I asked after Mrs Spikesy, and since they had already bought three of my pictures, I told him I was extending my range to include studies of the Downs themselves, especially around Firle and Ditchling, and not just their churches.

'But I hope there will be one featuring the Wilmington Giant,' he said. 'The wife would like that.'

I said that I hadn't really considered the Long Man as it had been done so often.

'Ah, but not with your special touch,' he replied gallantly.

I laughed and said that in that case I would do one especially for them – and naturally free of all charges. In this, I hasten to say, I was being perfectly sincere. However, such gestures are always helpful when one is after information.

We talked a little more, and then, glancing at my watch, I took the bull by the horns. 'I gather that grisly business involving the Erasmus matron has ended rather inconclusively. Death by misadventure, I gather. At least that's one thing less for you to bother about,' I added brightly.

'Well, it was never really my case; it was mainly the Brighton lot's. And when old Carstairs replaced me for a while, he was so keen to take his early retirement that he wasn't exactly champing at the bit to investigate beyond the obvious. It could have prolonged his service no end.'

'And the obvious being?'

He shrugged. 'Suicide, I expect. The poor woman was either drowning her sorrows or more likely did it deliberately. There was the additional drug, you see.'

'But somebody could have slipped her that as a Mickey Finn.'

'Hmm. I shouldn't think so. Normally when that happens there's a sign of . . .' He paused and cleared his throat discreetly. 'Uhm, well, some kind of sexual activity. But there wasn't any.'

'So how did she get hold of the drug?'

He shrugged again. 'Probably got it from a doctor at some point and then stored it up. It's a very potent sedative, a sort of relaxant, so she might have been having difficulties of one sort or another.'

Still probing, I said as casually as I could that Mr Winchbrooke had mentioned something about the police having taken some papers from her room.

'Yes, but there wasn't anything much, and they were handed

over to Carstairs. Some photograph of an angel and something
about tides turning . . . Oh yes, and there was a small notebook
with nothing in it except the words "A cheap little gold digger
and a cruel Lothario" plus an exclamation mark. Don't know
what that was supposed to mean. It was in inverted commas, so
probably a quote she fancied or the title of a novel. Anyway, as
said, that was for Carstairs' pigeon to make sense of – if it had
any.'
      Out of the corner of my eye I could see the garage man beck-
oning me to admire the newly spruced car. It was time to go.
Spikesy too had been hailed and, bidding goodbye, we walked
to our respective vehicles. 'Don't forget the Long Man!' he
shouted.
      'It's first in line,' I cried. It would be too. After all, he deserved
some thanks for being so open about the Memling affair . . . that
additional detail about the gold digger, et cetera, was rather
intriguing. I would tell Ingaza, should he be remotely
interested!
      As I sped towards Brighton, I started to reflect on what Spikesy
had been saying, but the mystery of the missing hipflask kept
interrupting. Despite my efforts to kick it away, the wretched
thing kept coming back into my mind. Nag, nag, nag. It was a
bit much!

I was able to park on the seafront only a few yards from the Old
Schooner. Ingaza was already there, perched on his habitual high
stool at the lounge bar. Always natty, today he looked especially
svelte in what I took to be a new and impeccably tailored suit;
a purchase no doubt to celebrate his victory over the city planners. And even from a distance I thought I could detect an air
of smug satisfaction in the way he wafted his cigarette and beamed
at the barman. Seeing me, the beam grew wider, and detaching
himself from the stool he executed a neat bow.
      'Primrose, dear girl, delighted to see you! And what a lovely
blouse!' he smarmed.
      I told him that he wasn't looking bad himself, but that perhaps
his hair could do with the teeniest trim.
      He leered and, running thin fingers through the brilliantine,

said, 'Ah, but that's the casual look these days; it doesn't do to
appear too military.'

The idea of Nicholas Ingaza ever appearing military was laugh-
able (although Francis had once whispered that he thought he
had been at Bletchley in the war, but perhaps civvies were
permitted there). Anyway, he bought me a double of something
and led the way to a table in the dining room. Having ordered
lavishly from the à la carte, he embarked on his recent triumph
re the gallery extension and the planners' eventual submission.
'Ran circles around them,' he preened, 'and in the end all their
defences were down. So, full steam ahead now!'

He proceeded to wax lyrical about the purpose, style and
proportions of the new building. It was a lengthy spiel and I fear
that my mind occasionally wandered back to the hipflask. I
suppose I must have been looking a trifle abstracted, for Ingaza
ceased and exclaimed impatiently, 'You haven't listened to a
word I've been saying; my brilliant description was totally
wasted!'

'Oh no,' I said hastily, 'I have heard quite a lot – it's, er,
fascinating.'

'Balls. There's obviously something distracting that questionable mind. What is it?'

'Well, if you want to know, I have had rather an odd experience recently, and—'

'Huh! Nothing new about that. Most of your experiences are
odd, and that's putting it nicely. So what is it this time? Not that
bloody Memling business, I trust.' He flicked his ash and frowned.

'Er, no,' I replied, 'it's to do with me actually – my mental
state. I think I may be—'

'Oh Christ, that's all we need!' He groaned. 'Still, I suppose
you had better tell me if you must.'

I toyed with my drink, took a gulp and then related the saga
of Douglas's intrusion and the vanishing flask. 'So there you
are,' I concluded. 'I think your charming friend may be going
quietly bonkers.'

'Nothing quiet about you, Primrose. If you were going bonkers
you would do it dramatically with one hell of a fuss.'

I bristled. 'Nonsense,' I exclaimed indignantly. 'I should

succumb with the greatest decorum . . . Anyway, if I'm not mad then what's the answer?'

He thought for a few moments and then said, 'Well, there are two possibilities: either your intoxicated friend did return and sneak in via the French windows and is now too embarrassed to own up – or it's old Scragarse.'

'Maurice? Whatever do you mean?'

'I wouldn't put anything past that cat. He'd nick the crown jewels if it suited. A nice piece of shiny silver on the sofa, what could be more enticing?'

I had a momentary image of Maurice crouched upon the cushions purring softly, left paw extended to make quizzical little pokes at the fresh novelty. But I shook my head. 'No, Nicholas. You may be right about his acquisitive nature, but despite being an expert at toting dead mice around, even he couldn't carry a thing like that in his mouth.' I was about to go on to say that perhaps it had been Douglas after all when Ingaza interrupted.

'But Bouncer could,' he said. 'Underneath that massive fringe there's a sly mind at work. He probably thought it was some new-fangled bone and grabbed it to bury in the garden. You'll see.'

We laughed and turned to other matters: the state of the nation, his new tango partner, Eric's invitation that I should join him for a darts session and – because I felt things were now sufficiently eased – my recent conversation with Inspector Spikesy.

'You see,' I said, 'it may sound far-fetched, but if my hunch about her having harboured a grudge against someone is right, and that in her role as punishing angel she was sort of hounding them, then that line about the cheap little gold digger and the cruel Lothario may be significant. Spikesy thought it might be the title of a book or a quotation. Maybe, maybe not. But apparently she had put an exclamation mark against it, so it must have meant something to her. The linking of the two types sounds as if two people were involved.'

'Really?' Ingaza said. 'It sounds a bit ambiguous to me. Why two people? It could be one person combining both tendencies, i.e. someone who exploits others for money and also happens to be a promiscuous lover.'

I thought about that. Technically he was right, of course, but I wasn't convinced. The adjectives 'cheap' and 'little' suggest something sneaky and petty (and though perhaps unfairly, were often applied to women); whereas a 'cruel Lothario' conjures a different image altogether: masculine and ruthless. I shook my head. 'No,' I said, 'I don't think the two harmonize. I am sure they refer to two different people, and probably of different sexes: a woman and a man.'

'Hmm,' he murmured, tucking into the first course, 'you could be right. It has been known, I suppose.'

How gracious! I too switched my attention to the plate of grilled mussels, and for a short while there was silence. And then he said severely, 'In your tête-à-tête with your beloved Spikesy, I trust you didn't mention Eric and what he had told you about Fred seeing that chap going upstairs with her. That was strictly off the record and Eric shouldn't have mentioned it. With his background the last thing Fred wants is to be involved with the police.' He paused, and then added more lightly, 'As none of us do, Primrose. You may recall, dear girl, that there are one or two unfortunate episodes in the past with which we have both been associated. It wouldn't look too good if those were disinterred, would it? I don't know about you, but personally I am looking forward to a quiet old age unencumbered by officious law officers.' He replenished his glass of Chablis and refilled mine.

I appreciated this last gesture and accepted the warning but was irritated by his reference to Spikesy. 'Inspector Spikesy is not beloved by me,' I replied coldly. 'We merely get on well. However, *dear boy*, I can assure you that I told him nothing of Fred's comments, nor shall I. After all, that is entirely hearsay and what Eric's pal chooses to do or not do is nothing to do with me.'

'Exactly.'

'Nevertheless,' I went on, 'you must admit that it is rather intriguing, isn't it?' And I gave an encouraging smile.

It wasn't quite reciprocated, but very nearly. 'If you say so,' he replied. 'But for God's sake, be careful. If someone really did murder this woman and they learn that you are sniffing about and on their trail, they may object and take pre-emptive action. On the *whole*, I suppose that might be a shame.'

And on that merry note we fell to the rest of our lunch, and in hushed tones began to dissect the oddities of our fellow diners.

When I reached home, though eager to get back to the studio, my mind was still fixated on the lost hipflask. And, stirred by Ingaza's idea that Bouncer may have been the culprit, I had been fondly imagining that as I opened the front door lo and behold it would be there staring me in the face. Often when bored with a particular plaything the dog will leave it in the middle of the hall to be retrieved later (or tripped over by me). This time, needless to say, the hall was immaculate.

I went into the kitchen to make a coffee to take up to the studio. From the window I could see my two companions peaceful in the garden: Maurice curled up by the sun dial and Bouncer lolling by the wooden railings, tired no doubt from monitoring the sheep in the adjacent field. As I waited for the kettle to boil, I happened to glance at his empty basket. It wasn't a pretty sight and I could see that the worn blanket needed a good wash – or better still, disposal in the dustbin. Fortunately, I had bought a replacement only the other day, and with its owner quiescent outside, it seemed a good time to make the swap without any grumbling protests. Thus I quickly bent down and stripped off the less than salubrious covering. It was there: right in the middle of the under rug.

The expression 'I couldn't believe my eyes' is surprisingly exact, as for a couple of seconds I literally felt I was seeing things. But in the next instant, realizing that I was not, I emitted a gasp of relief. Delight and fury battled together. Oh, how marvellous! Oh, wretched, wretched hound! I grabbed the article, put it on the highest shelf and pelted into the garden to remonstrate with the villain.

In retrospect, I think Bouncer must have sensed that something was amiss and not to his advantage. For before I had a chance to say anything he had leapt up and was hurtling towards me, tail wagging fit to fall off. There was a collision and, standing on his hind legs and amidst yelps of excitement, he proceeded to buffet and nuzzle me as if I was his long-lost playmate. It is difficult to withstand such an approach, and if he had hoped to disarm me he certainly succeeded. I patted his head and weakly told him that he was very naughty and very sweet. These had not been the words originally in my mind.

TWENTY-NINE

The Primrose version

My main relief at finding the missing article was to know that I was neither going out of my mind nor being jinxed by some poltergeist. Nevertheless, there still remained the problem of what to do with the thing.

So far there had been no enquiry from its owner, and I was hesitant to initiate contact in case Daphne had returned from visiting her brother. Were that the case, I rather doubted if Douglas had told her of his disorderly visit. It had been an embarrassing episode for both of us and possibly not something he would care to mention to his wife, or indeed to anyone. Thus, acting on Pa's old advice – when in doubt do nothing – I did exactly that. If Douglas wanted the flask returned then he would jolly well have to ask for it, and in his own good time. Meanwhile I would keep it somewhere safe and well away from roving paws and jaws! If required, at least I was now in a position to produce the damn thing. Thus I wrapped it in paper, went up to my bedroom and placed it carefully in one of the hat boxes on top of the wardrobe. Let that be a challenge to the dog!

I now had another task to perform: tea with Emily Bartlett. In a moment of thoughtless altruism I had promised I would try pulling the odd string with Winchbrooke to increase her salary. I've always felt that he was a bit stingy, and while Emily can be irritating, as his secretary she is indispensable. Being Winchbrooke, he may not always realize that. So far there hadn't been a chance to bend his ear, but I most certainly would. (Never let it be said that the Oughterards are slow in coming forward – except for Francis, of course.) Anyway, I rather suspect that Emily's invitation was a gentle prompt to pursue the matter.

I debated whether to take Bouncer with me but decided against it. I have noticed Emily twitching when in the presence of the dog. Can't think why. After all, when he isn't nicking other people's property or bellowing at the sheep and the cat, he is a most genial hound. But he certainly seems to unnerve Emily – though, of course, a lot of things do.

As she lives only half a mile away, I thought a brisk walk would do me good. So I set off smartly at four o'clock to reach her at the precisely instructed time of a quarter past. Her compact house is neatness personified and everything there is clean and orderly. But it is what you might call a blend of the bland and bizarre . . . bizarre in that you are met with a stone gnome in the porch with beard and fishing rod, while its brother keeps vigil by the garden door. Other than these two sentries, there is nothing either to offend or to gladden the eye.

However, what did gladden me was to see Bertha Twigg lolling in a deck chair: an occasional example of three being company and two rather less. To my surprise, she was deeply engrossed in painting her nails – a glittering crimson (unlike the pallid pink flaunted by our hostess a couple of weeks previously). Leaving Emily busying herself over kettle and teacups in the kitchen, I went to join Bertha at the garden table.

'What are you doing that for?' I asked. 'Stepping out on the tiles tonight?'

'No, worse luck. I'm practising.'

'For what?'

'Well, you know that new tracksuit I was going to buy?'

'The one with the gold stripe down the leg?'

'Yes, and it fits like a dream and shows off every curve, and so—'

'But I thought tracksuits were supposed to be loose.'

She gave a throaty chuckle. 'Not this one, it's really stream-lined. Anyhow, I think that to complete the job I should wear something eye-catching on my nails.'

'For the school inspection?'

'Oh, blow the inspection! No, for when I compete in the All-Schools Gymnastic Competition. I'm down for the wall bars and horse vaulting sections. I came third out of twenty last year, and this time I'm determined to jolly well win!' She paused, and then with a leer, added, 'And if not win, then at

least I'll dazzle 'em with my nails!' Waving her fingers in the
air as if conducting an orchestra, she collapsed into peels of
mirth, interrupted by Emily bearing a tea tray with doilies and
minuscule scones.

During tea a number of subjects were touched upon – mainly
to do with the school and the misdemeanours of its inmates, but
Emily also talked gaily about her and Hilda's plan to take a trip
to Le Touquet, at least twice adding the proviso: '*if*, of course,
funds permit!' Clearly this was aimed at me and my promise to
nobble Mr Winchbrooke. The hint was reinforced when, turning
to Bertha, she said pointedly, 'Don't you find that sometimes
our illustrious headmaster rather overlooks the hard work we
do?'

If a reply was expected she didn't get one, for Bertha was too
busy trying to wipe cherry preserve from the semi-dried varnish
on her thumbnail. The process clearly required exquisite dexterity
but, alas, seemed to produce only a sticky mélange of jam and
polish. For one ghastly moment I thought she might try to lick
it off, but politely and covertly she continued to use the white
linen napkin. Emily was sitting on the opposite side of the table
and I think the finer details of the process may have escaped her
notice. Later, of course, the result would be only too plain, for
contrary to the popular saying, not everything comes out in the
wash.

However, the little tea party continued to run smoothly and I
made much of Emily's sprucely cut lawn and predictable petunias.
She accepted the compliments with grace and said that the latter
had been a gift from Mrs Dragson. 'She won them in a raffle,
and not being a gardener, gave them to me. She said she didn't
like them anyway.'

Bertha gave a snort of laughter. 'Typical of the Dragon, she
doesn't mince her words, does she!' She turned to me and said,
'I told you, didn't I, what she said about Miss Memling being a
threat and so on. She certainly had it in for her. Can't think why.
The woman always struck me as being half asleep except when
she was prosing on about South Africa or that time gabbling in
the telephone box and then saying she was going to be the star
turn for some interview or other.' She paused again, then, leaning

forward and with a broad wink, murmured conspiratorially, 'Who knows, *maybe* it was Mrs D and that fancy man who did her in at the Majestic!'

'Oh, really, Bertha,' Emily exclaimed, 'your mind! Besides, that's all over and done with now. It's been established that what happened there, though most distasteful, was hardly sinister. And as for the so-called fancy man, just because she's been seen chatting to some gentleman in a mackintosh doesn't mean she is engaged in a *liaison*.' She wagged a cautionary finger. 'That's how rumours start, you know.'

There was some truth in Emily's words, but Bertha was quite unabashed and replied cheerfully. 'Ah well, stranger things have happened. Just mark my words . . . I say, these scones are jolly good. Have you got any more?'

Emily's frown turned to a smile of pleasure, and she went off quickly to fetch replenishments.

With our hostess safely out of earshot, Bertha leered and said, 'And that's a prime example of the way the least likely things can happen, because the last time I ate scones in this garden they were awful, all dry and hard. But these are really nice. It just shows, there's something to be said for shop-bought ones over the home-made variety, even if they are titchy.' She winked.

The early evening was still warm, and as I walked home from Emily's I chose to take the longer and prettier route. This involved passing Needham Court – not that I had any intention of paying a call. But not far from the entrance, I suddenly glimpsed Daphne walking the little poodle. It was evidently in dawdling mood, pulling on the lead and stopping at every opportunity. Seeing me, she waved and was clearly ready to chat. A little hesitantly, I crossed the road wondering what, if anything, Douglas may have mentioned about his unscheduled visit.

'Ah,' she exclaimed, 'I've just got back from seeing Rufus in London, and what's the first thing I have to do? Take this little tyke for a walk!'

'Isn't the garden big enough?' I laughed.

'Yes, but last week we planted some lily bulbs which will look superb when they come up – *if* they survive. For some reason

Tarzan won't leave them alone and keeps scrabbling in that corner. I suppose the novelty will wear off soon, but for the moment I don't trust him an inch, so the garden is temporarily off limits. Huh! Dogs, who'd have them?'

Thinking of Bouncer's recent exploit, I was inclined to agree, though I could hardly tell her of that. Instead, I asked after Petal, enquiring if he too was keen on lilies.

She shook her head. 'No, it's crisps and soft toys with him – can't get enough of either. But at the moment he's indoors with Douglas; they are both just lolling about being totally useless. A bit of a bore really. Mind you, after London I could do with a bit of lolling myself. The crowds were frightful!'

We prattled on for a while and then went our separate ways; she cajoling the lily-loving Tarzan and me homewards for a lively gin as antidote to Emily's weak tea.

With gin in hand and feet up, I reflected on the afternoon. On the whole it had been pleasant. Emily had done her best to be an attentive hostess and Bertha had been on good form. Meeting Daphne, too, had been useful, in that from what I could make out, Douglas had not apprised her of his drunken visit – or at any rate he hadn't so far. She had rather implied that he was not at his liveliest, so perhaps the memory of that faux pas, plus whatever else was worrying him, had produced a temporary inertia. Oh well, that was their problem . . .

As I mused on this, Bouncer came trotting in toting his dessicated toy rabbit, which he generously laid at my feet. He sat back on his haunches looking, I imagined, suitably contrite.

'You are a great big bad boy,' I said – words which immediately prompted a muddy paw being thrust on to my knee. For a few moments we gazed at each other in solemn silence, though God knows what he was thinking.

Then, removing his paw but leaving the rabbit, he pottered out again, presumably to entertain Maurice in the kitchen.

I closed my eyes. And for some reason Bertha Twigg and her absurd comments about Mrs Dragson and the Majestic came into my mind. I smiled. What an ass that girl was!

*   *   *

I think I must have dozed off for a couple of minutes, for when I opened my eyes I found myself gripped by an absurd thought: supposing that ass of a girl had been right? Was it conceivable that the upright and formidable matron of Erasmus House had indeed been responsible for Aida Memling's death? What fantasy, what rubbish!

As if for distraction, I found myself scanning the room, taking in the comforting sight of mahogany bookcase, sprawling sofa, heavy damask curtains, the Tientsin rug, and Pa's portrait glaring from above the fireplace. These were authentic all right, nothing delusional here: concrete objective facts, solid reminders of the real world, not fragile potty dreams . . . And yet slowly, bit by bit, the idea took hold and continued to nag at my mind as I prepared supper and fed the cat. And inevitably, the more I dwelt on it, the more insistent it became. And sitting at the kitchen table tucking into bacon and eggs, I began to review the 'evidence'.

According to Bertha she had harboured a rooted dislike of her colleague, going so far as to describe her as vindictive and dangerous and nursing a heartless hate; she had unexpectedly declined attendance at the victim's burial, indifferently declaring that she had better things to do. Coincidentally, she had used the Shakespearean expression about being hoisted by one's own petard, the same one referred to in Memling's anonymous note from Penge. According to Bertha there had been occasions when she had been seen with an unknown man – and indeed there was my own sighting of her at Victoria, dressed rather smartly and waving to a chap in the crowd. In itself, of course, that meant nothing, but what about the two boys' account of her meeting a mysterious man in the school grounds at night *and*, according to Sparks, his allusion to a job having been well done and that though regrettable would give no more trouble? Had this nocturnal visitor been the same one she had waved to at Victoria station – or the one seen by Fred accompanying the squiffy Aida Memling up the stairs at the Majestic? Was it conceivable that Mrs Dragson was an accessory after the fact – or indeed, had *engineered* the fact? Could it be possible that she had been a target of the avenging angel's 'mission' and was impatient to rid herself of such tiresome attention? Hmm. As Bertha had remarked in Emily's garden, stranger things have happened . . .

I stared down at my now empty plate. It was, of course, utter speculation, but speculation whose details would seem to hold a kind of coherence. For a moment I was tempted to phone Nicholas Ingaza and run it past him, but I immediately banished the urge. He would drown the idea with buckets of scornful and freezing water.

As I brooded on these things, I realized that the kitchen had gone strangely quiet – not that there's ever much noise, but generally at this time of day one hears the odd creak from Bouncer's basket or a contented purr (or irritable mew) from Maurice. But the only sound was the ticking of the clock. I looked up and saw the two of them staring fixedly at me, the dog with its ears cocked and the cat as still as a statue but with that piercing gaze that used to unnerve my brother. I too was a little unnerved and hastily left the table to wash up the supper things.

The next day, the weather being fine, and eager to keep my promise to Spikesy about a picture of the Long Man of Wilmington, I drove over to Windover Hill to make a few preliminary sketches. With these under my belt I could tackle the rest later in the studio, and with luck produce it in time for his wife's birthday.

It was a pleasantly productive morning, and although I had passed the giant figure numerous times, to be sitting up close to this legendary enigma was both restful and intriguing. As I gazed and sketched, I wondered about the two long staffs grasped so firmly either side of the massive hips. Were they props to aid him as he bestrode those ancient hills? Or in a far-off glacial age had he perhaps been an inveterate skier? But whatever he was supposed to be – whether god, giant, skier, fertility symbol or two-sceptred king – he was now enmeshed in the web of Sussex folklore, and I had much enjoyed his company and would try to do him artistic justice.

On my way home I stopped off in Lewes to do a few errands and, coming out of the post office, bumped into Mrs Dragson

– minus the lipstick when last seen in London, but neat as always. She bid me an affable hello but said she couldn't stop as she was off to stay with a friend in Beckenham, but before that was dropping in on Plumpton Racecourse.

'To ride a horse?' I said jokingly.

'No, silly, to place a bet. I'm backing Jester Boy for the two thirty. Now if you don't mind, I must dash, otherwise I shall miss both horse and train.'

I didn't mind, but was slightly dazed all the same, and watched as she strode purposefully down the hill to the station. 'Really, Primrose,' I muttered inwardly, 'you *are* an idiot. Fancy imagining for one moment that Mrs D could be a . . .' But even as I dismissed the idea, it did occur to me that even matrons and murderers are not averse to a bit of horse racing.

At that moment I saw someone else: Douglas Hamlyn. My instinct was to go over and make tactful enquiries about the hipflask. But he was in close conversation with a man I vaguely recognized as a member of the local angling club, so it hardly seemed the appropriate moment to broach the subject. He glanced in my direction and I hastily turned my face to stare into the window of the fishmonger's. After all, never let it be said that Primrose Oughterard causes embarrassment!

It may have been a trick of the light, but he seemed thinner than when last encountered. Was he still grappling with whatever it was that had made him collapse drunk and disordered in my drive? Once more I wondered how I could conveniently raise the matter of the forgotten flask without making things awkward for him, or indeed for any of us. Probably my initial instinct was right: do and say nothing unless approached.

As I was driving home, my mind returned to Mrs Dragson. I smiled, hoping that Jester Boy had triumphed in the two thirty and won her a nice little packet. But I also recalled her ultimate destination: Beckenham was somewhere in south London – Bromley, wasn't it? So obviously she had managed temporary time off from the school. In which case, with her assistant defunct, the boys would be bereft of a matron for the night. I couldn't see Emily stepping into the breach and doubted whether Bertha

Twigg possessed the patience to administer laxatives and cough medicine – and in any case, she would hardly be the most soothing of nurses. Ah well, perhaps their new geography master would volunteer. I gather he was eager to find favour with Winchbrooke.

But such vagaries were suddenly eclipsed by a recollection so stark that I nearly overshot the turn into my own drive: the Bromley area may contain Beckenham, but the latter is almost adjacent to *Penge*. Thus a note posted in Penge could well have been penned by a resident of Beckenham . . . *or* by someone occasionally travelling there from Lewes. Was Mrs Dragson in the habit of visiting that suburb? Enquiries would be made!

THIRTY

The cat's version

P.O. had been out all day and the house mercifully quiet. However, in the early evening she returned. And after the customary libations in the big room, she came into the kitchen and with much clatter busied herself with supper. I detected a state of some excitement . . . admittedly not unusual for our mistress, but as I knew that one of her day's tasks had been to visit the Emily person, I couldn't quite see wherein lay the stimulus. Perhaps she had also encountered others of a livelier bent. Anyway, she was clearly hungry and demolished the eggs and bacon with a zest not unlike Bouncer's when ravaging his bowl.

And talking of Bouncer, I noticed that he too was watching her carefully. So, after she had washed the supper things and gone upstairs, I said to him, 'Well, what's got into her, I wonder? Something is agitating that dubious mind; she had been relatively calm at breakfast. It's probably to do with the school incident that Lola had gabbled about, or perhaps she is still brooding on your absurd game with that man's silver case. So, what do you think, Bouncer?'

The dog looked vaguely surprised and said he thought I would know. 'After all, Maurice, you know most things.'

I told him that knowing most things did not constitute every-thing, which was why I was seeking his opinion.

Bouncer snuffled and frowned, and then said firmly, 'She's going doolally again.'

I pointed out that all humans are in a state of semi-doolally so I did not think his diagnosis especially helpful.

He looked a bit truculent, then said with a growl, 'Well, you could tell she was chewing on something because she kept tapping her left hand on the table and wiggling her right foot. That's always a sign that something's bugging her.'

'Hmm. Are you sure it was her left hand on the table and not the right? I mean to say, a lot of dogs wouldn't know the difference, would they?' I enquired gently.

Yes, a thoughtless remark no doubt, and it is small wonder that the dog leaped from his basket and confronted me with hackles up and teeth bared. 'SHUT UP, MAURICE!' he roared. 'Or I'll make catmeat of you and use my *right* paw to shove your fat head in the dustbin!'

I retreated hurriedly to the back of the Aga and mewed smooth apologies. 'A little joke, Bouncer,' I explained.

'Some joke,' he grumbled. But then he brightened and said, 'Talking of jokes, that joke of mine worked well, didn't it? You know the one, when I filched Chummy's drinking toy and hid it in my basket. That got her in a right old tizz – though I felt a bit rotten afterwards and was worried that when she found out I'd get a tanning. So I gave her lots of licks and hugs, and after that we both felt better.'

Careful not to provoke a further outburst, I agreed that his performance had been masterly and his apologetic overtures most tactful. 'After all,' I mewed, 'from what we have both observed there is definitely something disturbing that wayward mind, and it doesn't do to stir it further with jolly japes . . . brilliant though yours was,' I added hastily. 'We know from experience that when she pursues one of her madcap projects all manner of things can go adrift – our food, for example. You may recall the time when she was so embroiled with bringing that putrid Latin master to justice that she omitted to supply us with victuals for a whole day and a half. Disgraceful!'

Bouncer looked puzzled. 'Supply us with *what*, Maurice?'

'Vic . . . my fish and your meat. We can't risk that happening again.'

'I should think not,' he said stoutly. 'Like what you said, disgraceful!'

'And,' I continued, warming to my theme, 'there are other things that could be jeopardized too, like my woollen mouse and your toys – that gormless rabbit for instance with the pink eyes, and—'

The dog lifted his paw. 'Steady on, Maurice, I'm not quite

clear. What's my toy rabbit got to do with the Prim and her – her *projects*?'

'It has to do with her because if, as a result of her nosiness, she should blunder into a danger worse than her previous ones, we could suffer: i.e. we might be bereft of home, toys and all decent sustenance.'

'What was that last thing?'

'Food, Bouncer, *food*!'

'Cor,' he muttered, and started to scrabble down below. It is an unsavoury sight, but something he tends to do when thinking or worrying. And then, lifting his head, he said slowly, 'But it's more than that.'

'Oh yes? What more?'

For a moment there was silence. And then he said, 'Well, like with F.O. the vicar, she's nice, isn't she? She gives me cuddles.'

I blinked, nonplussed. And then I too lapsed into a thoughtful silence. Scenes of our life with F.O. and now with P.O. danced before my eyes and I felt a rare sentiment. Thus stirred, I gave a soft miaow and agreed with the dog. 'You are quite right, Bouncer. Despite being totally barking, each has afforded us much pleasure and entertainment.'

'And so she's nice?' he asked eagerly.

'Yes, Bouncer, she is nice . . . And that being the case,' I added briskly, 'it is our bounden duty to ensure that things do not go amiss. It would be a shame to lose her. We must find out all we can. Now, I shall devise a scheme. Meanwhile, here are my instructions. Listen carefully.'

'Right-o,' he snorted sleepily.

THIRTY-ONE

The Primrose version

K een though I was to explore the possibility of a Penge–
Dragson link, for the time being such enquiries had to be
shelved for I received a telephone call from Agnes Penlow
inviting me to lunch the following day.

She and Charles had at last returned from their protracted
house-sitting stay in Dorset coping with grandchildren and the
family's cats (fun but exhausting, Agnes had said). But now,
somewhat relieved, they were back in Podmore Place and could
resume normal life. 'Besides,' Agnes had murmured slyly, 'I want
to get the low-down on that rum business to do with the under-
matron at Erasmus. It blew up just as we were leaving. Fascinating
really – quite a little drama, I gather!'

I agreed that it had indeed been a little drama but doubted if
I could supply much low-down on the subject, but based on the
little I knew would do my best.

'Splendid,' she gurgled. 'Oh, and by the way, Bouncer would
be most welcome because the Hamlyns are coming too and will
be bringing that squidgy poodle of theirs. He's quite a sparky
little fellow and it's time poor old Duster had some gaiety. I
don't think he found the cats especially entertaining!' Actually,
with or without cats, I doubt if gaiety is Duster's forte, there
being something unnervingly sober about the cairn – or so it
seems to a mere human. Perhaps to fellow creatures he is a fund
of sharp wit and dour anecdote. Who knows?

I was glad the Penlows were back as I had rather missed their
enlivening presence. However, I have to admit to being slightly
less glad to learn that the Hamlyns would be there as, not having
spoken to Douglas since the 'episode' and still not certain if
Daphne knew about it, I thought that things might be a trifle

awkward. Would either of them raise the matter? Given the social
occasion probably not, but one couldn't be sure. Oh well, so be
it.

The following day I spoke sternly to Bouncer, telling him that
he was to be on his best behaviour and that were he tempted to
filch anything from table or sofa he would forfeit all bones and
never be taken anywhere again. He gazed at me impassively, and
then with a slow wag of his tail sloped off to sit by the front
door while I fetched his lead.

Negotiating the long drive at Podmore Place was no smoother
than the last time; but shambling in second gear and scanning
for potholes, we arrived without incident. I hauled the passenger
from the front seat and was about to enter the porch when I
noticed a man – neither Douglas nor Charles – throwing a ball
for a small dog, the poodle Tarzan. He had obviously seen our
arrival for he waved and hurried over.

I was greeted effusively. 'You must be Primrose Oughterard,
the artist.' He beamed. 'Daphne has told me so much about you!'
He extended his hand and shook mine vigorously while, less
vigorously, Bouncer and Tarzan circled each other politely.

Why Daphne should have mentioned me to him I had no idea,
and as he was a complete stranger I was somewhat taken aback.
However, things quickly became clear. 'I am Rufus, Daphne's kid
brother,' he explained, 'or possibly you may know me better as
Henry de Vere. It's my stage name – been strutting the boards
for quite a while now.' He gave a mock bow. Despite its theatrical
resonance, the name meant nothing to me. But being not a bad
performer myself, I was able to give the required response by
looking suitably impressed and delighted. (Silent homage without
lying through my teeth.)

Leaving the two dogs to romp on the lawn, we went inside,
where Rufus took my coat. In the drawing room I was greeted
warmly by the Penlows and cordially by Daphne. Of Douglas
there was no sign. Perhaps he was coming later or had slipped
out to the downstairs loo. But it was evidently neither, for as she
handed me a dry sherry Agnes explained, 'Alas, I fear Douglas
cannot be with us, he's currently not too well.' She turned to

Daphne. 'I've just told Primrose about poor Douglas nursing that awful migraine; he's not at all himself, it seems.'

Daphne shook her head. 'No, I fear not. Rufus and I are getting quite worried. I mean to say, he hasn't even done much fishing lately; he seems to lack all energy.'

'Probably needs a good tonic,' Charles interposed. 'There *are* such things on the market, so I've been told. I imagine a chemist could recommend something. But better still, send him up to the Tweed for a week. That should sort things out. I have a chum who owns a stretch near Peebles – it was one of old John Buchan's haunts. New landscape, fresh challenges, the questionable banter of some of those Scots bailiffs . . . He's bound to become his old self again. If you like, I'll send a note of introduction. In fact, he could probably stay with my friend if he wanted. Oddly enough his name is Douglas too. A damned good sort.'

Charles's suggestion sounded rather good to me: whatever Douglas's malaise – physical or mental or a mixture of both – a trip to the Borders and a few days fly-fishing on the Tweed in cheerful company would surely bring both rest and stimulus. I was about to say as much but was cut short by Daphne, who said rather dryly that he would probably get excellent attention by booking in at King Edward VII's hospital in Marylebone or seeing a Harley Street psychiatrist. 'After all, he's not short of a penny and it would be simpler and less strenuous than haring all the way up to Scotland.'

It was a response that struck me as being curiously churlish, and the money comment distinctly gauche, and I could see that Charles was surprised. However, ever the impeccable host, he smiled and agreed that she was doubtless right.

At that moment Agnes joined us, eager to broach the Memling topic. 'I gather the case is all wrapped up,' she said. 'Such a pity; I thought there was going to be a mammoth scandal! I mean to say, the circumstances were rather bizarre, weren't they? Still, I suppose it gave the boys something to write home about. But tell me, Primrose, wasn't Spikesy handling it? He's pretty shrewd, I always think – not like that oaf MacManus who was here before. So if there was anything really suspicious, I suppose he would have spotted it.'

I agreed with her judgement of Spikesy but explained that the matter had been largely conducted by the Brighton police, and that in any case Spikesy had been needed elsewhere and his place taken by a substitute whose acumen may not have been as sharp. But I did agree that there may have been something more to it than met the eye. 'Things are not always what they seem.' I laughed. 'And it's not so unusual for clues to be ignored.'

'Not by you, I bet,' interposed Charles, also laughing. He turned to Daphne. 'There are no flies on Primrose, I can tell you! She has a sleuth's eye.' He chuckled some more.

Gallant of him, of course, and I smiled. Nevertheless, I was hesitant to voice a more obvious scepticism of the official verdict and instead agreed with Agnes that it had indeed been dramatic but, alas, such things happened. I pointed out that the deceased had been a lone woman originally from a faraway country with no apparent relatives or known friends and no obvious interests. Perhaps bored with such a bland life, she had felt an urge to break the mould, throw caution to the winds and embark on a kind of spree. Presumably enthused by the novelty, she had overindulged, and aided by that weak heart had suffered the fatal collapse.

Even as I presented this scenario, I was struck by how reasonable it sounded, and for a split second my own private suspicions faltered. But the moment passed. *Trust your instinct*, I heard Pa saying. Well, it certainly couldn't be denied that my instinct had been absolutely spot on re the Topping affair and the Elsbeth Travers drowning, so why should I doubt it now?

'Oh yes,' Rufus broke in, 'one does hear of such things. In fact, some years ago I was in a play in the West End which had a similar theme.' He mentioned the name of the play, but it had evidently escaped my notice.

'How sad not to have interests,' Daphne murmured. 'I mean to say, surely it's having interests that galvanises one. Take my history project, for instance. Never a dull moment!' She laughed, but then said seriously, 'And that's why I'm concerned about Douglas: he does nothing but laze around. Getting a bit forgetful too – keeps leaving things lying about all over the place. It's maddening!'

It may have been my imagination, but I thought she shot me a quizzical look. It had been an ordinary enough remark so perhaps I was being unduly sensitive. Anyway, not wishing to pursue the subject, I turned to Charles and asked how their splendid orangery was getting on. He waxed lyrical, saying that they now had five new trees to augment the original one, and all were healthy and flourishing. 'After lunch you must come and inspect. It's getting to be a veritable forest, and doubtless Agnes will soon be making marmalade!' Hmm. I just wish he could be as enthusiastic in caring for the drive. But I suppose fresh tarmac isn't quite as exciting as a burgeoning marmalade factory.

At lunch I sat next to Rufus, who explained that the reason he was staying with his sister and brother-in-law was that he was currently in a Shakespeare series at Eastbourne's Devonshire Park Theatre. 'They don't generally do Shakespeare there, but this is a special project to help the local schools with their literature GCEs. It seemed a good idea to me as the sooner the kids learn to honour 'the bard', the better. So I offered to come down and lend a hand. Naturally, one is doing a bit of acting in the series but nowadays my main interest is in *direction*. It gives one so much more scope!'

Personally, I would have thought that either activity offered scope, but if what Douglas had slyly hinted about the latter's frequent 'rest periods' was true, perhaps directing was the better option. Rufus was pleasant enough and not bad looking in an unmemorable way. But despite the impressive stage name with its nod to Irving, I couldn't really see him in a commanding role. Like T.S. Eliot's poor Prufrock, he was no Prince Hamlet – his talent useful but secondary . . . Thus rather thankfully I confined my questions to the directing side of theatrical life. In this respect he was quite interesting – though even here I couldn't really see him having the necessary weight or tact to instruct a Gielgud or Richardson in their roles. A useful aide perhaps, but no more. However, we chatted amiably and he enquired politely about my painting, saying how much he understood the creative urge. Did he? Does anyone?

During our conversation the two canine guests wandered in followed by Duster. Possibly directed by the latter, they were evidently on their best behaviour, for they settled quietly under the sideboard staring intently at the table and at the five of us talking. Actually that's not quite accurate as most of their staring seemed directed at me. Perhaps Bouncer had told Tarzan I was a soft touch for food and at any moment would throw them a morsel. If so, no chance! But while enjoying both food and conversation, I sensed I was also the focus of another pair of eyes: Daphne's. She had been talking animatedly with Charles and Agnes but when I happened to look up I saw her gaze riveted upon me. I assumed she had heard something Rufus and I were discussing and wanted to join in. I flashed a receptive smile but it was not reciprocated and she immediately returned her attention to the Penlows.

As promised, after lunch we were taken to admire Charles's pride and joy erected just over a year ago: the exotic orangery. (Well, compared with most people's garden sheds it was certainly exotic, and for a few magical moments it was as if we had been transported to Spain or Italy.) On our way back to the drawing room for coffee I noticed the teetering Tarzan sniffing at my ankles. I laughed and, turning to Daphne, I pointed this out. 'Oh yes,' she said vaguely, 'he does that sometimes with people he's not certain of.'

Not *certain* of? Why should the creature be uncertain of me? It struck me as an odd sort of comment, but I added jovially, 'And when he's not pulling up lily bulbs, I suppose.' The allusion elicited a perfunctory smile and a quick glance at her watch.

Over coffee we discussed the usual things – the inanities of the government, the absurd effrontery of the opposition, the weather, England's cricket prospects and the soaring price of whisky – Charles going so far as to suggest that he might set up a private still behind the orangery.

Then, having put the world and whisky to rights, it was time to be going. Rufus shook my hand as effusively as when we had met. But when I asked Daphne to give my best wishes to Douglas, I thought I detected the merest hesitation before she replied, 'Of course I will. He's bound to be delighted.' *Bound to be delighted?* Warm words, cool tone.

*   *   *

Back in the car I congratulated Bouncer on his good behaviour and, reaching into the glove box, offered him a crumbling biscuit. Rather to my surprise this was disdained, his attention evidently taken by the slowly passing trees as we trundled back up the drive.

Once on the open road I reflected on the last three hours. It had been a pleasurable luncheon and I was glad to see the Penlows on such good form, though it was a shame about Douglas. I would have liked to make further enquiries, but though expressing her concern, Daphne had not seemed in the most receptive of moods. In fact, I couldn't help feeling that with me at any rate there had been a definite froideur. I wondered if Douglas had indeed said something of his visit, or parts of it at any rate. If so, did she resent this? Was that reference to his forgetfulness a covert barb to show that she was aware of what had happened?

Well, if so it was far too late for me to do anything about it – even had I wanted to. I turned my head to the dog. 'Don't you agree, Bouncer?'

He burped and continued to stare fixedly out of the window.

THIRTY-TWO

The dog's version

I had been feeling for a couple of days that something was up with our mistress (my sixth sense nudging me again). But when Maurice asked me what I thought it was, I was a bit surprised because generally the cat knows most things. So that's a turn up for the bones all right! I mean to say, it's pretty rare for the cat to admit he doesn't know something, so I got a bit twitchy. And I got even more twitchy when he warned me that if the Prim was getting another bone in her bonnet – like she sometimes does – then we would both be for the high jump. Mind you, I don't always believe what the cat says, but he seemed very definite. And what he said didn't half put the frighteners on me!

He said that if she got into danger (like she has sometimes in the past), then we mightn't get any more nosh or toys. And then he hinted something even worse than that: that she could even disappear for ever! Crikey, it was bad enough the vicar leaving us and going to that Happy Hunting Ground in the Sky, but it would be a bit rotten if she went as well! In fact, I don't mind admitting I became a bit FRORT and told Maurice that I wouldn't like that at all, as although I'd miss the bones and nosh I *liked* being with her. Don't know why that is really, but I suppose she's a bit like our old master used to be: a sort of cosy warm blanket, always there. (Though, mind you, even cosy blankets have their rough spots!)

When I told Maurice what I thought, he went sort of silent. But then after a bit of scrabbling and muttering he said he absolutely agreed with me and that we must find out what was bugging our mistress and see that she was SAFE. It's not often that the cat agrees with me, so I was pleased and just about to curl up and go to sleep when he screeched, 'So these are your instructions, Bouncer!'

In a way the cat is like P.O. – won't let up! Which is why, just when I was about to have a quick shut-eye after a lot of bounding about, he started to tell me where to go and what to do. Still, it's all in a good cause: to protect us and the Prim. So I didn't really mind and listened obediently.

He explained that he was going to wander up to the school and talk to that big white cat Lola who lives there. He doesn't like her much – thinks she's a smart-arse (not his words, mine) – but as P.O. often visits there he thinks she may be useful as a look-out. Meanwhile, he says I must be extra chummy with Petal and Tarzan because they belong to that man who was here the other night who was flopping about and whose thing I took. Mind you, that wasn't the first time he had been in the house, because he and his wife had come with Tarzan and those other people when P.O. was feeding them food and drink and they were all making a lot of noise yacking and gobbling.

Maurice says that the more we observe the Prim's mates and her movements, the better chance we have of learning what's going on with her. So, Bouncer's going to be Special Agent Number 1 again! It's time he had another sniffing job on the go. It doesn't do to get out of practice – like those daft dogs who don't know a bone from a fish head. Yes, Bouncer's himself again!

A few days later – at least I think it was days, I get a bit muddled with time – Maurice gave me my first ASSI-NINE-MENT. He said he had overheard the Prim on the phone babbling to some friend or other, and from what he could make out it sounded as though she was going out for a nosh the next day. 'If you are polite enough, Bouncer,' he said, 'she may take you with her, and then you can keep your ears and nose open and see what you can pick up.'

'Like a bone?' I asked.

The cat didn't like that and hissed that my damn-fool jokes weren't funny and would I kindly be serious. So I lowered my head and put on my mournful look. He then said that if she did take me with her that I was to watch every move, and that if by any chance Tarzan happened to be there – wherever it was – I should see that he did the same. 'You can tell him I said so,' he purred. 'He is bound to take notice.' Maurice thinks that the poodle admires him. *I* think that Tarzan is a slick little sod who knows which side his toast's buttered on. But I'd be a fool to say that to Maurice. There would be an awful FRAK-ARSE!

Anyway, that evening I did my extra best to be good; and as the cat had predicted, the next day P.O. put me in the car and we drove off. My sixth sense was on top form because I felt straightaway that we were going to that great big place where Duster lives. I like it there because there's plenty of long grass and rabbit holes and sometimes the tall man gives me a biscuit or some of those nice crackly things that humans eat when they are throwing drink down their throats. Duster says he can't stand the noise of 'em . . . but then that's Duster. He's a bit like Maurice: picky. Or what the cat would call FASTIJUS!

When we got there P.O. let me out, and we were just going towards the house when this man came up and the two of them starting jabbering. But then I suddenly saw Tarzan, and while the humans were busy jawing we said hello and had a good sniff. I remembered what Maurice had told me – to monitor the Prim and not let her out of my sight, and also to tell Tarzan to do the same. Well, I don't know about the cat, but I can't do two things at once. So I decided to stay with the poodle while Prim and the chap went inside. We played about a bit on the lawn, and then I gave him Maurice's instructions: to watch everything like a lynx (or like Maurice). 'Oh, of course,' he yelped, 'and do give your feline friend my very *best* wishes!' (Smarmy little tyke!)

After that we went into the house and met Duster in the hall. The cairn actually wagged his tail and muttered that we were most welcome. 'Och aye,' he said, 'I see you're here agin.' I explained that we had a mission: to watch my mistress, and try to pick up *signals* as to what she was up to. 'Oh, God help us,' he growled, 'not another of those spying games; it was bad enough last time. I had to take to my basket for at least two days afterwards!' From what I remember (which isn't a great deal), Duster's part in that business hadn't been very much. I think he had been a look-out, but that was all. Still, cairns are funny creatures and being Scotch maybe he had played a cannier role than I had noticed.

I was all ready to go into the big room where Prim and her mates were babbling when Tarzan sidled up and explained that his master wouldn't be among them. 'He's at home with Petal,' he said, 'lying on the sofa with a cloth over his eyes and holding his head.'

'Oh yes? What's wrong with Petal's head?' I asked.

'*No*, not Petal. The master! He's not well. Petal is worried and says he should see the vet, and I agree. But it's difficult to tell with humans.'

'You can say that again,' I agreed. 'Come on, let's get on with the snooping.'

And, hoping to catch titbits of gossip *and* get some biscuits, I was all ready to bound into the party, but Duster stopped me and said we had got to be very quiet, well behaved and UN-OB-TRU-SIVE. I thought that was a bit rude as Bouncer is never UNOBwhatsit! And I very nearly bit his ear. Tarzan tittered and whispered, 'Come on, Bouncer, do what he says.' And then he turned to Duster and gave a sort of poodle bow. Typical!

Inside the big room we sat quietly and watched. There was the usual thing – masses of smoke from those long white things they put in their mouths and a lot of loud laughs. The tall man threw me one of those crunchy things which I ate *very* quietly – though Duster didn't think so as he kept tut-tutting. Anyway, after a bit more smoke and drink they must have got hungry because they trooped into another room and sat round the table, and with a lot of oohing and aahing started to gobble their grub. Duster made us sit under the sideboard, which was quite good as we were able to survey everybody but especially the Prim, and we hardly took our eyes off her. Tarzan whispered that the man she was sitting next to was his mistress's brother who was staying with them for a while. I thought he seemed all right but I could see that P.O. wasn't all that taken. You can always tell when she's not sure as her nose twitches and a faraway look comes into her eyes – even when she's smiling. (The vicar, our old master, was a bit like that but he smiled less and his nose twitched more. Still, I expect he is smiling all right now – basking up there in the clouds with all those angel things flying around and giving him fags and humbugs!)

But it wasn't just P.O. that I had in my sights but also Tarzan's mistress – Daf something or other. At times she seemed very merry, like when she was talking to Duster's people; but sometimes she was . . . hmm, what's the word that the cat uses? Uhm, oh yes, WARY. That's it. Wary and watchful. And the person she seemed the most wary of was our Prim! I kept my eye on both of them and could tell that something wasn't quite right. I mentioned this to Tarzan, who said he had noticed it too. He said that the Daf lady could be quite nice but that sometimes she got tetchy. Mind you, if I lived with the poodle I think I might get tetchy too. But living with Maurice I just go bananas – no nagging niggles, just plain rage. So that's all right.

After the humans had fed themselves, they trooped out to look at that great big glass thing the nice man had put up. There was a lot of oohing and aahing again, but it gave us dogs a chance to chase about and have a romp. I shoved my nose down a couple of the rabbit holes, but no luck. They were probably asleep or out on the razzle.

When we followed the humans back to the house, I have to admit that I was quite impressed with Tarzan. He kept so close to the Prim's heels that I thought that at any moment she would tread on his titchy snout. In fact, when we got back inside I gave a friendly woof and said he had the makings of being a good agent. This pleased him as he started to prance around squeaking, 'Hooray! I'm a spy! I'm a spy!' I told him to shut up and keep his ears pricked and that real spies didn't make a song and dance about it.

After the party was over and we were back in the car, I sat in the front seat as I like to do and watched the trees go by. My sixth sense told me that P.O. was a bit tense and I *think* that she may have asked me a question. But do you know, I was so busy

RE-VU-ING things, and planning what I was going to report to Maurice, that I can't be sure . . . Anyway, when we got home the cat was out. And so, after I had been given a Bonio and told that I had been a good boy, I settled down snugly in my basket and dreamed of spies and bunnies.

THIRTY-THREE

The Primrose version

As things turned out, my recurring thoughts about the hipflask incident and what, if anything, to do about it became an irrelevance. For the item would never be needed again, or certainly not by Douglas.

Its owner was found dead, half submerged in the River Ouse, a mile or so out of town. Rod, tackle and a packet of cigarettes were strewn on the riverbank some yards from where the body was found. The deceased was fully clothed and with stones stuffed into the jacket pockets. It was evidently a classic case of suicide.

Indeed, when the news filtered through, my horrified mind recalled a similar event in 1941 – the writer Virginia Woolf, unable to stand whatever it was she had been struggling with, had also resolutely taken her own life by wading into the placid Ouse a little further downstream. Had Douglas Hamlyn known of that or had it been yet another of life's ghastly coincidences? Well, whether the earlier death had been an 'inspiration' or not, it didn't matter. The poor man was gone.

As in most such cases the question of foul play was raised but quickly dismissed: all the marks were of deliberate self-destruction although the local press had made no mention of a suicide note – not that that meant anything. Though usual, such notes are not always left, and even if there had been one, Daphne may have felt it too private to show. As I brooded on the news, I naturally recalled his absence at the Penlows' lunch, Daphne's concern about his health and her remarks about his growing lethargy. Had that lethargy been part of a dulling despair, some gradual and insidious breakdown? Clearly those earlier purchases of sleeping and migraine tablets at the chemist had been a vain attempt to alleviate such symptoms. I also recalled his having said how much he enjoyed those lone sojourns on the riverbank 'communing with nature'. Had they been simply for pleasure, or as a means of escape and ease from some nagging burden? Quite possibly. Daphne had said that the fishing jaunts were becoming less frequent, as if he couldn't summon the energy. So had that final excursion, equipped with rod and tackle, been a desperate hope to recover routine, to resume normality . . . a hope destroyed by a sudden overwhelming impulse? Or had the whole thing been carefully prepared, with the river being both a practical means and a nostalgic reminder of happier times? Who could tell? Unless a note were discovered, or produced, it would remain a painful mystery.

Well, such speculations were pointless. The deed was done, and I tried to rid my mind of those fateful hours. However, while the river images might disperse, a particular picture did not: Douglas embarrassingly drunk, sprawled in the middle of my drive and later dazed and unhappy in the drawing room. Apart from that brief glimpse in Lewes, it had been the last time I saw him. And the memory, so vivid, would not go away.

What *was* it he had been going to tell me that evening? What had been weighing so heavily on his mind that he could find no release except by water and the dragging weight of those stones in his pockets? He had seemed on the brink of divulging something, and I was irked by the thought that, had it not been for the intrusion of the cat and dog, he might have found some relief and helpful sympathy. Sometimes, I ruminated, even the smallest of words or actions can tip the hand of fate for good or ill. And regarding the latter, I fleetingly pictured Francis on that bright June morning and his chance stroll in the wood which had brought such alarming consequences.

But then, wrenching my mind back from the dead to the living, I thought of the bereaved Daphne Hamlyn. Whether or not there had been some 'marital disorder' (which Douglas had seemed to imply), her husband's suicide would have been a terrible blow – particularly in view of her recent delight over the history project. It just shows how, in the midst of gaiety, grief can be so appallingly close.

*   *   *

But another aspect of the tragedy – and one that clearly appealed to the local press – was the occasion of its shocking discovery: an early-morning nature ramble comprising four boys and a master from *'a renowned Sussex prep school close to the area, and whose junior matron was, alas, recently found in fatal circumstances in one of Brighton's best hotels'*. Doubtless the manager of the Majestic was none too pleased to see this gratuitous reference so soon after the other business, but I have it on the authority of one close to him (i.e. Emily) that Winchbrooke was – to speak figuratively – engaged in banging his head against every desk and wall he could find. The school inspectors were due the following day.

One gathers the walk had been suggested by the biology master, Jenkins, who also taught nature studies. He had been keen to point out to his charges the delights of the living world at sunrise and in birdsong. Most of the class was unenthusiastic about this, preferring the more comfortable delights of bed. But four boys had shown interest and been given special permission by the headmaster to go on the little jaunt. According to Emily, when Jenkins had mooted the idea to Winchbrooke he had said it might help to impress the inspectorate as he knew that one of its team was a keen ornithologist who would often go out at dawn to listen to 'our feathered friends as they herald a new day'.

Apparently the headmaster had seized upon this, for he is said to have exclaimed excitedly, 'Yes, and it'll just show them how enlightened the school is. Not only does Erasmus House instruct its pupils in the finer points of contemporary art' – alluding, of course, to those painful daubings currently adorning the main corridor – 'but also in the beauty and benison of nature at its most tranquil, untainted by raucous noise and crudity.' Coming from Winchbrooke, not given to romantic excess, the fulsome imagery of those last words was surprising and I wondered from where they had been culled . . .

Anyway, other than the pleasing sound of birdsong, the young dawn-walkers may have been sheltered from noise but they certainly witnessed crudity. What a terrible way to have their morning idyll so harshly shattered! I asked Emily if the boys had been very upset. She said that Jenkins had reported two of them being in tears, but once back at school they ate a hearty breakfast and couldn't wait to tell the stayabeds what they had missed.

But to return to the crucial matter: the victim's sad demise. Naturally, as soon as I had heard the shocking news, I sent Daphne a letter of condolence to which – and slightly to my surprise given her somewhat curt attitude at the Penlows' lunch – she had been quick to respond, and in a tone perfectly cordial. Perhaps at the time concern for Douglas had made her on edge, or I had been unusually sensitive and seeing slights where none existed. It could have been either or both.

She wrote that the funeral would be private and held not here in Lewes but in London where she had two or three close friends, and where she would be staying with Rufus – an 'absolute rock' – until it was all over. She said that her brother had greatly admired the older man and was 'knocked out' by the news, and his upset almost as deep as her own . . . I have to admit that in view of Douglas's rather scathing allusion to the actor's resting capacity, I was a trifle surprised by that comment, and doubted if the latter's regard had been fully matched. Perhaps to be supportive of his sister Rufus was playing to the gallery a little, or maybe Daphne was exaggerating her brother's reaction in order to comfort herself. Mourning can sometimes muddle perspective.

Anyway, in the circumstances her decision to hold the funeral out of Lewes seemed sensible. Although settling in well, the Hamlyns were still relative newcomers and their social circle comprised amiable acquaintances rather than old friends. An intimate service in London with a select few would probably bring greater comfort. I wondered how long she planned to be away. A short absence to cover the funeral itself? Or perhaps longer, to recuperate quietly before returning to deal with the inevitable and sad practicalities.

Either way, I did rather wonder what would happen in the interim to the two dogs. But presumably arrangements had been made, probably for the local kennels to take them for a period, or maybe to stay with Richardson the vet, Bouncer's friend. If the latter, I just hoped the goats would cope. It was one thing for them to have Bouncer studying them in awed silence, but would they be so skittish if their audience was the mammoth Petal?

And thinking of the mastiff, I also hoped that he wouldn't be too upset by his master's death. You never know with dogs and loss: sometimes they can seem to be fairly unmoved, but often are deeply disturbed. From what I gathered, Petal had been especially close to Douglas, and it worried me to think that he might now be suffering. In fact, the more I thought of that huge, devoted creature bereft and moping, the more anxious I became. Frankly, truth to tell, I think that the dog's likely distress started to bother me more than that of its mistress.

How unseemly! Thus to alleviate guilt, I mixed a particularly lethal Sidecar and went up to the studio to daub more paint on the Wilmington Giant.

A week passed, during which I continued to apply myself vigorously to the Wilmington picture and other projects (I fear I am not a disciplined artist and indulge only when mood or muse dictate). However, after an arduous spate it was time I took time off and did some essential shopping in Lewes. While there I happened to encounter the chairman of the History Society and we got chatting. He told me that he had heard from Mrs Hamlyn, now back from her husband's funeral, and he gathered she was intending to eventually quit Sussex for America.

He must have seen my surprise, for he explained that apparently Lewes and Needham Court retained too many memories of her husband which, fond though they were, were also painful. 'She wants to start again,' he explained, 'and is seeking "fresh woods and pastures new". So as a preliminary she and her brother are shortly off to do a three-month reconnaissance of the States with a view to her settling there permanently, preferably the west coast.'

'Oh dear,' I said, 'the society will be the poorer. Wasn't she going to give a talk on Anne of Cleves next year?'

'Yes, most unfortunate. We shall miss her lively interest. But that's life, isn't it? Sometimes we are overcome by events and have to act accordingly.'

I thought of Francis and his event and agreed wholeheartedly.

THIRTY-FOUR

The Primrose version

In the studio I was at the Long Man again and was just in the middle of brush-stroking a particularly tricky piece of gorse when I heard a ring at the front door. I wasn't expecting anybody and it was an interruption I could do without. But reluctantly I laid paints aside and went downstairs to investigate.

A man stood in the porch whom I vaguely recognized as Mr Colvert, the local postmaster. He was holding a small satchel and looked slightly sheepish. 'I do apologize, Miss Oughterard, but I'm afraid I have an admission to make.'

'Oh dear, I'm sorry to hear that. What is it?'

'Well, it's these, you see.' And from the satchel he withdrew a small batch of letters secured by a rubber band and thrust them at me. 'I've been in charge of the sorting office here for nigh on ten years and nothing has ever gone astray before. Can't think how it happened! Only found them today, in a totally different pigeonhole from the usual one. I'm afraid they're over a week late. Hope you weren't expecting anything urgent.'

'I shouldn't think so.' I smiled. 'Bills probably. Please don't worry. One slip in ten years is hardly major!'

He thanked me for my patience, assured me that it wouldn't happen again and went off, clearly relieved.

Before returning upstairs, and shooing Maurice off the hall chair, I sat down and glanced through the envelopes. Nothing of consequence, it seemed: a couple of bills as predicted, plus a postcard from Scotland, the Courtaulds' monthly newsletter and an envelope, the writing on which I didn't recognize – maybe an invitation to something, in which case it would need a prompt reply. I opened it quickly as I was in a hurry to get back to the studio. Inside was a sheet of paper, undated, but bearing the address of Needham Court. The letter read as follows:

My dear Miss Oughterard,

I write to apologize for my disgraceful intrusion the other evening. As you will have realized, I was far from being my normal self. Nevertheless, such behaviour was inexcusable, and I sincerely hope you will accept my deep regrets.

I fear that I was extremely garrulous and foolishly disclosed certain things which should never have been said. Actually, such had been my physical and mental state at the time that I cannot exactly recall how much I <u>did</u> say or imply, but suspect I may have burbled about an episode in South Africa. If so, would you please ignore that. I like to think I can rely on your friendship and discretion.

But one thing I do clearly recall is leaving that silver hipflask on your sofa. Tiresome for you I am sure, but annoying for me too, as ages ago it was a present from my spouse, who will be displeased were she to learn of its loss. Would it therefore be possible for me to call again – in seemly state this time (!) – to retrieve it? I'll take the liberty of telephoning you shortly to fix a time at your convenience. Again, with all my apologies.

Yours sincerely,
Douglas Hamlyn

I read it a second and third time. And then, quite untypically, burst into tears. What shook me was the letter turning up *now*, after his death. For suddenly the man was alive again, had become a breathing reality. I could hear his voice, see clearly those rather thin features. He was no longer an unfortunate acquaintance of the past but a living presence – there in the hall beside me. And I couldn't bear it.

I think Maurice must have observed my reaction for he jumped on to my lap, and after a few hiccuping sobs I felt a rough tongue scraping my knuckles. The cat rarely licks and I even more rarely cry, but now we were acting in tandem.

However, tears had never been encouraged in the Oughterard household ('a waste of time', my father had robustly counselled). And so, after blowing my nose on the hem of my smock, I pulled myself together and went into the kitchen for a coffee and cigarette. Here, under the gaze of the cat, now settled on top of the Aga, I ruminated.

Evidently the distress he had shown during that visit had grown intolerable and he had relieved it in the only way he could. But what increased my dismay was to learn that, far from being indifferent or calculatedly silent, Douglas had been acutely aware of his gaffe and eager to explain and apologize. He had expressed a touching faith (or so it seemed) in my friendship and discretion. Had my failure to respond been the last straw in prompting his suicide? I felt tears welling again as I confronted that awful possibility.

But reason prevailed. No, an immediate answer had not been expected; he had said that *he* would telephone to fix a time to collect the flask. The initiative was to have been his (presumably to ensure that Daphne wouldn't overhear or pick up the phone), and sadly he had not taken it. Naturally, had I received such a phone call I would have been readily receptive . . . after all, *I* hadn't wanted the damn thing and the sooner it had been returned to its owner, the better.

Once more I studied his words. One didn't have to read between the lines to see that all had not been well with husband and wife – or 'spouse', to use his own rather legalistic term. For in addition to what he had earlier hinted about a rift in their relationship, it seemed pretty obvious that her gift was no longer of any sentimental value – his only concern being that *she* might be displeased by its loss were she to find out. Was the South African 'episode' – whatever that may have been – the root cause of their problems? Possibly. But did it matter? Not really. As far as I was concerned, the poor man's tragedy was over . . . and I was left with its silver remnant in my hat box.

But I was also left with the current quandary of what to do about Daphne when she returned from staying in London for the cremation. After all, I was in an awkward position: her husband's visit itself and now this letter made me a kind of retrospective confidante. In the circumstances it wasn't the most relaxing role and certainly not one I had chosen. Still, to reveal anything to Daphne would be madness: upsetting for her, embarrassing for me – and a betrayal of the deceased's trust in my silence. This time it was my mother's warning voice I heard: *Some things, Primrose, are best left unsaid.* I nodded and put the letter back in its envelope.

Fortunately there was something else on my mind to which I could return without fear of personal embarrassment: the Memling matter. Talking with Inspector Spikesy at the garage had pushed my thoughts further in that direction. And given the ghastly shock of Douglas's death, such diversion was no bad thing. It was something I could ponder in a detached way without feeling any emotional concern. Thus, curiosity untinged by sadness would now be my main pursuit. How to deal with the Daphne situation could wait till after her return.

But meanwhile, and in addition to the Aida Memling mystery, there was a further matter needing close attention: the Erasmus House inspection and the fate of my pictures currently banished to its cellar. I gather that the inspectorate descended on them for three days, made copious notes, annoyed the masters, perplexed the boys, upset Emily, and then departed po-faced.

You would have thought that once their reconnaissance was over the school would know its fate. Not a bit of it! Apparently it would take a full month for its officials to study their findings and to complete the report. Mr Winchbrooke does not possess the patience of Job – or of anyone, biblical or otherwise – and he is not a happy man. Naturally, *my* principal hope has been to have my pictures restored to the main corridor. But Winchbrooke was hesitant, saying that until the report was received it was best to allow those frightful replacements to stay *in situ* 'in case in the meanwhile they send an undercover agent to confirm that the school's character remains just as they had left it and with no sudden changes'. Well really, how paranoid can one get!

Considerably more so, it would seem. For Bertha Twigg has just informed me that their chaplain has undergone some stupendous religious crisis and is now convinced that the rest of his days should be spent chanting and fasting in a Tibetan monastery. To this end he has packed his bags, discarded his copy of *Hymns Ancient and Modern* and has gone to catch the Golden Arrow

from Victoria, change at Paris and then on to Lhasa via
Kathmandu. Needless to say, bets have already been placed as
to how long it will take him to recover his senses and return to
the safety of Lewes and the Anglican church.

But paranoia is not confined to school chaplains and headmas-
ters. Aida Memling also suffered from it, and in her case with
fatal results. Increasingly I was convinced that her obsessive
mission to wreak vengeance on some quarry was surely the cause
of her death – either by a total dissolution of her senses exacer-
bated by drink and dope *or* by the hand of that quarry. And the
various indications – the cryptic yet subtly threatening note from
Penge; her scribbled draft reply to a request for an interview, in
which she declared her eagerness to expose some injustice; her
excited words to Bertha outside the telephone booth also about
getting publicity – seemed to suggest the latter. Contrary to the
official verdict, she had surely been the victim of murder – murder
by someone determined to quell her and her missionary zeal for
ever. And Primrose Oughterard was going to get to the bottom
of it!

THIRTY-FIVE

The Primrose version

The afternoon had been taken up by the chore of letter writing. There were several pending and something had to be done to stem the flow. But my dutiful efforts were interrupted by the telephone. Rather to my surprise it was Daphne asking if I would be free that evening as it would be so nice to have a cosy natter over a drink. I say 'surprised' as I had thought she would be busy preparing for her American reconnaissance with her brother. However, it suited me quite well, as having penned four letters I was already bored and would welcome a diversion. Thus I accepted gratefully, and happily calling a halt to epistolary labour, I went upstairs to make myself presentable.

As it was a dry evening I decided not to bother with the car. And in any case, a short walk would do me good after sitting at my desk for so long. I hesitated, wondering whether to take Bouncer, but as it hadn't been suggested, decided not to. (Nothing worse than having children and pets foisted on one unsolicited!)

At first sight Needham Court looked shrouded in darkness, almost as if empty, but as I drew nearer I could see Daphne's car in the drive and glimpsed curtained light from the ground floor's sitting room. The door opened and I was greeted by Rufus. This surprised me as I hadn't realized that he was down in Lewes again and Daphne hadn't mentioned it. Perhaps they were off abroad sooner than I had thought.

He ushered me into the sitting room. A log fire smouldered in the grate and the room had a mellow ambience which was welcoming after my rather chilly walk. 'It's so good to see a proper fire and not just an electric one,' I said appreciatively, 'especially now that the nights are drawing in. So much nicer!'

Daphne smiled, offered me a sherry and said that there was

no point in doing things by halves. 'When in need, do the job properly. That's what I always say.'

'Hear, hear,' Rufus chimed and passed me a bowl of peanuts and potato crisps. I declined these as I had left a rather substantial casserole waiting in the Aga and which, sherry apart, didn't need preliminaries.

I agreed with Daphne about doing a job properly and said that our beloved town clerk had now taken to wearing a decent suit instead of his usual slacks and an ill-fitting jerkin. 'At least he looks better now,' I remarked, 'but is just as obstructive!'

Rufus laughed and said that he was probably practising for an interview to higher things – mayor of Worthing, for example.

'Town crier more likely,' Daphne quipped. 'He's got the lungs for it.'

They asked after Bouncer and I said that despite having his coat trimmed and now less dishevelled, as with the town clerk nothing really changed, for he too could be just as difficult. 'It's like people – looks can alter but temperament doesn't.' And as an example, I cited Petal, saying that his bulk surely belied his docile nature.

'Docile?' Rufus exclaimed, 'You can say that again! He's too idle to hurt a fly. He may look the part, but he's no guard dog. As soft as soap, that creature is! Typically he's fast asleep now, flopped at the top of the stairs.'

He got up to stoke the fire, while Daphne said that it was a long time since they had last seen me and hoped that the pictures were going well and were raking in pots of the 'hard stuff'. 'I bet you've got a nice little set-up going there,' she added. 'Probably makes you a mint!' She laughed. Personally I did not find this especially risible, feeling that the reference to my private finances was vulgar and the words crude. Naturally I have a healthy regard for matters economic – as my dear brother had been fond of pointing out – but such a bald allusion was jarring, especially from a mere acquaintance. However, remembering *my* manners, I smiled politely and said that things were going very well and I trusted that her history project was also flourishing.

'Well, it *has* been, but one's become rather sidetracked of late. Too many other things to think about . . .' She broke off to light a cigarette and I watched the smoke as it curled above her head, wishing she had offered me one too. 'Oh dear, I can imagine,' I said sympathetically. 'So much to do after that dreadful business with poor Douglas. It must be so difficult for you.'

'Not half as difficult as being plagued by an officious neighbour,' Rufus said quietly.

I frowned. What an odd thing to say. What did he mean and whoever was the neighbour? But in the next instant I knew, for when I looked up it was to be met with an unsmiling face and an accusing stare.

'Oh yes, Miss Oughterard,' he murmured, 'I fear that is you.' The words hung in the air, sharp and scathing.

I glanced at Daphne who gazed back silently. Then, after carefully stubbing out her cigarette, she said, 'Yes, my brother is right – you have been a bit of a bore, haven't you? And frankly it has become rather tiresome.'

Despite the fire's relaxing warmth, I felt suddenly chilled to the bone. The welcome given to me on entry and the ease of our light chit-chat had vanished, its place taken by a cool hostility. What should I say? I had no idea. Not normally lost for words, I struggled to find a useful response. But other than a feeble, 'I'm sorry, I don't really understand . . .' nothing came.

'Oh, but I think you do,' Rufus said sardonically. 'That's the problem: you have understood rather too much and it's getting disturbing. Disturbing for us of course – but, er, well it could be for you too . . .'

The last words trailed off lightly, but it was those that held more than a whiff of menace. And even in my state of shock I was intrigued to see how radically his whole manner had changed. Far from being the easy personable chap whom I had originally met at the Penlows', he was now curt and hard and – I sensed – dangerous. The sudden switch from nice to nasty made me think that perhaps he was a better actor than I (or Douglas) had assumed. Maybe that long accumulation of bit parts had generated not so much 'a talent to amuse' as a talent to adapt – and, if necessary, to instil fear. And it was a creeping fear that I now felt.

But I felt something else too: family pride. The Oughterards were not the sort to bend to this kind of attack – Ma and Pa would have been most displeased. Even Francis had had a kind of resilience. And having been his older sister I would now show the same, and more. I would not be intimidated!

I looked at the pair of them: Daphne lounging expressionless on the sofa; he standing grim-faced and arms folded. They were no longer pleasant acquaintances but enemies – and, collecting my handbag, I stood up to go. 'I think this charming evening has come to an end,' I said coldly. 'You obviously have some peculiar axe to grind, but I have better things to do than to remain here listening to its noise.' I started to move to the door but Rufus intervened, barring my way.

'Sorry, Miss Oughterard, but that can't be allowed. Sit down, please. You might like another sherry perhaps.'

His voice had taken on a mocking note which enraged me. 'Don't be such a damn fool,' I snapped. 'Kindly let me pass.' But even as I said it, I knew that he would not. To have tussled with the man would have been foolish and undignified, and so I shrugged and returned to the chair.

I glanced around at what a few minutes ago had been a very warm and comfortable room. It was now a war zone, bleak and booby trapped. And despite my anger I was at a disadvantage, being confused and not knowing where a grenade might land.

'Well, what is it?' I asked with cold indifference.

Daphne sighed. 'As said, you are a troublemaker, Primrose Oughterard, and it's beginning to get on my wick. Everything was going absolutely perfectly until you and Douglas started playing up.'

'Me and Douglas!' I exclaimed. (Playing up? Hell, did the woman think I had been having an affair with him?)

'Yes,' she said bitterly, 'his stupid nervous breakdown, mutterings about the police, and then coming to you to pour it all out. Lost his nerve and then the fool had to yap about it!'

Police? What did she mean? I cleared my throat. 'Er, had to yap about what?'

'Oh, don't pretend you don't know,' she snapped impatiently. 'That bloody little hound Aida Memling of course.'

The words struck me like the proverbial thunderbolt, and in a flash things became clear. Hurtling out of the blue like that, the name itself was shock enough, but the adjunct *hound* sent my mind reeling. Oh my God, not only had I been right about the woman's 'mission' but now I knew her quarries: Daphne and Douglas Hamlyn, one's friendly neighbours. So, *they* had been the targets of the Angel of Vengeance! But, shocked though I was, I managed a steady face (learnt from years of playing poker with Pa). Sometimes rampant curiosity trumps all.

Thus, ignoring the Memling reference, I said, 'Ah, I see. But if you don't mind my asking, how do you know that he paid me a visit?' (Presumably, as I had rather feared, he must have mentioned it after all.)

'He wrote to you and I happened to read his letter, or at least its draft. Douglas was like that – very exacting about his letters. For the important ones he would always keep a pencilled copy. He had left it lying on his desk – careless really. But he was getting like that – forgetful – as with the hipflask he had left with you.' (This was said with a sneer.) 'Anyway, there was a scribbled date of about three days earlier, so it had obviously been sent.'

As she spoke, my racing mind was putting things together and I knew that my suspicions made sense. Slurred and hesitant, Douglas had spoken of South Africa and of two women, one of whom it would seem had been called Eunice – Eunice Mel something, he had mumbled. Or *had* it been Mel? He had been so indistinct that I may have mistaken the l for an m. Yes, the surname must have been Memling! I remembered what Spikesy had said of that photo with the initial E on its back and which the police had confiscated from her bedroom along with other scraps. Could E have stood for Eunice, and was Eunice the sister of Aida? Aida for whom Daphne clearly had such contemptuous loathing . . . And yet despite the latter's outburst, neither she, nor Douglas, nor indeed Rufus, had ever uttered a word about knowing the woman. After all, there had been enough speculation locally about the matron's death, but nothing from that quarter. Strange, to say the least.

The Hamlyns had come from Durban, South Africa. She too was from Durban, and despite Douglas's earlier denial of knowing

the family, there must have been some link which they had been
reluctant to disclose. Yes, South Africa was the key. Something
had happened there involving the Hamlyns and the Memlings
which in all likelihood had prompted Aida's vengeful pursuit.

But gripped as I was by these past images, I had not forgotten
the present reality and I didn't like it. I didn't like it at all.
    And I soon liked it even less. Clammy horror slid over me as
I grasped the full implications. *They* had killed Aida Memling.
It fell into place: her pursuit, their anger and then retaliation.
'Tides turn,' the note from Penge had warned. It had also
contained the petard reference . . . Oh yes, the woman had
followed her mission all right, and they were the victims. But
the victims had struck back, had contrived a rebuff which sent
the persecutor and her explosive weapon sky-high in the most
dramatic way. The realization sickened – and, I may say, frightened me. No longer was their hostility merely unnerving; it had
become a danger possibly imperilling my own safety.
    The room held a steely tension broken only by the ticking of
the clock and an occasional crackle from the fire and its flickering
flames. They were watching me closely as if making some kind
of assessment. I could almost sense them thinking, waiting, planning their next move. What sort of reaction were they expecting
from me? Bluster? Tears? Violent fury? A sudden move to rush
out of the door? There would be none of this. If I were to escape,
it could only be by stealth and a detached calm.
    Some months earlier, Inspector Spikesy and his nice wife had
invited me to supper and I had flogged them one of my paintings
(a couple later given as presents). One of the things we had talked
about had been the police interviewing technique of suspects.
Spikesy had said that the essential thing was not to be hectoring
or accusatory but to show an interest in *them* and their feelings
and problems. Far from being confrontational, one should display
a quiet empathy. This could disarm and relax and often appeal
to their vanity and, while not necessarily producing full confes-
sions, would often reduce their hostility, making them more open
and pliable.
    Surely this was the only way: to be civil and relaxed. To be

sharp and aggressive would only antagonize. I thought of Ma's words: *Don't answer back, Primrose, it doesn't suit you.* She had been right. At the moment it suited neither me nor the situation! Thus, in the hour of maximum danger as this most certainly was, I should need to be the essence of tact.

I leant back in my chair trying to look as relaxed as possible. 'But for goodness' sake, Daphne,' I said, 'just because Douglas visited me and made a few indiscreet remarks, does that really make me such a danger? You are being a bit oversensitive, aren't you?'

'Oh, you were a danger before then: your doubts about the verdict, saying you thought there was something fishy about the whole thing and that Memling had perhaps been a threat to a person or persons unknown, that she had been pursuing some private grudge . . . You had said these things jokingly. But some jokes are funnier than others, and this wasn't one of them. I had got your number, Miss Oughterard, and knew that you meant what you said and wouldn't stop sniffing around until your suspicions were satisfied.' She gave a sardonic laugh and added, 'In fact, now I come to think of it, not unlike Aida Memling – alert and rabidly persistent.'

Naturally, I was incensed by the comparison. But composure being vital, I ignored this and continued with what I fondly imagined to be my charm offensive.

THIRTY-SIX

The Primrose version

A ctually, I am not sure that charm is my strong suit, but I can certainly show interest (as Ingaza endlessly remarks, albeit using a different term). Given the situation, such interest was both genuine and contrived; for while satisfying intellectual curiosity it could also be a lifesaver . . .

'You know, what puzzles me,' I began conversationally, looking at Daphne, 'is why Aida Memling should have been so intent on hounding you and your husband like that. I mean, clearly she was a crackpot and saw herself as some sort of avenging angel, but I can't see why she should have felt so provoked – or for that matter why you should have found it so vital to . . . well' – I coughed discreetly – 'to take those particular steps. I mean, it must have been pretty risky.'

Rufus laughed (almost good-naturedly, but not quite). 'Oh, that was me. I set her up with red roses, booze and dope and took her out on the town in Brighton. It worked like a dream – though nightmare might be a more accurate term. It was one of the most boring and embarrassing evenings of my life. She kept shrieking with laughter and pawing at my jacket. Frightful!'

I smiled in mock sympathy. 'So how on earth did you do it? Must have been tricky.'

He gave a modest shrug. 'Ah, that's where my acting experience came in. I contacted her at the school and spun a tale about being a journalist with a special interest in South Africa, and wondered if she could help me with an article I was doing. I said that as a journalist my particular remit was exposing cases of personal injustice and that I'd heard about her poor sister who had been deeply wronged, gone to the dogs and committed suicide – through no fault of her own.'

'Oh dear,' I murmured.

'It wasn't "oh dear" at all!' Daphne broke in indignantly. 'That sleazy little tart had brought it entirely on herself. She was loud, stupid, vain and vulgar, and made a monkey of Douglas. And if he hadn't met me, God knows how he would have coped. He was always impressionable and she really led him a dance. Her behaviour in public was increasingly outlandish and she had become like a limpet and wouldn't let go. She was angling for marriage and money. Which was where I came in. I caught his eye and we became lovers. He then dropped her and married me. She didn't like that and took up with a very dubious crowd, filled herself with drink and drugs and then eventually nose-dived off Athlone Bridge shrieking, "I'm a pretty bird". She drowned. The whole thing was utterly absurd and unsavoury. Of course, it made the papers and was a nine-day wonder, but then was forgotten. Or so we thought.'

Daphne paused to light another cigarette (again without offering me one), and then continued. 'But we hadn't counted on the younger sister, Aida,' she said bitterly. 'She was totally different – as different as grey chalk from rancid cheese. Both Douglas and I had met her very occasionally but she had made little impact; humourless and dull. I had no idea what made her tick and didn't care.'

At this Rufus gave a caustic laugh. 'But you came to care, didn't you, Sis! That little grey mouse turned into a venomous shrew!'

'And that's an understatement,' she snorted. 'She wasn't just venomous, she was also clever – far more so than Eunice. She became obsessed with the idea that Douglas had betrayed her sister and was responsible for her suicide. She hated us both, although at the time we had no idea of this and it took a good five years for us to realize what was going on.' She broke off, staring at the fire, and murmured as if to herself: 'Remarkable really. You wouldn't have thought she had it in her . . .'

'Had it in her?'

Daphne looked up. 'I mean that she had the guile and sheer

bloody persistence to try to ruin our lives. She conducted a slow campaign of attrition, a means of delivering pain to us and justice to her sister . . . little by little, threat by threat. It was masterly really and very nearly worked. But not *quite*. We saw to that, or at least Rufus and I did.' She glanced at her brother, and with a faint smile said, 'You see, sometimes the boy can be quite useful.'

He smiled back and replied modestly, 'I do my best.'

Somehow, this fleeting exchange between brother and sister disturbed me more than their portrayal of the murdered woman. The latter and her schemes were dead, but these two were very much alive and I was unsettled by their collusive intimacy. They seemed so sure of themselves, so confident. I felt as if I was outnumbered not by two but by twenty. Still, there was nothing for it but to remain cool and go on as best I could. Besides, I was fascinated by her reference to Memling's campaign of attrition and was curious to know the logistics.

'What do you mean when you say "little by little"?' I asked in only mock puzzlement. 'It must have been an awful strain.'

'Not to begin with, but it certainly became so. Eleven months after our marriage and exactly a year to the day of Eunice's suicide, Douglas received a note posted from Jo'burg. It contained a single word: *Killer*. Nothing else. It was totally stark – not even an exclamation mark – so wasn't blatantly hostile, just nasty and meaningless. At first, we didn't see the significance of the date – that it was the anniversary of Eunice's death (not something we had bothered to note in our diaries!) and it was only a week later that the penny dropped. That was a shock, of course, but as nothing further came, we shrugged it off as being the work of some kid or crank, got on with our lives and dismissed the whole thing . . . Until the next one arrived exactly a year later.'

'With the same word?'

'No. It said, *Happy Days!* Just like that. And this time there was an exclamation mark, so it was presumably intended to mock.'

I nodded. 'Hmm, sounds like it. And was this from Johannesburg too?'

'Oh, that would have been far too repetitive,' she said acidly. 'Clever Clogs sent it from Cape Town.'

'Goodness, she got around, didn't she?' I said, genuinely surprised.

'Oh yes. Like a bloody springbok,' Daphne replied tightly.

'Hah! That's not the half of it,' interrupted Rufus. 'That girl got everywhere. All over the place. It was part of her plan. Anything to put the frighteners on old Douglas *and* the wicked wife!' He gave a loud guffaw.

'Shut up, Rufus,' Daphne exclaimed. 'I'm telling this.' She turned back to me and continued.

Despite my fear, I couldn't help being amused by her reaction. It was almost as if Rufus had stolen her thunder and she was piqued by the intrusion. I must have been the sole person to whom they had revealed the story, let alone the part they had played in its dénouement. Maybe talking at last to a third party was a form of catharsis. If so, the more I could spin things out and seem vaguely empathetic, the greater the chance of them relaxing their guard. Yes, I must try to engage their trust, or at least be an attentive audience. To this end, therefore, I enquired politely if I might be permitted another sherry.

'Of course,' Rufus replied graciously. 'We'll all have one.' He crossed to the side table and poured the three glasses and gave one to each of us. Such was my optimism that for one bright moment I thought there might be a toast. An absurd thought, naturally, but at least my request had not been spurned. There was a brief silence as we sipped. And then, pushing her glass aside, Daphne quickly resumed her narrative. There was to be no lingering over sherry; she was obviously too absorbed in her tale.

'Well, after that second note Douglas became agitated and said he was damned if he was going to spend the next twelve months waiting for a third piece of nonsense from this joker.'

'So you didn't suspect Aida?' I asked.

'We had no reason to. She had gone from our lives, and we had never seen much of her anyway. Besides, she hadn't given any trouble before and the two letters had been sent from such a wide area, not from Durban but two cities so far apart . . .

Anyway, Douglas was upset and said that since the insurance business was looking for someone to manage their GB firm – in Eastbourne of all places – we should go back to England. He had never been to Sussex, but I had known it as a child and if they needed someone to run a branch there and liaise with their London headquarters, I was all for it. So that's what we did: decamped from sunny South Africa to sunny Eastbourne.' She smiled, evidently recalling the move. 'As you can imagine, it wasn't quite what we had become used to in Durban, but very nice all the same.'

'Oh yes,' Rufus interrupted again, 'and their Devonshire Park Theatre is splendid. You used to go to plays there, didn't you?'

'Yes, we did occasionally,' she agreed. 'And we did a lot of other things too, including tennis and venturing on to the golf course. It was all very nice. The branch flourished, Head Office congratulated us, and money was made – quite a lot actually. That bit of the south coast is filled with the rich and elderly, all eager to buy the most exorbitant insurance for their health and Bentleys or to protect themselves when tottering up the steps to its Grand Hotel. So, for about eighteen months, all went well, with no nasty notes.' She tried her sherry again, and grimaced. 'My goodness, Rufus, this is a bit dry, isn't it? I thought we had some Amontillado left.'

'Oh, very sorry, My Lady. Will do better next time.' He gave me a wink, and again I felt a surge of hope.

'So what happened?' I asked eagerly. 'What went wrong?'

'What went wrong was that as Douglas was walking past the bandstand one morning, he encountered Aida Memling. She was coming from the opposite direction, looked straight at him and then walked on. Assuming he had been mistaken or a trick of the light, he didn't mention this to me. But a fortnight later it happened again. He was just coming out of our office in Terminus Road and there she was, studying one of the notices in the window. Just as before, she glanced at him and then moved off without saying a word. This time he was convinced it was her – fuller in the face and different hairstyle, but definitely the same woman we had known in

Durban: Eunice Memling's boring sister. Three weeks after that, another anonymous note arrived but this time addressed to both of us, not just Douglas.'

'So where did this one come from?' I asked. 'Timbuktu?'

'Huh! As good as: Dungeness in Kent.'

'But that's an outpost of Romney Marsh!' I exclaimed. 'Quite a way from Eastbourne. What was she doing there?'

'Presumably the same as she had been doing in Jo'burg and Cape Town – sending cryptic notes to baffle, disturb and demoralize. And this time there were actually three words on it: *Nemesis draws nearer*.'

'Extraordinary,' I murmured.

'Yes, but it worked. We were terribly rattled. It was obvious that someone was stalking us from every direction, and Douglas's sightings of Aida meant that it might conceivably be her. Frankly, I was less certain. Mistakes are easily made and some people can look surprisingly alike. Still, the whole thing – the third letter and Douglas's conviction that the woman had been Aida – was enough to sour Eastbourne for both of us. Douglas had done well in the firm, inherited a fat legacy from an aunt and was in a position to take early retirement. We both loved Lewes with its fishing and historical associations, and on a whim we decided to quit the south coast and move somewhere less busy and popular.'

'You'd have done better to have tried the Australian outback or the Outer Hebrides,' Rufus said. 'Much safer.'

She sniffed impatiently. 'Doubtless. But we wanted somewhere civilized, with culture and moderate weather, not to be living as recluses in arid heat or freezing cold! We wanted *normality*. It wasn't too much to ask, surely!'

Inwardly I agreed with her but said nothing, not wanting to stop the flow.

Daphne gave a bitter laugh. 'For the first four months after the move it was lovely, and everything was as we had hoped. And then Douglas had another sighting: he saw her *here*, in the middle of Lewes, can you believe it, coming out of the dentist's. He told me he had felt sick and nearly collapsed.' She paused for a few moments, and then added, 'Frankly, I

didn't believe him. It all seemed too much of a coincidence
. . . and you see, it struck me as being odd that it had always
been *he* who had seen her, not me. I began to think he might
be hallucinating or going round the twist – after all, one does
hear of that happening.'

'So when did you learn that he had been right, that she was
definitely in Lewes and at the school?'

'I was in the local library and overheard two women
discussing the new matron. One of them said she had had a
temporary job assisting the dentist, and that it was to be hoped
she could cope with the boys as a couple of the rascals had
just sabotaged the gym's vaulting horse by unscrewing one of
its legs . . . I thought that was quite funny, until I heard the
other say, "I think she's called Memling, or some such, and
comes from South Africa." I can tell you, that took the smile
off my face!'

'But not as much as her coup de grâce, that last message,'
Rufus said. 'After that you rampaged like a mad bull.'

'I did not rampage,' she retorted angrily, 'I merely decided
that we'd had enough and that this woman and her effing high-
jinks should be dealt with.'

Had she been standing she would have stamped her foot; sitting
down, all she could do was upset her sherry. It trickled slowly
down the side of the sofa. It was quite a decent sofa, and I
watched its journey in some dismay. I asked Rufus what message
he meant.

'The one delivered to our door *by hand* at six in the morning,'
Daphne answered. 'I had gone downstairs to let the dogs out,
and there on the mat was this white envelope. At first I thought
it might be the newspaper bill, but that always comes on a Sunday
and this was Thursday. Anyway, I opened it. This time there were
seven words: *And nearer. Funny old world isn't it?* My God, she
was getting verbose!'

'So the adverb "nearer" was linked to the previous message,
"Nemesis draws nearer",' I said helpfully.

She shot me a dirty look. 'What a brilliant mind you have,
Miss Oughterard. Yes of course it was.'

Chastened, I retreated into a submissive shell.

'But this was a step too far,' she continued, 'and something had to be done. There was no point in going to the police as she had been so crafty: letters from diverse places, long time lags, enigmatic minimal words, no dates, and importantly no overt threats. We had nothing to accuse her of. It was all conjecture and deduction; no proof of anything. Still, if she wanted to play that game and plague us with snide little notes, we could do the same. Or I could. Douglas was far too disturbed and was becoming quiet and withdrawn. He had lost all his old spark – not quite the chap I had married. So, I composed an anonymous message of my own, issuing a warning that she could expect her comeuppance. There was a friend of mine in the London suburbs who I was going to visit, so I posted it on my way there.'

'Penge,' I muttered.

She looked surprised, and then said mockingly, 'My, you have done your homework,' before turning to Rufus and saying, 'What did I tell you? Charles Penlow wasn't exaggerating when he said she had a nose like a Pointer!'

Presumably Charles had meant this as a sort of compliment, but in the circumstances I could have done without it. However, I said nothing while also wondering what had been Memling's final goad: what had she done or written that tipped Daphne over the edge and resulted in murder? Something must have flicked the lever.

It had. And she told me without prompting. 'I enjoyed writing that note,' she confided. 'It gave me immense satisfaction. At long last she was getting a dose of her own foul medicine. And it was a way of showing that we were undaunted and that her malicious tricks could rebound. For about three weeks we saw and heard nothing, and I thought that my threat had worked and that she would realize the game was up and slink away.'

'But she didn't,' I said quietly. 'By then she was so immersed in her role as warrior angel, so wedded to that mission of righteous destruction that she couldn't give up even if she had wanted to . . . So what was her fatal mistake?'

'Her fatal mistake,' Daphne replied slowly, 'was saying hello

to me at twelve o'clock midday in the middle of Lewes High
Street.'

It's funny the way the mind plays tricks, for I suddenly heard
Winchbrooke's voice declaring, as he often did, that the most
trivial events can unleash enormous consequences; that out of
the prosaic could spring the dramatic . . . Well, if I ever saw the
headmaster again, I would suggest he use the encounter of Daphne
and Aida as a prime example.

'You mean she actually greeted you, face to face?' I asked.

'Yes. The last time we had spoken was in Durban years ago,
and that was only briefly. And now, after all her mad manoeu-
vres, she had the gall to stand there and bid me good morning
as if it was the most natural thing in the world. No sign of guilt
or shame, no attempt to side-step and skuttle off. On no! She
actually barred my way, saying how nice it was to see me and
hoped things were going well. Then after some fatuous remark
about the weather, she said she was terribly busy and must be
getting along . . . I was stunned. It was as if she was being
quietly defiant, tacitly taunting me; and it was quite obvious
that my retaliatory note had been useless. I knew then that we
would have no rest until that woman had been expunged from
our lives.'

There was silence, broken by a slight cough from Rufus. 'And
there you have it, Miss Oughterard – well, the bare bones at any
rate. Rather a strange tale, I think you'll agree.'

I nodded. 'But a sad one too,' I murmured, for the ghost of
Douglas dead in the river had floated before me. I turned back
to Daphne. 'Yet in death she still wielded power, didn't she?
Douglas's suicide was so tragic.'

She regarded me steadily and then said curtly, 'Yes, tragic.
But it was also a godsend. I mean to say, if he was going to start
getting drunk and babbling to all and sundry about Eunice and
events in South Africa, we'd have really been in the cart. Like
an idiot I had told him about our plan for Aida, and initially he
had gone along with it. But then he seemed to get cold feet and
became increasingly morose. And after the thing itself, he broke

down completely and muttered about suicide and confessing to the police. I didn't take him seriously and told him not to be such a melodramatic fool and to pull himself together . . .'

She paused, drumming her fingers on the sofa arm, and then shrugged dismissively. 'Well, he wouldn't – or couldn't. You know the rest. Another of Aida Memling's little achievements,' she added bitterly. 'I am *so* glad we destroyed her.'

THIRTY-SEVEN

The Primrose version

I considered those words. Aida Memling may have been the root cause of Douglas's decline and death but it was surely his wife who had completed the work. Had she been less assertive, less impatient and more tactful in her handling of him, he might have survived. As it was, she couldn't have reacted more badly. It was a salutary lesson. And I made a mental note that, were I to escape this awful evening, in future I really should try to be nicer to the town clerk . . .

But even as I made that resolve, another thought suddenly struck me: the dope in Memling's gin. I turned to Rufus. 'So what about the drug – where did that come from? Inspector Spikesy seemed to think it was pretty rare, virtually unknown in this country and certainly not on the market.'

'Phew, Penlow was right,' he snorted, 'you *are* inquisitive! Still, since you ask, I can assure you that much as I love all things thespian, the theatre isn't exactly a money spinner – unless you happen to be one of those beloved old ponces at the top of the tree. I always knew I wouldn't be among them, so I made other arrangements. Being a man of several parts, I have certain sidelines which produce—'

'Shut up, Rufus,' Daphne snapped. 'We've got things to do.'

She returned her gaze to me and said thoughtfully, 'Things to do with you, Miss Oughterard. You should have stuck to your painting smock, not donned a deerstalker. It doesn't suit you. We have already dealt with one pest, and if necessary we can do the same again.'

Both her words and tone made me realize what a fool I had been. I had thought that by listening to their tale and appearing sympathetic I was being so clever. But obviously my pathetic efforts had changed nothing. They were determined to shut me up just as firmly as they had Aida Memling. I gazed at her impassively, my mind in a whirl.

'However,' she went on, 'not being a creature of habit, I would prefer another method, something less painful and more . . .' She broke off, seeming to search for a word. 'Yes, that's it, more *businesslike*. Simpler and easier all round.'

I had no idea what she meant, but the term 'businesslike' sounded distinctly sinister. What were they planning for me? Something brisk, slick and ugly? I gritted my teeth and waited.

'You see,' she continued, 'we could come to some sort of accommodation, make you an offer.'

Accommodation? An offer? I was bewildered. 'What on earth are you talking about?' I exclaimed.

'What my sister means,' said Rufus casually, 'is that we could cut you in. Poor old Douglas has left her a nice little packet. You like money, don't you, Miss Oughterard?' He regarded me quizzically.

I could hardly believe my ears. The scoundrel was actually offering me a bribe. How crass could he get? Never have I been so humiliated! 'I don't know what you mean,' I replied furiously. 'The last thing I want is to accept anything from you or your mercenary sister!'

He sighed. 'Hmm. I thought that might be your reaction. Well, think about this instead . . . Supposing it was put about that your brother, the late Reverend Canon Francis Oughterard of Molehill, Surrey, had murdered one of his parishioners, the *charming* Elizabeth Fotherington. How about that? It wouldn't sound too good, would it?'

This I was totally unprepared for, and such was my shock that without thinking I cried, 'But you have no proof!'

There was silence as brother and sister exchanged glances. And then Daphne giggled. 'Proof? No, we have no proof, but from what you've just said it sounds as if some may exist. Could be interesting – or others might find it so.'

I glowered, all show of sympathy gone. 'Rubbish,' I retorted, 'a total figment of your imagination. You said yourselves that you were abroad at the time and knew nothing about the case. That tramp did it. The case is closed.'

'For lack of further evidence,' Rufus murmured. 'Certainly the situation suggested the tramp, but he died before the case came to court. At the time we had a hunch which we found rather amusing. "'Twas the vicar what dunnit", we used to laugh. We didn't take it seriously, of course, it was just a joke. But sometimes hunches, however absurd, can be right. You had such a one about the death of Aida Memling – that she had got in someone's way, had disturbed their lives and was killed for it. You happened to be right. Just as we might be right about your brother. It only needs a few words here and there to get people thinking. It could even open the case again.'

'But there is no truth in it,' I lied.

'Huh! Truth doesn't matter.' Daphne laughed dismissively. 'It's what people *believe* that counts. And if they come to believe that there was something sinister about that case, that the real perpetrator had been a *vicar*, then it wouldn't do much for the name of Oughterard, would it? Mind you, I bet it would increase the sales of your pictures no end. I can hear the gossip now: "My dear, I've just bought this charming pastoral painting – they say the artist's brother was a murderer! Rather unusual, wouldn't you say?"'

Daphne had assumed a slyly drawling tone. She was rather a good mimic, and I inwardly winced, envisaging the scene.

'My sister is right,' Rufus said. 'Whether or not your brother was responsible we don't know and it hardly matters. Once an idea catches the public imagination it tends to linger. Rumours of that sort can spread quickly and do endless harm – as we know only too well. Your reputation could be irreparably damaged. You wouldn't like that, would you?'

While having a healthy self-regard, it wasn't the loss of my reputation that I feared, so much as my brother's. I had spent years trying to conceal his crime and protect the family name, and the idea of it now being dragged into the public eye, proof or not, was intolerable. Unlike their calculated and viciously organized assault on Memling, Francis had acted impulsively in a flash of wild panic, and no one could have been more horrified by the result than he. Later he had sacrificed his own life for that of another and had died honourably. I couldn't bear the thought of that honour being stained.

Thus for one agonizing moment I wavered. But reason and anger prevailed. If I accepted their offer I should be in their grasp, but equally they in mine. It would be a trading of secrets and such arrangements are invariably fragile and slippery: silence is never assured. Besides, the Oughterards do not take bribes, and this was blackmail. Disgraceful! And if they tried to rake up a case against Francis or tarnish his name, I would fight them, or anyone else, all the way.

'You are speaking to the wrong person,' I said coolly. 'I don't play those games.'

'A pity,' he said dryly. 'It would save us a lot of trouble, and you of course. There will have to be a dispatch, and a quick one too. You see, we're off to Seattle tonight. Can't afford to miss the plane; poor Daphne really needs that holiday!' Absurd though it all sounded, the term 'dispatch' stabbed me like a knife in the dark, and I knew that he meant every word. They were going to kill me.

Yet desperation drives, and even now I thought I might somehow deflect them and make a rush to the door. Oh my God, how to delay?

Panic mounted, but I heard myself saying, 'But you can't kill me now; it would be far too complicated. How will you cope with my corpse? You can hardly leave it here. A bit dangerous surely?'

'Easy,' Rufus replied nonchalantly, 'we'll bung it in the car boot, and then en route to the airport drop it off in some delightful Sussex ditch. There are plenty about.'

I swallowed and started to feel faint, but somehow managed to say, 'Oh yes? And kill the dogs too I suppose. Simpler than all that quarantine palaver!' My eyes slid towards the closed door; so near and yet so far.

He shrugged. 'The kennel people are coming to collect them in the morning. They'll stay in the shed tonight and be taken from there. They will be quite all right . . . unlike you.'

I opened my mouth to babble something else. But no sound emerged, for I saw something that froze me utterly. Slowly, Rufus had started to unbuckle his belt, and at the same time I heard a faint rustle and realized that Daphne had moved from her chair and was standing right behind me. As I gazed at the unfurling belt, I thought he was going to strike me. And then from the way he was holding it I saw that he meant to do something far worse: to strangle. As he advanced, I tried to move, but my feet were paralysed and I could feel Daphne's hands gripping, pinioning my arms. He stepped forward. 'Close your eyes,' she whispered softly.

Instinctively I did as she said, but I could hear my breath heaving in great gasps, and then caught the whiff of his sweat . . . And then, worst of all, I felt the warm touch of leather encircling my throat. Tightening and tightening.

THIRTY-EIGHT

The cat's version

U nlike on the two previous evenings, my customary prowl had been most productive: a deftly caught newt from the vicar's fishpond, mayhem wrought among the blackbirds and two grossly fat field mice. The latter I would place under the kitchen sink – my trophy spot – for P.O. to marvel at in the morning.

However, there was a penalty for such vigorous exercise: while negotiating some barbed wire I had hurt my left paw and it was painful. Still, being a cat of stoical disposition, I made no fuss and settled down for a restful night's sleep under the stairs.

Restful, did I say? Hardly! About an hour later, just as I was dreaming of caviar, cream and trout's head, I was awakened by a squeaking noise and a tug on my tail.

'Good Cod,' I miaowed, 'what is it! Who's there?'

'It's me,' a small voice yapped. 'Wake up, sir! Wake up!'

Now, I may be well disposed to Tarzan in the general run of things, but to have the creature barging into my private lair like this was a bit much. What on earth did he think he was doing? 'Why aren't you at home?' I hissed. 'And how did you get in?'

'Through the cat flap,' he said breathlessly. 'You must come quickly – and Bouncer too. Something nasty is happening at our place, and your mistress is there and it's all . . . it's all nasty!'

'What do you mean "nasty"?' I demanded.

'What they are saying to her. It's not nice! I don't like it!' Tarzan twirled around in frantic circles, and then raced into the kitchen.

Clearly something was very wrong. I caterwauled for Bouncer asleep in his basket. 'Bouncer,' I screeched, 'come here immediately.'

The dog came floundering into the hall.

'P.O. is in danger. These are your instructions: follow Tarzan and go to her aid. Immediately!'

'I can't,' he growled.

'What do you mean, you can't?' I hissed.

'The poodle is having a pee on the Aga door. I'll have to wait for him. Why don't you go on ahead?'

'Because,' I said furiously, 'I have hurt my best paw. I am incommoded. Now, go to her rescue immediately with or without the peeing poodle!' He bolted off and I was left fuming. Really, what one has to go through with these canines, let alone the humans!

However, piqued though I was, I was also worried. Had our earlier fears been realized – that our mistress had got herself into some dire situation which could turn fatal? I felt my fur stand on end. Disagreeable for her. Dreadful for us! I paced about (well, limped actually), for once bereft of all thought. But naturally, my mind quickly restored itself and I summoned Tarzan from the kitchen, presumably by now much relieved.

'How did you get out?' I asked.

'I was out already, in the garden shed. The Roof person had put me there to be collected by the vet in the morning, and I was waiting for Petal to come and join me, but he was taking so long. So I slipped out and crept into the house by the front door. The Roof man hadn't shut it properly. When I was in the hall, I knew that your mistress was there because I saw her coat. Then I heard a lot of talking going on in what they call the sitting room, so I listened carefully. I'm quite good at that – especially now that I'm a spy!' He paused for a quick scratch.

'And then what?' I mewed.

'As I listened, my sixth sense told me something very bad was happening and that there was *danger*, and that the lady might get hurt or worse!'

The little nose had begun to twitch again and I could see he was still agitated. But I was somewhat agitated myself to hear of his sixth sense. I had thought that this was something peculiar to Bouncer, or rather to his imagination. But perhaps it is something with which all canines are endowed – or think they are.

Tarzan started to whimper. 'It's nasty,' he sniffed again, and started to chew his paw.

'Yes,' I said sternly, 'you have already made that observation. Now collect yourself. Good spies do not lose their nerve. We must think carefully.'

'Yes, yes of course, sir. But I might be able to think better if I had one of Bouncer's biscuits. Do you think he would mind?'

'Whether Bouncer minds or not is irrelevant. His biscuits are far too big for your small mouth and you would choke on it,' I said severely.

'But not if I just had a *little* nibble, just a titchy one.' He hesitated and then said, 'I say, sir, I see you have hurt your paw. That must be so painful, but I expect it happened when you were doing something very brave – a sort of war wound.'

I blinked, slightly nonplussed. War wound? Well, I suppose the effect of leaping over a piece of wire might be thus termed. After all, I think human military types referred to such a barrier as being *a barbed wire entanglement*. Anyway, I considered Tarzan's compliment most courteous. He deserved something in return. 'I think you can do better than nibble at one of Bouncer's questionable biscuits,' I remarked. 'Our mistress keeps some dainty wafers in the drawing room. You might care for some of those.'

'Ooh yes,' he yelped, 'my favourite!' There followed much twirling and scrabbling about and he nearly did a somersault, but I stopped him just in time. 'Do not,' I said hastily. 'That will tire you out and you will be unable to assist Bouncer.'

I slipped into the drawing room, relieved the side table of some of its store, and returned to the poodle. 'Eat this and then follow Bouncer. He will give you instructions. But whatever happens, I shall expect you to report to me.'

There followed some rather distasteful munching sounds. And then with snack finished, Tarzan shot off to do as I had directed. I sighed and settled down to await developments.

As things turned out, Tarzan did not report to me, for he had been overtaken by events. After he had sped after Bouncer and arrived at Needham Court, matters had already been taken in hand – largely by Petal, of all creatures. He told Bouncer that he had duffed up the nasty man and that our mistress was alive and that the two beastly people had run off, jumped into their car and zoomed away. Bouncer then took charge, ministered to the Prim, and told Tarzan that for the time being his services were no longer required.

I gather that the poodle was not unduly perturbed by this and raced down to the garden shed (from which he had originally escaped) to await the arrival of Petal. From what I can gather, the two are now being looked after by the vet Richardson and surrounded by mountain goats. Not to my taste exactly, but I suspect that as long as they are together Petal and Tarzan can adapt to most things.

That night, our mistress returned accompanied by Bouncer and looking considerably the worse for wear. Her voice sounded funny too. Anyway, she muttered something totally incomprehensible to me – though I think kindly meant – and retired to her bed.

Since then both she and I have been keeping low profiles. Eventually I trust that sanity will return, but until then I shall keep quiet . . . though doubtless the dog will have a few things to say. He generally does.

THIRTY-NINE

The Primrose version

The choking began. And at the same time a sound of tempestuous roaring consumed all my being. *So this is death*, I thought, *not soft but thunderous . . .*

I awoke to find myself sprawled on my back, throat on fire and barely able to breathe or swallow. Dazed and disorientated, I could just discern the ceiling above and hear the silence all around . . . but a silence broken by an odd chomping noise. Painfully I turned my head and saw a massive mound of black fur a few feet away. It was Petal.

The chomping stopped and the dog too turned its head and stared at me with solemn eyes. And then, slightly to my surprise, it went back to whatever it was doing. The next moment I was even more surprised. For from outside came the sound of loud barking and a mad scrabbling at the window pane, and even in my confused state I knew that it was Bouncer. Unlike before, the sitting-room door was now wide open and, levering myself up, I stumbled through the hall and out into the porch. Here I was once more attacked – not by a malevolent human, but a joyous dog. Such was the force of Bouncer's frenzied buffeting that I nearly collapsed again, but managed to steady myself and calm him down.

I then saw that Daphne's car was gone. Obviously, having dealt with me, they had made a dash for the airport. But I was puzzled for, of course, I hadn't been dealt with – or at least, only up to a point. By now I should be dead, so why wasn't I? What had stopped Rufus from completing his task? I looked at Petal who, presumably diverted by Bouncer's noise, had now joined us. He held something firmly clamped in his jaw. I switched on the porch light and he dropped the object at my feet.

It was a mangled brown suede shoe – one of a pair that I had

noticed Rufus wearing. I gazed in shocked horror. What had the
dog done? Savaged the man and ripped off his footwear? I recalled
the nightmare sound that had split my ears as the belt was winding
round my neck. So perhaps not the noise of death after all, but
of Petal, the docile creature, 'as soft as soap', as Rufus had
declared. They said he had been asleep at the top of the stairs.
If so, perhaps roused by sounds from below he had gone to
investigate, and hadn't liked what he saw. Somewhat nervously
I told the mastiff that his gift was much appreciated. He gave a
slow wag of his tail, bent his head and, after some snuffling,
picked it up again. Evidently not a gift but a brief loan. At that
moment there came a faint yapping from the distant garden shed:
Tarzan, closeted overnight and awaiting the vet's arrival the next
day. Petal cocked his ears and, toting the shoe, lumbered off
down the path.

I was left with Bouncer, and together we returned to the now
mercifully silent house and I collected my handbag and coat.
Glancing at the telephone in the hall, I wondered if I should
contact the police. Absolutely not! I had experienced more than
enough drama for one night and couldn't face any more. All I
wanted now was peace, bed, throat tablets and aspirin. 'Come
on, Bouncer,' I croaked, 'let's get home.'

There wasn't much I remember about that walk except that
Bouncer stuck to my side like a leech. Even when the tabby cat
Tiddles crossed our path, he didn't deviate an inch.

Once safely indoors, I nearly tripped over Maurice. What he
was doing in the middle of the hall floor at that time of night, I
couldn't make out. He is usually either in his lair under the stairs
or affrighting some creature outside. As I made for the kitchen
to pour a glass of water, he lurched towards me, miaowed loudly
and started to pull at my laces. I think it was a kind of welcome,
and noticing the limp I gave him a sympathetic stroke and resolved
to investigate in the morning. But just then I was in no condition
to do anything except take the pills and crawl into bed.

I don't think I have slept so long since I was a child, and when
I did wake it was after ten o'clock. I lay staring at the ceiling

(this time my own, thank God) and started to go over what had occurred the previous day. It was probably a kind of delayed hysteria, for when I thought of Rufus and the fate of his shoe, I started to giggle. I assumed that one of their suitcases in the back of the Jaguar had contained a spare pair, otherwise he would have received some very funny looks from the officials at London Airport. If Petal had attacked him, and maybe Daphne as well, they must have fled in terror, perhaps using the car as a sort of sanctuary from the ravening hound. Dwelling on this, I recalled that the front door, though closed, had not been locked. A curious oversight for anyone leaving their house for three months – unless consumed with panic and their mind on other things, i.e. saving their skin!

For a little while I savoured the scenario, a convenient means of dodging what to do next. Report it all to the police? The repercussions could be endless and filled me with gloom. I probably wouldn't be believed, and instead branded as a mad mischief-maker (like Aida Memling). But even if I were taken seriously, the two of them would deny it or make counter-charges – even drag in the Francis allegation – and the whole thing would become an utter nightmare. It was bad enough coping with the throbbing throat, let alone having to face future upheaval. The benison of sleep was beginning to wear off and once more I lay there exhausted, dreading the prospect in store . . .

The telephone shrilled in my ear. Wearily, and warily, I lifted the receiver and tried to say hello. Hardly a sound came.

'Hello, hello,' Charles Penlow said. 'Is that you, Primrose?'

'Yes,' I croaked faintly.

There was a pause. And then he said, 'I'm sorry, it's rather a bad line. Can you speak up?'

'Not really,' I breathed, 'I've got laryngitis.'

'Ah, sorry to hear that' (he didn't sound especially so), 'but I wondered if you had heard the news.'

I closed my eyes. What news? That the Lewes rugger team had beaten Hove? Erasmus had failed its inspection? The church tower collapsed? Emily Bartlett had run off with the town clerk?

'No, not really,' I muttered.

'Ah, well, brace yourself. I fear it's rather sad.'

Brace myself? Lying semi-comatose in bed, it was the last thing I wanted to do.

'Sad, you say?'

'Yes. It's Daphne Hamlyn and her brother. You know they were flying to Seattle – well, there's been a plane crash. Soon after take off, in mid-channel. All safe, crew and passengers, except for them. Frightful, isn't it!'

For a few seconds I was silent. And then I asked him if they were really dead.

'Oh yes. It was on the wireless this morning. Such bad luck, don't you think?'

'Oh yes. Frightful,' I agreed.

After he had rung off there was only one thing I could do. I turned on my side and went fast to sleep again.

My slumber lasted for several hours and when I finally emerged to bath and dress the room was filled with sunlight. Normally if I stay abed Bouncer will come to tug at the eiderdown and demand I let him out. This time there had been no such summons. Presumably the dog, like myself, had been worn out by the night's exertions and was still lolling in his basket. I examined my neck in the mirror. Not a pretty sight. There was a large bruise starting to appear and a couple of small red wheals. Some discreet covering was definitely needed. Well, that could be dealt with later. Meanwhile I was ravenous.

I went down to the kitchen where, as expected, the dog was dozing. He opened a lazy eye, snuffled and shut it again. Despite the horror of the previous evening I had remembered to take the stew from the oven before going to bed. Though cold it looked rather good all the same. Could my throat stand a few morsels? It could – a somewhat masochistic experience, but satisfying nevertheless.

From the window I could see Maurice crouched on top of the chinchillas' hutch, his tail dangling in front of the wire. He does that when he's in a good mood, so presumably the injured paw wasn't too bad. Still, perhaps he should see the vet. Thinking of the latter, I was reminded of Petal and Tarzan whose temporary guardian he was supposed to be until Daphne's return. He was scheduled to pick them up from the shed earlier in the day. I wondered if like Charles he too had heard the news of the plane crash. If so, would the dogs take up permanent residence with the goats?

Briefly I brooded on this, and then turned to the fate of Daphne and Rufus – which inevitably brought my mind back to Aida Memling. 'Nemesis draws nearer', her penultimate note had threatened. Hmm, I thought grimly but not without satisfaction, Nemesis has had a busy time recently. Were he of the sporting fraternity and enjoyed the pursuit of game birds, he could be said to have scored a neat left and right . . . Actually, though sitting there at the kitchen table in safe surroundings, I still couldn't quite believe they were dead. An awful thought struck me: perhaps Charles had been wrong. Maybe he was getting deaf and had misheard the wireless bulletin. Supposing it had said, "All dead *except* for two passengers". Heaven or Nemesis forbid! I leapt from the table and rushed to catch the lunchtime news.

Aah . . . all was well. The announcer's voice was most soothing; there had been no mistake. Thoughtlessly I lit a cigarette and inhaled deeply. Agony!

What the future held for Needham Court and the owner's projected plans for its sale, I couldn't care less. As long as Primrose Oughterard wasn't involved, nothing else mattered. But I thought of Rufus and idly wondered if *The Stage* would print an obituary for Henry de Vere. Perhaps a passing reference but probably no more. But then I recalled his saying that 'being a man of several parts', he had had a lucrative sideline. So when not strutting the boards and conning susceptible idiots, what else had he been engaged in? Flogging hamburgers on Bexhill beach? Again, as with the business of Daphne's estate, I really wasn't interested. Beastly cad!

I glanced at the clock. Almost three o'clock, and although mid-November the sun still shone. I would drive into Lewes and amble about in civilized normality. Why, I might even purchase those flowers for the town clerk . . . On second thoughts, no. One can do too much of a good thing. Can't one?

Selecting my best and widest silk scarf, I draped it round my neck (not tightly!) and set off to enjoy the rest of the afternoon.

Emerging from the bookshop, I encountered Mrs Dragson, and in view of the recent revelations I felt a bit ashamed. My earlier suspicions had been wide of the mark. Still, it just shows how easily mistakes can be made. I flashed my best smile and asked winningly if she had been successful at Plumpton Racecourse. 'Oh yes,' she replied airily, 'Jester Boy made a nice little packet. I could give you some tips. Mind you, I shan't be in Lewes much longer.' The stern face twitched into a broad smile. 'I am getting married. Second time around. So nice!'

I gave my congratulations and asked if she and her fiancé would be retiring. 'Oh no,' she replied. 'Robert runs a splendid business demolishing and renovating old sheds and cricket pavilions. And I'm going to help him – not physically, of course, but taking orders for materials and so on. In fact, I've already persuaded Mr Winchbrooke to give us a commission to overhaul that awful old, battered thing in the school garden. It's such an eyesore. Robert has surveyed the thing and is sure he can do a grand job on it. Mr Winchbrooke is thrilled.'

'How nice,' I said tightly, thinking of wretched Sickie and Sparks and their nocturnal espionage tricks. 'And, er, where will you be living? Somewhere in Sussex?'

'Oh no – Penge. A most salubrious place, and Robert has just opened a new office there. It's all very convenient and near enough to whizz down to Lewes in the van. So, toodle-oo for now, Miss Oughterard . . . and, er, good luck with the paintings. I expect you will have heard the news.' She looked vaguely amused, winked and went on her way.

I gazed after her. Wouldn't you know – blooming Penge again! And what had she meant about the news? The plane crash? Unlikely. It must be something else, but what? Huh! I would find out.

As I approached the car park, another familiar figure appeared: Inspector Spikesy. 'Ah,' he said cheerfully, 'haven't seen you for a bit. How's the Long Man? The wife and I are really looking forward to it. You must come to lunch when it's finished.'

I thanked him and assured him it would soon be done and wouldn't take much longer. And then very cautiously I said that apparently Lewes had lost a couple of locals in a plane crash.

He frowned slightly. 'Well, one was local, Mrs Hamlyn of course, but the brother was not. Lived in London mainly.' He paused, glanced around, and then muttered, 'A bit of a shame really, it rather messed things up.'

'Messed things up? Well, I suppose he might have felt that too. I mean to say, death does tend to have that effect.'

'Ye-es, but that's not quite what I meant.' He lowered his voice further. 'You see, I was on to him and was about to make an arrest. Pipped at the post, you might say.'

Spikesy sounded rueful and I was distinctly intrigued. 'In what way?' I murmured.

'He ran a nice little line in the drugs trade: a dealer in the obscure and lethal. Not nice . . . Ah well, he won't be doing that any more.' Spikesy spoke with the resigned voice of one who had been cheated. But then more robustly he said, 'But I am sure you'll keep that under your hat, won't you, Miss Oughterard?'

'Oh absolutely,' I declared.

He smiled and nodded. And then looking at my scarf, said, 'A very pretty design, if I may say so; most unusual.'

Spikesy's slightly indiscreet remarks about Rufus would of course be kept a deadly secret. And in any case, I didn't really want to dwell on either of that pair again, least of all what I had undergone at their hands. Nevertheless, there must have been some urge to 'unburden' myself, as the popular pundits say, for Nicholas Ingaza came to mind. Yes, he was the one person in whom it was safe to confide. I grinned. Little did he know what was in store for him! I would alert him the moment I got home.

FORTY

Emily Bartlett to her sister

My dear Hilda,

Just to keep you updated – as the modern idiom goes. I am sure you will be delighted to hear that thanks to Primrose O our little trip to Le Touquet is definitely on! Yes, she has dropped a persuasive word to Mr Winchbrooke about my deserved salary increase and – believe it or not – he has actually listened to her and done the decent thing! So, my dear, start packing, and do buy a French phrasebook and get your hair cut. I don't think that long plaits at fifty-four are much favoured by our Gallic friends. They prefer a more 'with it' style, to again use the popular jargon.

And talking of jargon, Erasmus has at long last received the inspectors' report. Hurrah! We have done remarkably well! In fact, the only black mark has been for the pictures in the main corridor. They are apparently deemed to be 'excruciatingly boring, incomprehensible and ugly, and a most unsuitable introduction to decent English art'. Primrose has said nothing (she is currently suffering from a nasty attack of laryngitis), but one can tell from her smug expression that she is delighted. Perks the janitor and the new geography master have been instructed to resurrect the originals from the cellar. Mind you, I don't imagine that the dubious Mr Ingaza, the Brighton art dealer, will be too pleased. No doubt he was making a pretty penny from their rental.

You ask about the Memling case. No, there is nothing more to say on that score, and a good thing too. The verdict of misadventure remains, and as you can imagine, Mr Winchbrooke is much relieved. Indeed, he is almost light-hearted, and only the other day complimented me on my pink nail polish . . . though I <u>think</u> he was joking when he *suggested I get some pink hair spray and eyeshadow to go with it.*

Oh, and a little bit of gossip. Rumour has it – largely put about by Bertha Twigg – that Mrs Dragson is engaged to be married. Her husband to be is a renovator of garden sheds and has already inspected and delivered fresh fittings for the rather dilapidated one in the school's garden next to the playing field. When I asked Bertha if the newlyweds would be staying on here in Lewes, she said that she suspected they would be de-camping to Penge near London where they both have relations. Of course, this is all very nice for Mrs Dragson, but I fear she will be missed by the boys. She is a firm disciplinarian but a fair one, and will be a considerable loss to Erasmus House. Let us hope that the next matron will be as good . . . and may we be preserved from any questionable <u>*assistant*</u> *ones!*

Well, Hilda, I must sign off now. A busy bee as always! Give my love to Mother – should she be interested – and for goodness' sake, before we go to France do warn the care home about her little habits, otherwise their bill is likely to be exorbitant.

    Your devoted sister,
    Emily

P.S. Don't forget the haircut!

FORTY-ONE

The Primrose version

Once home I fed the dog and prepared to ring Ingaza to fix a time for my 'outpouring'.

Ideally, I thought, he should come here. After all, with so delicate a revelation to be discussed, privacy was essential. Besides, my throat still being tender it meant I could concoct a suitable menu – an abrasive steak for him and soup and junket for me. But so absorbed was he in the gallery's extension project and other profitable exploits that he might think a trip to Lewes surplus to requirements. Still, it was worth a try, and I could bribe him with a bottle of Talisker from Pa's legacy in the cellar.

In fact, no such inducement was needed for it turned out that he was already scheduled to be in Lewes the following day. Why? To visit Erasmus House to retrieve those execrable pictures currently displayed to impress its inspectors. Apparently, their report had arrived sooner than expected, and such was its criticism of the paintings that Winchbrooke couldn't get rid of them soon enough.

'So, mine are going to be restored to their rightful place?' I asked eagerly.

'It would seem so,' he replied with little fervour.

'Oh, excellent,' I chirped, feeling greatly cheered.

'Hmm. Maybe excellent for you, Primrose,' he remarked dryly, 'but less so for me. I had rather hoped they would be extending the loan period. That batch of substitutes has been earning the gallery a nice bit of pocket money. Still, win one, lose one, I suppose.'

As Ingaza's winnings are considerably greater than his losings, I can't say that I was bothered.

'Exactly, Nicholas,' I said cheerily, 'and if you come to lunch

I will open a bottle of Pa's special Scotch and you can take the rest back with you. I am currently off that particular wagon and will stick to wine. My throat is a trifle sensitive these days and I fear whisky is too sharp for it. Such a bore.' I laughed.

In a brighter tone he said he had thought my voice was sounding rather hoarse and assumed this was due to over-exercise.

I retorted that I feared it would soon be taking further exercise, as I had *much* to recount, which he was bound to find interesting. I then added that not only would his visit bring joy to me, but that Maurice too would be enraptured by the prospect.

I think he muttered 'Cripes' but it could have been a stronger term.

Normally Ingaza arrives in his beloved old Citroën Avant, but this time he drew up in a smart Land Rover, presumably better suited to accommodate the pictures whose frames I could just see piled in the back.

On entering, his first words were, 'Where's Scragarse?'

I told him that Maurice sent his sincere apologies but was currently engaged elsewhere. 'Nothing apologetic about that cat,' he said grimly, 'but at least it's not sitting glaring at me.'

I took him into the drawing room and, as a preliminary to my discourse, filled his glass lavishly with the promised whisky. He took a couple of sips, nodded appreciatively and enquired what particular snippets of gossip I had to impart. *Snippets of gossip?* Little did he know what was coming! I then launched into my account, during which he sipped steadily and looked increasingly attentive. In fact, rarely have I seen him so curious – or shocked.

'Good God, Primrose!' he exploded. 'I warned you to steer clear of that business and that it could be dangerous. But of course, a total waste of breath. Always is – nothing changes.' Yet even as he remonstrated, I could see that he was shaken by hearing of the events at Needham Court. And when Bouncer trotted in to say hello, he absent-mindedly stroked his head.

We went into lunch, where over wine, his steak and my soup we ruminated about various aspects of the case and the psychology and motives of the three deceased. We tried to analyse Memling's insatiable obsession to demoralize and expose those whom she deemed her enemies, and the ruthless tactics used by Daphne and Rufus to retaliate – and in my case, to stifle further enquiry. It wasn't the most riotous of feasts.

'It rather knocks poor old Francis's blunder into a cocked hat, doesn't it?' Ingaza murmured.

I sipped my wine. 'Almost,' I replied.

When he departed, having carefully slipped the Talisker into his briefcase, to my surprise he gripped my shoulders and said quietly, 'Look after yourself, Primrose bloody Oughterard – one doesn't want to lose you.' He turned and walked quickly to the car, but not before making the V sign at Maurice crouched on its bonnet. Scragarse leapt to the ground and glowered.

The next day there was a phone call from Eric.

'Wotcha, Prim,' he yelled, 'I've got an idea.'

'Oh yes,' I replied somewhat nervously, 'you would like me to come to your next darts match?'

'Nah – better than that! His Nibs and me are going to take a little trip next month to Tangier. You could come wiv us if you like.'

I don't think I have ever been so startled in my life (even by the ordeal at Needham Court) and at first I thought I must have misunderstood.

'Yes,' he continued, 'old Nick seemed a bit worried about you when he got home yesterday, sort of glum, and he said you'd got a bad neck or something and weren't eating much. So I said that perhaps you could do with a holiday and suggested Tangier. Just up your street, I shouldn't wonder – a lot going on there of *interest*, one might say!' He bellowed a laugh and I winced. 'Anyway,' he went on, 'Nick looked a bit po-faced but said I could give it a try if I must, but he would lay me a tenner you'd say no . . . So, wotcha think, gal?'

Totally nonplussed, the gal thought nothing for a few seconds. And then, determined not to let Nicholas Ingaza win his bet, she said, 'How very charming of you. Yes, I should love to come.'

*   *   *

Back in the kitchen and in a haze of disbelief, I looked at Bouncer sitting quietly in his basket and said, 'Holy hell, old boy, your mistress is going mad!'

He regarded me steadily. And then burped in what I took to be agreement.

.